PORTOBELLO EH15

Dave Bliss

Printed in the United Kingdom

ISBN 978-1-78723-257-0

Published by CompletelyNovel.com

First published 2018

For those who were there along the way

"We are fallible, we all know that. We will make mistakes. But I hope and I believe we will never lose sight of what brought us here: the striving to do right by the people of Scotland; to respect their priorities; to better their lot; and to contribute to the common weal."

Donald Dewar at the opening of the Scottish Parliament, 1 July 1999

CHAPTER ONE - THE HOMECOMING
(Late September 2013)

Pantechnicon was a very long word. He knew that because he had recited it many times in his head as he had walked to primary school as a young boy growing up in a small village in the Yorkshire Dales in the north of England in the early 1970s. He would repeat it again and again until it had lost all rhythm and by the time he arrived at school the word would have dissolved into a collection of meaningless syllables.

Portobello was a similar word that he'd tried the same trick with and repeating it ad infinitum meant that it too had begun to lose its sense. But, unlike what he had learnt was a rather antiquated word for a large lorry, Portobello never quite lost its real meaning for him. For along with other words such as Corstorphine, Craiglockart, Musselburgh and Joppa, it represented the place where he had first understood love. They were place names that had tantalised him and teased him when he had first seen them as a child.

Back then they were exotic destinations on the fronts of maroon buses that criss-crossed the city to which his father had moved. They were unlike his other childhood vocabulary of place names such as Countersett, Aysgarth, Askrigg and Hawes. These were the towns and villages within Yoredale, places that represented a harder way of life, places that his family had called home and places from whose grasp his father had escaped to enrol at university in Edinburgh.

On occasions when he had first visited his father in the city with his mother or grandparents, one destination on the front of the city's buses had teased him more than others and had lived long in his memory: Portobello. It had become a special place for him, where a bus journey could take you to the seaside. To him and the other children of the Dale, seasides were for holidays, for endless car journeys, for sand, sunburn and picnics. Yet Portobello was a seaside right in the city where you could play on the sands and watch the ships out in the Forth waiting to take their turn in the harbour at Leith.

Portobello was a magical place for him as a child, for along with the zoo, it was a favourite destination for a young family enjoying the opportunity that the city provided. Yet they had only ever been passers by in its evolution. They had never lived there together. They were only ever visitors.

He had always wondered what it was about the city that had captivated him in those early years, for it was a place that always pulled him back no matter where else he had been. There were the iconic landmarks of the Castle, of Arthur's Seat, of Princes Street and many others, and there were other places that had become special to him as he had returned to the city over the years. There were the flats he had rented during the Festival, favourite bars, the green spaces of The Meadows and Calton Hill, and the ski slope at Hillend. All were special to him in their own way. He had known for some time that although it had been part of his life for as long as he could remember, he'd only ever known it as a visitor, or worse, as a tourist. What he'd always regretted was never having lived in it, never having paid council tax in it, never having called it home.

Until now that was. Because now there had been a change in his life: a change that had been sudden, almost reckless, even for him. His friends often suggested that he ran his life by making last minute decisions. They sometimes despised him for it. He needed to be more organised like them, plan things in advance, be committed. He'd listened to them over the years but had never changed. Why should he, he had always argued. Let them change if they wanted to, but for him his life had always been like riding the wave, letting it take him where it might. But there was an enigma to him as well. His carefree, lackadaisical approach was his outward appearance. Inside, he was different. Inside he wanted to make decisions based on all the facts and would put things off if he wasn't sure of himself. Sometimes getting it altogether pushed things to the wire. This had until recently infuriated her, the person who until a few weeks ago he had thought he would be spending the rest of his life with.

She had often complained about his indecisiveness, the most recent being only a few days earlier when he had starting assembling a few things to leave the home that they had bought together. He had had to leave with what he could carry and that had proved a challenge to him. Even though he had arranged to put some of his possessions into storage, particularly the books that he had accumulated over the years, there was still far too much to get into the two large suitcases that he had hurriedly acquired. In the end her exasperation forced her to intervene and she had said that she would send the rest on by courier. But at the end, when she'd driven him to the station, she was quite gracious, though he reflected later that that was possibly because she was still living in their house and was still driving their car. When they said goodbye, as he had boarded the train for London, there was none of the animosity that had come to dominate their relationship over the last year or so. Instead they'd parted amicably, both of them agreeing to keep in touch, though neither having any expectation that they would.

He had stayed with his sister overnight in London. She had tried not to judge, or so she had said, although in his experience she always did. She had been forthright in her questioning about the move. Was it permanent? Was he moving by himself? Was *she* going to be joining him? What was happening to the new house that they'd just bought in Bath? He had tried to convince her that the decision to move north was largely impulsive. He'd seen an advert in The Guardian for a job in Edinburgh and had gone for it. It was an opportunity to run his own department, a step up from where he had been at Bath, but more importantly it was in Edinburgh, something that, as she knew, he had always dreamt of. Things weren't quite what they had once been in Bath and if it hadn't been this opportunity, something else would have driven them apart, he'd told her. Much as though he still had a soft spot for that city and probably always would, whether it was the colour of the buildings, the slightly faded gentility of the place, or the atmosphere that they exuded, there was nothing to keep him there now.

A day later, the realisation of what he had done struck him as the taxi pulled up outside his rented flat. Bath Street, Portobello, EH15: there was an irony, he reflected, as he thought of the years he had been happy in that city of that name, indeed where, until recently, *they* had been happy. *They.* There was no *they* now. He was alone for the first time in his life and learning to live by himself was not something that he had planned at a time in his life when there should have been more certainty and someone to share it with.

The taxi left him on the pavement with all that he had been able to carry. He paused. What was he doing here? He fumbled with the keys that he had collected from the agent's office after getting off the train. Unlocking the street door, he climbed the polished stairs to the third floor of the red sandstone tenement building. He really was starting again he thought, as he stood on the landing.

Unlocking the door to his new abode, he stepped inside. The flat was much as he remembered it from when he had viewed it a week earlier on his flying visit to the city to find somewhere to live. His possessions, few as they were, now stood beside him in the hall, making little impression on the high ceilinged room. It would be a few weeks before he could arrange to get what was his share of the divided spoils. What they'd decided was his had now been consigned to a metal storage unit at the other end of the country. Until then he was going to have to manage with what the suitcases held, together with the fresh bedding that he'd hurriedly bought at a department store on Princes Street before getting the taxi.

The flat smelt of someone else, someone he would never know. The agent had talked highly of the previous tenant; had said that they would be sorry to see him move on; that their job would be so much easier if only all tenants were as good. He had felt as though this was either some sort of coded warning or challenge, although he wasn't quite sure which, let alone the implications if he got it wrong. He opened the windows to air the rooms and change the atmosphere: he was the tenant now. Checking through the agent's inventory he photographed readings from the gas and electric meters on his mobile phone. Money was going to be tight, at least to begin with, and he wasn't going to pay for someone else's fuel usage, no matter how much of a model tenant he had been. Making up the bed was next and then what? How was he going to fill the rest of the evening? What's more, how was he going to fill all the evenings to come, now that she was no longer part of his life?

There was a knock on the door. Who even knew he was here, he thought, as he peered through the spy hole in the front door. A short grey haired old lady stood outside on the landing. He took off the chain and opened the door.

"Hello, I hope you don't mind me interrupting you. I know you must be busy unpacking and everything but I just wanted to introduce myself. My name's Mrs McNiven and I live along the landing. When I say I, I mean we. I live with my husband Bill, but he's deaf, watches the tv all the time. He wouldn't know if someone new had moved in next door or if Jason was still living here."

He could hear the Countdown clock coming from a television deep inside the neighbouring flat and judging by the volume deduced that if anyone was sat in close proximity to it then they were either already hard of hearing or soon would be.

"I hope you like living here," said his neighbour. "We liked having Jason here. We were sad when he moved." She handed him a plate with some home made scotch pancakes on it. "I've made these this afternoon. I hope you like them."

There was a call from inside the adjacent flat.

"He'll be wondering where I am. I'd better go. You can let me have the plate back another time."

With that she was gone and he was left standing on his doorstep holding a plate of pancakes and feeling slightly puzzled. This was compounded by the realisation that he hadn't even introduced himself. There would be another day for that he concluded, as he closed the door behind him. He smiled to himself as he contemplated the welcome to the city that he had just received.

He put the plate down in the kitchen and went through to the living room eating one of the pancakes. He'd left the window open and sounds from the street below distracted him. He looked out. A group of young people were standing around some communal wheeliebins, one of them astride a motorbike. As he peered down the rider revved its engine making it sound more like a demented wasp he thought than a serious mode of transport. He hoped that he hadn't moved in opposite the meeting point for the area's disaffected youth. The engine revved again. He sighed. The agent hadn't put that on the particulars of his new home. His new home! Everything had happened so quickly: the break up, the advert, the interview, the move. Now here he was about to start a new life in the city that he had loved since a child.

....

Waking up the following morning, he was disturbed by the noise of gulls mewing and calling to each other outside. They were a menace to many people, but they also had a certain majesty, particularly herring gulls which as he had often noticed were never in awe of their surroundings, always on the look out for opportunity. That was him now, on the look out for opportunity. He lay in bed, taking in the lay out of the room and pondering his surroundings more generally. Opportunity was what had brought him to the city, he reflected, that and probably the most uncomfortable long distance train service that the franchised rail system could provide. He laughed to himself. Voyagers they were called. They might look like leftovers from a Star Trek convention with their swishing striped doors, but they were grossly uncomfortable and notoriously short of luggage room, particularly for such a long journey. He'd once got chatting to a driver whilst waiting for a late running train, who'd told him how it gave him a sense of purpose to see people waiting on platforms to meet others on his train. Maybe so, he sighed, but there had been no one to meet him when he had arrived in the city the day before.

He opened the curtains and peered out over the rooftops. At least it wasn't raining. Auld Reekie had at least spared him that on his first day in her midst. It might as well have been though. The haar was in. He closed the curtains again. There'd not really been an opportunity to do any shopping the previous evening, he consoled himself, and there was nothing in for breakfast. He had a bottle of water and a couple of biscuits left over from the train, as well as the last of Mrs McNiven's pancakes. They tided him over as he got washed and dressed.

There was no answer from his neighbour so he decided to return her plate later. Making his way downstairs, he opened the door onto the street. Turning up the collar on his jacket, he was immediately reminded that the haar is an insidious sort of weather, something that he had forgotten about living in the west of the country. It was no laughing matter as it greeted him with its clammy embrace. He recalled memories of family holidays on the east coast of Yorkshire that had been blighted by the haar's southern cousin, the fret. No sign of the demented Wasp's owner this morning though, he noted, as he stood in the cold clawing mist contemplating which way to go in search of provisions. What to do? Thinking that he would find a supermarket later, he turned right towards the sea that he couldn't quite make out but knew must be there.

On the corner of the sea front were two establishments. One was open: the Espy. Of course, he thought, short for Esplanade. It advertised that it did breakfasts and was open all day. Part pub, part café, one thing struck him immediately: it had an Australian feel. He was going to like Portobello he thought, living by the sea. By the sea! He suddenly realised that he'd never lived by the sea. That was going to be something different.

It wasn't a traditional Scottish pub that was for sure. Away from the bar there was a group of women sitting together drinking coffee. They looked like young mums on leave from the school run, taking time out before the dilemmas of the rest of the day. Staring at the old pictures of Portobello that hung on the walls, he was suddenly aware of neither wanting to appear too casual, nor too much of a tourist. He ordered an Americano with cold milk and a pain aux raisin. How civilised that you could go to the same establishment by day to relax as you could to partake of something altogether stronger later in the evening. It reminded him of some of the trendier bars in Bath that they had occasionally visited when they were new in the city and looking for places to go, not that they had done much of that in more recent times.

His phone buzzed in his pocket. Funny, he thought, for his father to have used one when he had first moved to the city all those years ago, he would first have had to find a phone box, then make sure that he had the right collection of assorted coins. It was a text from the office. Had he arrived safely and was he coming in to see them later on? *'Yes'* he responded. That would keep them happy until he'd finished his pastry and coffee. He wasn't due to start work until later in the week as he wanted a couple of days to settle in. His phone buzzed again. It was his sister: had he remembered it was their parents' wedding anniversary. 'No' he thought, but with a memory for dates like she had, what would be the chance of him ever forgetting. Whilst he was glad of the interest that others showed in him, he felt that his space, his new space, was oddly already being invaded. He'd buy a card and post it later.

One of the coffee drinking mums smiled at him. She was probably slightly older than the others he judged. Her coffee clearly finished she was sitting slightly apart from her friends. He noticed her light brown hair loosely but fashionably tied back in a pony tail and her red dress: some of his friends wouldn't have worn dresses that smart for a wedding let alone a mid-morning coffee, he thought. He sort of smiled back, more of a facial movement than a full smile but an acknowledgement nonetheless. What were they talking about he wondered. Their voices were getting louder and more excited. One of them was showing the others something in a magazine. Fashion? Celebrity? He couldn't make it out. People watching was what they had done on holiday, making up stories about those around about them.

The woman with the ponytail stood up and made her way to the bar. She smiled at him as she went by. He smiled back and his gaze lingered as she passed him. She laughed with the staff behind the bar as she paid her bill. Conscious that he didn't want to seem to be too distracted by her he picked up his phone and looked at the screen as if checking for texts or emails. She walked back past him.

Time to move. He needed to explore. Outside, the haar was still as dense with its all embracing greyness. A ship sounded out in the estuary. Maybe one of the cruise ships that sailed up to the Forth Bridge to allow passengers to stare in awe at its majesty. Not that they would see much today, he chuckled. He walked up Bath Street towards the High Street in search of a bus to take him into the city. He'd need to get to know bus times as he couldn't afford to use taxis all the time.

In the lurking clammy air it seemed a little seedier than he remembered from his first visit. But that suited him. Apart from the Espy he passed an organic café as well. Eating out wasn't going to be an issue. There was also a once proud art deco cinema now turned into a bingo hall. Well if he needed company, it was always there. Crossing the High Street in front of the Town Hall, he made his way to the bus stop proudly displaying the sign 'to the city'. Out of the swirling mist came a No 26 maroon bus. Edinburgh was proud of its buses. It was one of the few places where the global giants of public transport had so far failed to get a hold. It remained to be seen if the city's residents could develop the same love affair with the trams that had taken six years to arrive and which had seemed to dominate every comedian's jokes at the Fringe that they had come to for the last few years. That would be something else that would change. *They* would not be attending the Fringe next year. The Festival, the Fringe, the time of year when Edinburgh becomes a cultural melting pot, or a chaotic Hades, depending on your point of view. He'd be there by himself next summer.

He boarded the bus and took a seat upstairs. He could always lose himself in the bustle of the city centre for a couple of hours. As it was, Princes Street was itself partly embraced by the sea mist when he got off the bus and the attraction of shopping left him. Ignoring the Gardens and The Gallery he pulled up his collar again and headed up The Mound towards the city's University. He crossed the High Street, dodging the rickshaw drivers plying for trade amongst the tourists who weren't put off by the increasingly dreich weather. Edinburgh was one of those places where tourists congregated no matter the weather or time of year. In fact it had become adept at attracting them and providing opportunities for them. As he passed Greyfriars Bobby, the small statue of a faithful dog that was part of Scottish folklore, a gaggle of Japanese tourists asked him to take a photograph for them which he obliged.

Ahead of him lay the beating heartland of the University. This was an area he knew well, having been to many shows here on the Fringe over the years. It was strange though, not to see any posters advertising the season's latest shows or any young people pushing flyers into your hand for unknown comedians.

The Centre for Excellence in Children's Services, strangely abbreviated he thought to CECS, was located in a large former town house on a tree lined square. The building in which CECS was based was also home to other Research Units which together were part of an Independent Institute. CECS occupied the attic area that at one time would have been the servants' quarters. He walked around the square noticing a number of University offices. Nearby were the French and the Political Sciences departments, which should make for some challenging discourses he thought. There were also a number of blue plaques adorning the walls of some of the buildings referring to distinguished former University staff and students who had either lived or worked there in times gone by. He laughed to himself. Perhaps one day they'd put up one to him.

CECS had become a highly respected organisation, partly funded by government grants and partly by research commissions. Its aim was to promote best practice within children's social work throughout Scotland. The former Director had recently taken on responsibility for the Institute itself, hence the post that had arisen for which he had successfully applied. Going forward there were to be two full time researchers and a Co-ordinator based in CECS as well as a number of associates across the country, led and managed by the Director. The Director. It had sounded somewhat grandiose when they had phoned him to offer him the job, but it hadn't taken him long to accept. Over the couple of months since the interview he'd got used to it, it had had chance to become real. He had tried it out amongst friends and found that it fitted. A couple of his former colleagues had teased him about it, suggesting that he was off to Edinburgh to direct a play at next year's Fringe. His mother had been particularly impressed although hadn't fully grasped what the Centre's role actually was. She had kept asking him what it was that he was going to be directing.

After a few minutes of standing opposite the building and inwardly smiling to himself, he walked across the street and up to the front door. He read the name plate once more, somehow doubting himself as to what it said and what he was really doing there. Pressing the intercom buzzer he announced himself: "Hi, this is Matt. I think you're expecting me."

"Aye, we sure are. Come on up," said a disembowelled voice from the intercom.

The door buzzed open. It was time to face his future in the very city in which his father had fashioned his own.

CHAPTER TWO - STARTING OUT
(Summer 1970)

He had been five when he had first heard the word Edinburgh. It was 1970 and his father was going to university there as a mature student. It hadn't been his plan. Back then there were opportunities to work in nearby Teesside in the pharmaceutical industry and a relative had got him a job there on leaving school. Growing up in the post war period though had meant that the need to do national service had got in the way of his career before it had even started, for even as late as 1960 the country still required its young men to give up nearly two years of their lives to undertake largely futile training in the arts of war. Some had become involved in military action during the country's post colonial period; others had been unwitting guinea pigs at the sites of the nuclear bomb testing that went on during the period; whilst rumours abounded that others had spent their required time undertaking menial and largely pointless tasks. By the end of the 1950s though there was pressure to move on from what was increasingly seen as anachronistic and a hark back to a darker period in the country's history.

However, the white heat of the technological revolution that was the 1960s had not yet taken control when Matt's father's turn came to receive his call up papers. They had appeared like every other young man of the times did in the form of a brown envelope through the post from the Ministry of Labour and National Service. He had been expecting it for some time. Others that his father knew had had theirs and although one or two had been called away to distant RAF bases, most made the comparatively short journey to Catterick Camp, the army's main base in the north of England, to report for their period in uniform. For him though, there had always been an alternative; one that required him to be at least as resolute and strong as many of those who enrolled without question.

Matt's father came from an old North Riding of Yorkshire family with a longstanding non-conformist religious tradition. His grandfather had been a conscientious objector towards the end of the First World War. Instead of fighting he had joined an ambulance train, something which was far from an easy alternative, having come under shell fire in spite of its clear Red Cross markings, with many of those on board being killed. Following in his own father's footsteps, Matt's father had therefore applied for exemption from military service. Although the outcome wasn't a foregone conclusion, the fact that everyone knew that national service was coming to an end had helped to persuade the judge at the tribunal in Leeds. He had given Matt's father three choices: to work in a hospital, in forestry or on the land. Not having a fondness for the sight of blood he'd chosen the land and had subsequently found himself assigned to work on a large moorland estate in the northern Pennines. As a result, he'd had to move from his home on the edge of the Cleveland Hills to the south of Middlesbrough, forty or so miles to the west.

The Pennines form the backbone of England. At their southern end they are made of harsh dark gritstone with steep sided valleys and flat topped boggy hills. The industrial revolution took hold in the area. The fast flowing rivers and later locally mined coal provided energy to power the factories that sprung up in the valley bottoms, whilst the sprawling houses clung to the hillsides above. They were at times bleak though nevertheless strong communities each with their own sense of identity. By contrast, towards their northern end, the Pennines become mellower, made predominantly of carboniferous limestone though topped off in places by some inspiring gritstone summits. No less harsh in the teeth of an autumn gale or when the snow gathers in the depths of winter and cuts off upland farms for days at a time, somehow the pale more rounded stone promotes an optimism within the valleys, or Dales as they are known, that characterise the area. One such Dale, Yoredale, runs from west to east for about thirty miles from the high fells and lean pastures, carved through by the Settle to Carlisle railway, to the more gentle rolling scenery of the area around Hattonbridge. The area is renowned the world over for its white crumbly cheese often eaten at Christmas time with fruit cake. The village of Hattonbridge lies at the junction of a smaller tributary Dale, Hattondale, which is named after the river that flows down it and in turn gives its name to the village.

Matt's father had moved into lodgings in the village, or 'digs' as they were known at the time. Here he had not only completed his required period of national service, but also discovered his love of working on the land. When his two years was completed he had stayed on after being offered a job as part of the estate management team and all thoughts of a career developing new drugs in industrial Teesside were replaced by ones of tramping across the limestone wilderness that dominated that part of northern England.

He'd also found time to fall in love.

Matt's mother was from the nearby cathedral town of Ripon and after training had got a job as a district nurse in the area.

Her role was to support young mothers and elderly residents of Yoredale in what still felt like the new National Health Service. It hadn't taken long for Matt's father's future to become intertwined with that of his mother's when they married in late June in 1962.

Money was extremely tight to begin with and, although they had a tied cottage in the village, they were largely reliant on her wage to get by. It was the harsh winter of 1962 - 63 when they had first started trying for a family. It might have been the cold nights and the occasional power cuts that followed, or the relief of having completed his national service. But it was also the 1960s and the post-war era was at last behind them. In its place were opportunity, modernity and freedom of expression. Matt's mother was already working, unlike many of her friends, and, as the district nurse, had a position of respect within the community. It was nearly two years though before she had finally fallen pregnant and she had almost given up hope. Her mother had told her that she was working too hard and that she would need to give up work if she wanted to conceive. Her grandmother had, ironically, given her more support and encouragement and told her not to give up hope. Children were to be treasured, she would say. But like treasure, they're not always easy to find.

It was spring 1965 when Matt was born and there was great celebration in both families. He was the first grandchild and his grandparents were supportive of his mother. His early memories were happy ones, growing up in Hattonbridge. The cottage's small back garden with its apple tree and vegetable plot was his first playground. There were other young families in the village and the children became close friends even before they started school. There was very little traffic through the village at that time and the children were used to playing in each others gardens and on the village green in the shade of the large horse chestnut trees that grew there, under the watchful gaze of one of their mothers, or Sergeant Woodward, the village policeman.

Meanwhile, Matt's father had started to make a career on the estate and he had been encouraged to seek a qualification in order to progress further. Studying for a degree was not something that anyone from either of their families had ever done and when it was first suggested, there was much consternation. Why did he need to? Where would he go? How would his wife manage, particularly with a young child to look after? Theirs was a strong relationship though and they had found a way of supporting him to do it, with a combination of her salary, a scholarship that he successfully applied for and a small grant from the estate.

What was a surprise to everyone though was that he chose Edinburgh. It was the result of a chance conversation one day in the estate office when a consultant who had been called in, had spoken highly of the University and what it had to offer. Matt's father had made enquiries and liked what he found and the die was cast after he had visited for an interview. It was the late 60s and the city was alive, the Festival already a feature of the calendar. The Forth Road Bridge had been open for a few years and the Commonwealth Games were to be staged in the city at the newly built Meadowbank Stadium and Commonwealth Pool. There was a sense of excitement in that part of Scotland which he quickly aligned to. His family were still puzzled though as to why he needed to leave Yorkshire, or indeed the north of England. Surely, Leeds, York or even Durham could have offered him the same opportunity?

September 1970 finally arrived and the day came when he had to go. Matt's grandparents had been to visit them the day before and had wished his father well. But on the day when he finally left it was just the three of them. It was a fine late summer's Sunday morning, the day before he was due to start his course in Edinburgh, and Matt's mother had driven them to the station in Northallerton. In those days it was the county town of the North Riding of Yorkshire with a wide main street on which both the twice weekly market and the annual May fair were held. Trips to the town were special for Matt and his parents. They had been there only a few weeks earlier to buy him his first shoes for starting school and afterwards his father had taken him to the cattle market as a treat. For Matt it was a magical place, the air heavy with the smells and noises of the animals together with the chatter of the Dales farmers.

His mother had cried as they stood on the platform to say goodbye to his father. At that moment he did not know where Edinburgh was, although he knew that that was where his father was heading. The deep throated tone of the large Deltic diesel engine roared and the train started its journey north passing the milk processing factory buildings that adjoined the station. They'd watched it go, watched it into the distance towards Darlington until they couldn't see it anymore. Then they'd walked in silence back to the car before heading up the Dale and home, just the two of them.

It was a strange atmosphere in the house that evening. Something was missing: his father's voice. His mother had tried to make up for it by playing an extra game and reading him two stories before he went to bed. But lying there unable to sleep, he could hear her downstairs gently sobbing. Even though he was still young, it seemed that Edinburgh had a lot to answer for.

The next day he had gone off to school, reciting words in his head in the way that he did. He had tried Edinburgh before but this time it didn't seem right. He didn't want it to lose its meaning and had quickly changed it to others that he knew would soon become incomprehensible collections of sounds in his mind.

That day they had learned about Ghana, a place in Africa where chocolate came from, or so he had understood. They were to draw pictures of a cocoa pod and the best would be entered into a competition to win some chocolate. He wasn't sure what a cocoa pod was but thought it might be like a very large pea pod like the ones that his father had grown in their garden that summer. Mrs Simpson, his teacher, had opened up a map of the world to show them where Ghana was, but he had wanted to look at another map, one which showed him his own country, one which showed him where his father was. Mrs Simpson had explained to him that Edinburgh was in Scotland and was a long way away but not as far as Ghana. Apparently Ghana and Scotland weren't even on the same page in the book. That made Edinburgh sound like a long way away because chocolate came into the village in Mr Taylor, the shopkeeper's van - he'd seen it - and yet you needed a train to get to Scotland!

A few days later when he got home from school he found a postcard waiting for him. It showed a large bridge over which trains could travel. The bridge was red and looked as though it was made from Meccano. The postcard was from his father and it explained that he had arrived safely and that he was living with a family who were looking after him. Why did his father need another family to look after him, he thought? He had a family of his own here in the Dale.

He took the postcard to his bedroom that evening and put it on the table by the side of his bed. He lay there staring at it, imagining that the train that was visible on the bridge was the one that his father had travelled on to go to Edinburgh and that it was on its way back with his father still on it. He showed the card to his grandparents who had come up from Ripon to see Matt and his mother that weekend, but they were more interested in knowing how she was, than what was on his card. He'd taken it outside and had sat under the apple tree. Clearly if his father had chosen it and sent it to him then it must be an important place.

When he had gone back inside, his grandparents and mother were deep in conversation. He couldn't understand what they were talking about, but his grandmother seemed to be very concerned and she had her arm around his mother's shoulders.

"It'll be easier next time, my dear. It always is," he had heard her say.

"I know," his mother had replied. "That's what I tell some of my mums. But it won't make it any easier if I'm here by myself. And with Matthew to look after as well. How are we going to manage Mum?"

Matt stood by the back door holding the postcard from his father. He looked at it and then out into the garden and to the hills of Hattondale beyond. His life had changed, that he knew. What he didn't know was how it was set to change over the coming months and years.

CHAPTER THREE - EARLY DAYS
(October 2013)

CECS had been the brainchild of its founder and former director, Helen Goddard. Under her leadership it had achieved international renown, advising governments and councils about the care of children. She was well respected amongst her peers in the research community and academia. Matt knew that she was going to be a hard act to follow, particularly as she would also be his manager and still very much hands-on. However, Matt had known of her work for a number of years and had met her and heard her speak at conferences. In fact, although a key reason for applying for the job had been his need to leave Bath, the opportunity to work with Helen Goddard had certainly influenced his decision.

The former townhouse, within which the Institute and CECS were based, was on what would have once been a fashionable square to house Edinburgh's growing elite. Not quite as renowned as the New Town to the north of Princes Street, but in its day just as grandiose with wide streets and built around a private garden. Assigned to the attic area, the Centre's offices suited Matt: far enough away from the front door and the bustle of the Institute's main business, but still very much able to influence its direction. He was keen for CECS to be part of Helen's vision for the future and had said so at his interview. It would do neither its, nor his own reputation any harm.

Alison, the Centre's Co-coordinator, had shown him round when he had emerged from the haar earlier in the week, but today was his first day for real. It had been a struggle to get up and to get organised. He had worked mainly from home in Bath and the prospect of getting back into the routines and culture of office life was not something that he was looking forward to. However, he shouldn't have worried. Alison had gone out of her way to make him feel welcome. She had a cafetière of coffee already made when he arrived, the aroma wafting down the stairs as he made his way up.

"Don't think you'll get this every day," she said. "Unless you make it that is!"

By half past nine she'd introduced him to the Health and Safety notices; invited him to join an office sweepstake on who was going to be the next Rector of the nearby University - he'd get back to her later on that one, he said; showed him the battered biscuit tin that housed the tea and coffee fund; and the notice reminding everyone to do their own washing up. It was a notice which, judging by the pile of dirty cups and other lunch time detritus in the sink was, he observed, as ignored in this office as similar ones were in offices elsewhere. Why office workers seemed so unconcerned about hygiene issues was something that had always amazed him. Maybe there was another PhD thesis in there if only he could find the time.

Alison showed him to his office which looked out over the square and the garden that it surrounded. She said that Helen had had to go to a meeting elsewhere in the city first thing but would like to catch him later in the afternoon. Matt replied that he wasn't looking to stay late on his first day as he imagined that there would be plenty of time for that later and in any event, he had to confess, he really needed to do some food shopping or he'd be going hungry.

"Where was he living?" she'd asked.

"Portobello," he'd replied.

"That'll be EH15 then, very nice." Alison smiled as she left him too it.

He gazed out of the window onto the street below. He knew it from visiting the Festival, when in most years it became part of the Fringe. One year in particular, he recalled, a Spiegeltent had been pitched in the garden. They had been there to a recording of a radio comedy programme. For a moment he was wistful as he thought of the two of them chuckling together as the comedians on the panel game had vied with each other to make the audience laugh. In his mind's eye he could see the throngs of festival goers on the street below, the two of them amongst them.

In reality what he actually saw were groups of new students aimlessly milling around, unsure, like him, of where to go or what to do next. His father must have once been in that same position when he had first arrived in Edinburgh many years earlier. Matt sighed as he thought of how it wouldn't have been easy for his father, at least to begin with. He'd spoken to him from his sister's and, unusually for his father, he had offered him encouragement and said that both he and his mother were looking forward to coming up to Edinburgh to visit him once he was settled.

Later that afternoon, he was going through some files when there was a knock on the door. Helen entered, not waiting for a reply.

"Matt," Helen said. "It's good to see you here at last." She was a few years older than him and was married with two sons, both away at university.

"Good to be here," he replied. "I can't wait to get started. It's an important year with the new legislation and a new future for the country no matter what happens."

They talked of some of the work that was in the pipeline and that he would be involved in. Helen told him about the other staff who worked in the Centre and who were looking forward to meeting him. She also asked him about how much he knew of Edinburgh. He lied and said that he had a lot to learn. Although on saying so, he realised that that was actually true: what was it about the place that had taken so much of him and yet had come to represent so much to him over so many years?

After a while, Matt remembered that he had not really settled in to his new flat and that he needed to shop. Excusing himself and arranging to meet with the others the following day, Matt let himself out of the back door of the building. Standing momentarily, he sighed deeply. It was going to be different. In the distance beyond the tenement buildings of the south side of the city he could see the outline of Salisbury Crags emerging from the gloom of the haar that was finally receding. His sigh became a smile as he realised that for the first time in his life, he was at home, home in the city that for too long he had smelt and touched in his dreams and yet in reality had always eluded him. His smile turned to a grin. He was no longer a visitor. Looking up at the crags and the summit of Arthur's Seat beyond, neither was he the child that had climbed them with his father many years before.

There was a sudden urge though to explore his past and become that child again, even if only for an hour or so. He headed toward the Commonwealth Pool and into the parkland at the foot of the Crags. The road that skirts through the park is a rat run for those who know about it and at that time of the afternoon it was beginning to get busy with those starting their journey home. He took in deep lung fulls of cold damp air as he walked, gathering pace, down through the park towards the Dynamic Earth exhibition, the new Parliament building and Holyrood House itself. He paused outside the Parliament building admiring the optimism of the architecture and the vision for the country that it represented. The wild garden effect in front of the building which was clearly part of that vision was looking suspiciously overgrown no matter what the information board tried to suggest. He overheard the various languages being spoken by the tourists thronging outside the Palace gates, nearly tripping up three of them who were taking a collective 'selfie'.

He walked on, reluctantly becoming an adult again, to find his bus stop on Regent Terrace. The number 26 in its distinctive Lothian colours collected him and navigated its way through the early evening traffic towards the communities that fringe the shores of the Forth to the east of the city. He noticed that they passed a couple of large supermarkets on the way and he made a mental note of them in case he needed to do a big shop. On this occasion he stayed on all the way to Portobello, getting off just before Bath Street. He asked a young couple with a pushchair who were waiting to cross the road if there was a grocers or small supermarket in the town. They pointed him towards one in Bath Street itself which he had somehow overlooked. He managed to find the basics that he needed to get started.

"Muesli. That'll do you more good than the Pain aux Raisin you had the other day," a voice said, admiring his basket. It was the woman from the Espy; the one in the red dress; the one who he had thought had smiled at him. The red dress had gone, replaced by a more casual ensemble of jeans and a loose white blouse, though the hair was still kept neatly in place in its ponytail.

"You're probably right at that," he replied. "It was a nice place though. Nice coffee as well. It would be good to drop in every morning, but I dare say I won't get much chance given I've just started a new job in the city."

"We did wonder, when you came into the Espy."

"And you all get the time to meet up there?"

"Not every day. No. But it's nice when we can. We meet there after everyone's got school out of the way and before lunch. It's a sort of pre-lunch club really."

"Ah, I see."

"Are you new to the area as well, none of us could recall seeing you around before?"

"Yes, new town, new job, new flat," he said.

"... by yourself, or with you someone? Any children?"

"Yes, no and no. In that order," he replied.

"Sorry, that sounded rude."

He didn't hear the apology as it had immediately made him think of all the conversations that they had had over the last few years about starting a family. Not quite the right time. Too soon. Too late. Maybe next year. Maybe after the next job interview. Maybe never. It still seemed real and yet it was already also part of his past. "No, never been in one place long enough I suppose."

He excused himself, muttered something about having to get back, although for what he wasn't sure. He paid for his purchases and made his way outside, turning to smile and noticing once more the smart well groomed ponytail as well as its owner.

He made his way down Bath Street and from a distance gazed up at his flat window. He'd chosen well he thought. It commanded an uninterrupted view up the street. For the second time that day he found himself smiling.

It was cut short though. The Wasp had returned. He heard it before he saw it, but it was unmistakable. Its rider was sitting astride his warhorse revving the beast's throttle. He had attracted a group of other young people; some in awe of the image he presented; some just attracted by the group itself. Judging by the cigarette ends in the gutter he realised that it was a regular haunt and his spirits sank at the prospect of coming home to this little ensemble each evening. He crossed the road in front of them to the door of his flat.

Letting himself in to the hallway and shutting the noise of the Wasp and its admirers outside, he relaxed. There were a set of mailboxes on the wall each with a flat number on it. He was surprised to see a letter poking out of his flat's box. There weren't that many people who knew that he had moved. Eagerly, he opened the box and pulled the white envelope out. The address, with its EH15 postcode, was written in a distinctive handwriting, one he knew well. The Bath and Bristol postmark was all he needed to see. It was from her.

....

By contrast to Matt's recent move to the city, Aurélie Parmentier had arrived in Edinburgh the previous year. She was an only child from what she thought of as an ordinary family living in a village in the foothills of the Alps and far from metropolitan France. Living in the mountains was often romanticised she had come to understand. Outsiders came on holiday and in their minds never left, seeing only the landscapes and feeling only the sun and the pure air on their faces. For her and her friends though, the reality of living in the bottom of a valley was that it was often isolating. What looked picturesque on a postcard was a lot more foreboding on a long November night before the first snows and tourists arrived.

She had specialised in English literature at her local University in Grenoble. Like most young people in France going away to university was not something that she had considered. She had always envied British students and their desire to keep their families at arms length. Those that she had known who had come to work in the ski stations each winter, saw the years between leaving school and getting a job as a time to explore, to experiment with life and, as one of them had once told her, 'to find out where the world bites you on the bum' - something not easily achieved if you lived at home with your parents both in their fifties and a slightly senile grandmother in her early nineties. These young people were known both to each other and to locals alike as 'Seasonaires'. They arrived in the Alps each autumn in the short period between the end of the summer and the grape harvest and the coming of the first snows. They came from other northern European countries usually those which themselves did not get much snow. What was the attraction she and her friends had often wondered? It wasn't as though they were well paid and what little money they had, seemed to be spent on getting drunk. By contrast she had learnt to ski on Wednesday afternoons when, like other French children, she had had the opportunity to learn as part of the curriculum. Consequently she saw skiing as physical exercise rather than as a social activity.

In her third year at Grenoble she had used the opportunity of Erasmus funding from the European Union to study abroad. Her parents had forbidden her from applying for any London institutions. For them, London was too big and dangerous. She had plumped for Edinburgh as it was the only other city on the list that she'd ever heard of. She arrived in late summer 2009 just before the start of the University year and instantly felt at home. Arthur's Seat and the crags around the castle had welcomed her. Mountains in the city! She couldn't have had nothing on her horizon. The buzz around the city was not like anything that she had ever experienced in industrial Grenoble or in her quiet village, even in the height of the tourist season.

On her first day in Edinburgh, the Festival was still in full swing. Getting off the airport bus on Waverley Bridge she had felt an assault on her senses. She stood in the middle of the pavement amongst the throng of people simply breathing it in; immediately in love and yet a person obstacle with her bright red duffle bag and new red and black holdall, bought especially for her first trip outside France. Within minutes she'd been offered information about open top bus tours of the city, had flyers for any number of shows at that year's Fringe thrust into her hand and had had her ears assaulted by the noise of bagpipes coming from the nearby corner of Princes Street. She was in love.

In fact the year had passed quickly and when it was up, Aurélie felt bereft at the thought of leaving Edinburgh and the relative independence that she had had. It was no longer a foreign country. It was home. By the following year she had completed her studies in Grenoble and had vowed to return to Scotland as soon as practically possible after her graduation. She had taken extra classes in conversational English, built up her credits and sought out ways of getting work in Edinburgh, or 'Embra' as she had come to understand it was pronounced from the novels of Iain Banks, the Scottish author whom she had studied whilst at the University.

The day that she had received her letter of acceptance from the British Council confirming her role as a French language assistant at the University, there were mixed emotions within her family. Her mother had cried. She had assumed that Aurélie would return to the village after her studies. That was what young women like Aurélie did. There were many young men in the area for her to settle down with. Her grandmother had cried as well, but more because others were. Her father was perhaps surprisingly more supportive and told her to go and follow her dream. He promised that he and her mother would come and visit as soon as possible if they could find someone to look after her grandmother.

She had arrived back in Edinburgh again towards the end of the Festival and had again enjoyed the crazy vibrancy that is the Scottish capital in late August. Unlike her first baptism into the melting pot of Edinburgh festivals she had quickly got hold of a Fringe brochure and had managed to see a couple of comedians, although she did not understand all the accents let alone all the humour!

After first staying with a family, the Robertson's in Morningside, she had found her own flat. Although she had hoped to find somewhere in the Grassmarket, she had decided that the constant buzz and the noise of the traffic on the cobbles would be too much for someone used to drifting off to sleep to a deafening silence. She had found a small garden flat just to the south of The Meadows, an area with a student feel and yet only a short walk to the University, or 'le fac' as she still thought of it in French. Aware that her salary was not going to give her the security she needed she had advertised in local shops in the Bruntsfield and Morningside areas to give French language lessons to school children. She gambled that there would be some aspirational parents who would be content to pay her to help their offspring develop their otherwise dubious skills in the French language. Her gamble paid off and she was not short of extra work. It was a good way to get to know people and she enjoyed it even though she often wondered how many of the young people she taught would ever use the talent that she motivated in them; apart from maybe an odd winter as a Seasonaire.

Once she had settled into her flat she had very quickly developed a morning routine that saw her ready for work within an hour, showered, dressed, make up on and out of the house. Even though a year on she had now brought Hubert, her car that her parents had bought her when she had graduated, over from France, she still preferred to walk to work at the University. She could get across the grassy area of The Meadows thinking of home in the campagne, yet planning the day in the city. Like most French people that she knew though, there was always time for a coffee and a croissant. She had often been complimented on her ability to eat a croissant without dropping a single crumb!

That morning she was running late. Her mother had been on the phone the previous evening. Her grandmother was not well again and her mother was, as usual, worried. Would she please think of coming home and help to look after her, her mother had asked. She'd reminded her mother again that she had responsibilities and commitments in Edinburgh and that she couldn't just drop everything. Consequently she'd gone to bed restless and had slept in.

Fortunately she knew that there was a coffee bar on the street near the departmental offices, so she'd skipped breakfast at home thinking that she could get it there on her way into work. Aware that she was already late, she had stood slightly impatiently in the queue. With her double espresso and croissant in one hand she scrambled to put her purse away with the other. She turned, not concentrating on what or who was around her. Suddenly the coffee collided with an outstretched arm, whose owner was himself in the process of ordering his coffee. The hot liquid dispersed itself quickly, not only down the man's arm but splattering across the pavement and the front of the coffee bar. The young man shrieked as the hot coffee soaked into his jacket.

"Excuse moi, Monsieur!" Aurélie exclaimed, the suddenness of the incident causing her to resort to her native tongue. "I'm so sorry."

The barista from the coffee bar crawled out from his box as quickly as he could clutching a handful of paper towel thrusting it towards the young man who was gradually recovering his stance. Removing his coffee stained jacket he gratefully took the paper towel and animatedly wiped at his arm. Aurélie held her head with one hand and the dripping coffee cup and sodden paper bag containing her croissant in the other, whilst continuing to apologise profusely. "Let me take your jacket. I'll get it cleaned. How's your arm? Is it burnt? Do you need to get someone to look at it?"

"No, I think I'll live. But the jacket's a bit of a mess," the young man said.

"Look, here's my card," said Aurélie. "I teach at the French department over there," she said pointing at the terraced house at the other side of the square. "But I also teach French privately. This is my business card. It's got my phone number on it. Give me a ring and let me know what it costs. I'll pay for a new one if necessary."

"Thanks," the young man said. "My name's Gavin. I work in the laboratory down the other end of the square." He extended his hand, which Aurélie shook gratefully. "Don't worry, it was an accident. Just my luck to be stood in the way, I guess."

They parted with the young man promising to let her know what it cost and laughing saying that he might get her to give him some free French lessons in compensation. Aurélie looked at the soggy mess of cardboard, paper and croissant in her hand. She had gone off the idea of breakfast by this time and put the remnants in the bin by the side of the coffee stall. Hurriedly, she made her way over to the department building by now aware that she must be very late indeed.

By contrast, Matt had been up sharp that morning, determined to make an early impression amongst his new colleagues and aware that his usual owl like behaviour would mean that he was more likely to be late than early in future. She had been very much a lark, always wanting to be in bed when he had been thinking about a late night movie and opening a bottle of his favourite single malt whisky. Nevertheless, that morning he had managed to get to the department before anyone apart from Alison. He'd used the time productively, arranging things in the office, moving the desk closer to the window to give him more natural light as well as more of a view of the square below. He'd binned a couple of old calendars and taken down an old departmental phone list that still showed Helen as the Centre's Director. A rather dead looking spider plant had gone as well. The Centre for Excellence in Children's Services and he were alike he thought: they both needed to move on.

Content with his furniture moving he'd offered to make Alison a coffee along with one for himself in return for the mobile phone and business cards that she presented him with. Returning to the window in his own office with his coffee he admired his name on the new business cards. Although he was happy to give 'Director' a try, he hoped he could live up to it.

Matt gazed out across the square from his vantage point three floors up. There was an old police box at the corner. Like many in Edinburgh, this one had been retained and put to another use. It had become a coffee bar, clearly a honey pot for office workers like him and students from the nearby university as they hurried to and from lectures. There were a few people standing in front of the open hatch waiting their turn for the young barista to perform what always seemed to him to be an unnecessarily complex ritual to produce a cup of coffee. A young woman was at the front of the queue. She had long brown hair and carried a large red duffle bag over one shoulder. She had taken custody of the coffee and seemed to be wrestling with her bag. Suddenly the young man behind her was gesticulating wildly, thrashing his arms around. The barista had crawled out from behind the bar and was intervening between the two of them. Matt assumed that the young man had been trying to 'dip' the young woman's bag. There appeared to have been an argument between the two of them and the young man had taken his jacket off. Things looked to have become heated. In the end the young woman had hurried away clearly unnerved by her encounter. Matt noticed that she'd gone into one of the neighbouring University buildings and he thought he ought to follow to offer to be a witness in case she wanted to call the police.

Just as he was putting his jacket on to leave there was a knock on the door. Helen entered along with Anna and Dougie, the other two members of the Centre's staff. Helen introduced them all and called Alison through as well. Before long they were sharing experiences and contacts, names of others in the research field or across children's services throughout the country, some of whom Matt was already familiar with. Helen left them talking and offered to make a pot of fresh coffee. Thoughts of what he had witnessed earlier left him as they got involved in a discussion of the team's work and who was currently doing what and it was lunch time before Matt remembered his earlier intention to be the Good Samaritan.

CHAPTER FOUR - FIRST IMPRESSIONS
(Autumn 1970)

When Matt and his mother lived together in Hattonbridge in the early 1970s it was a small but thriving village with most of its residents living and working locally. Although a few cottages had become second homes there was still little in the way of a tourist industry. Yes, there were day-trippers at a weekend, but they mostly stood around the village green, or sat on one of the benches eating an ice cream from Taylor's Shop. Most had melted away by Sunday evenings. Things were changing though. Alf Braithwaite, the landlord at The Hattonbridge Inn had introduced basket meals, although some of the local farmers would challenge him that when he started serving soup in a basket they'd be impressed and take up his offer. Until then, they'd stick to their pints of bitter and pork scratchings.

The village was built around the green with a row of detached and terraced cottages on either side. At its top end was a farm, whilst at the bottom end stood the church. The main road from Ripon up Yoredale to the north-west skirted the bottom corner of the green before passing by the Hattonbridge Inn. The primary school was about half way up the green on its west side with a playground behind. Lying just outside the Yorkshire Dales National Park, planning permission had not been an issue and a new housing estate, called Pennine View, had been added in the year before Matt had started school. Most residents felt that it had changed the character of the village, but the number of young families who had moved in had at least meant that the school had stayed open. There were also three shops: a butcher's, a post office and Taylor's grocery shop. The road that led past the farm at the top of the green and the few cottages beyond very quickly became a single track road as it wended its way up Hattondale to Skelton and eventually south over the high tops towards Wharfedale and beyond to the industrial heartland of the West Riding of Yorkshire.

Their house was on the road to Skelton and just beyond the village boundary at the foot of Hattondale. Unlike the rest of the village which was built predominantly of sandstone, their cottage was made of local limestone, giving a glint in the sun and a sheen in the rain. Facing due south, Matt's bedroom window looked towards Skelton at the top of the Dale and the high fells beyond. As a growing child in the 1970s these quickly became his playground. In later years, when he'd left the Dale he would often long for its peace particularly when he needed space to think or make decisions.

Although it was a tied cottage, to Matt it was home: the family home; their family home; his family home. Even as a young child he had felt the warm glow and certainty of family life. There were routines that were inexplicable to an outsider, but to the family were just the way it was. Pikelets toasted on the open fire in the sitting room on a Saturday afternoon. Wash day and consequently hot water, every Monday and Thursday mornings and, if he was lucky, fish and chips from Leyburn on a Friday tea time that his mother would bring with her after work.

But in 1970 that had changed when his father left for Edinburgh. Matt and his mother had had to settle into a new routine, just the two them and to look after themselves. His mother had had to reduce her hours to ensure that she was at home by 3.30 every afternoon for Matt finishing school and with his father away, there was less money in the house and no fish and chips on Friday evenings.

It had taken some weeks for Matt to understand why his father had apparently left them and even then he wasn't sure. It was true that he would be coming home for holidays and in the mean time would regularly send his son post cards, at least one a week. But these were no substitute for having his father at home. Most of the postcards were of famous steam engines that he had never heard of. They were not like the Deltic diesels that pulled the Edinburgh trains out of Northallerton. They were from a different generation, or so he believed. His mother had bought him a scrapbook to keep them all in and from the very first he had stuck them in with glue thus permanently obscuring the text that his father had so conscientiously written out in a neat handwriting that his son would be able to read. His father recounted things he had done, places he had visited and the people he had met. He kept repeating that Matt and his mother should visit Edinburgh. It was a beautiful place, somewhere to fall in love with; but his mother had seemed less enthusiastic.

Matt knew that his mother was not happy and seemed to be crying when she was by herself. He heard her from the garden when he was out playing, or from his bedroom when the house was quiet in an evening. He'd asked her if everything was all right and she'd said yes, though he didn't believe her.

By late October the usual autumnal gales were ripping through the Dale, not only taking the leaves off the trees but in some cases whole branches, including those on the village green. Roads were flooded and the Yore had broken its banks in two or three places. One particular night the wind was very strong and the rain was lashing against the front of the cottage. Matt was unable to sleep and had taken refuge in his mother's bed. She had hugged him tight.

"Would you like to go and visit your Dad?" she had asked him as they lay in the dark.

"What, now?" he had asked back.

"No, in a week or so. There's something I'd like to talk to him about and I don't want to do it on the telephone."

The rain clattered against the window.

"I really want to see Dad," he said, "but I don't want to go anywhere now."

"No, not tonight. Not in that weather out there, silly. And anyway, there won't be any trains at this time of night."

It was a Friday in late November when Matt and his mother eventually stood on Northallerton station with their bags packed. She had taken the day off work and had told the school that Matt would not be in that day. It was a cold morning and there had been talk of snow in the Dale. They had had to catch a local train as far as Newcastle. Standing on the platform under the great canopy of the Victorian station Matt heard the unmistakable roar of the Deltic before he saw it. To a nearly six year old boy it was a leviathan, another one of his favourite words. His eyes were wide as it drew past them pulling its blue and white coaches.

They arrived in Edinburgh a few hours later and his Dad met them at Waverley station. There were hugs all round and both of his parents cried, something that he found hard to understand. Emerging onto Princes Street, Matt's eyes widened and his jaw dropped. Even though some of the postcards that his father had sent were of the city itself, he wasn't prepared for what he saw. Everything was big: the buildings, the people, the skyline. It was more enclosed than anything in the Dale. And the buses. All the buses were double deckers! He tried reading the names on the front of them. They were letters and words he couldn't understand.

"What would you like to do first?" his father asked.

His mother said that she was tired after the journey and would really like to sit down somewhere. Matt's father had arranged to borrow a camp bed and had agreed with the Strachans, the family that he was lodging with, that the three of them would stay in his room for the weekend. He explained though that it wasn't very large and they probably ought to find somewhere else to sit just now.

Matt had stood by his parents' side gazing at the sight in front of him. There was what appeared to him to be a church. Unlike the one in Hattonbridge it had a tall pointed spire but it had no walls. Inside it was a large white man sat on a similarly large white chair. But the man didn't move! Matt was confused.

His father noticed him staring. "What do you make of him then, Matt?" he asked. "That's Sir Walter Scott. A very important man in these parts."

"But he's sitting very still," Matt said.

His Dad laughed. "That's because he's a statue!"

Apart from the gargoyles on the church in the village, Matt had never seen a statue of a person before.

Matt walked past the Scott monument in Princes Street Gardens with a parent on each hand. To passers by, a very happy young family.

A short while later they were sitting in the café in Jenner's department store looking out over the same gardens. His father pointed out the castle and promised him that they would go there tomorrow. They all had soup and a bread roll, although it was not a sort of soup that Matt was used to and he found it a strange taste. Edinburgh was not only bigger than Hattonbridge, it also had different food.

His parents had talked, holding each other's hands, and Matt hadn't been able to understand what they were saying, although he was more preoccupied with the sights and sounds outside. The city was also a noisy place. After eating they made their way out on to Princes Street and caught one of the double decker buses. They went upstairs and Matt sat at the front with his father. It took them over the top of the station and past even more high buildings, eventually taking them to what Matt thought was a field, except there were no animals, just people and bikes. It was becoming a very unusual day.

"Welcome to The Meadows," his father had said. "Nearly there!"

They walked a short way before going into one of the buildings. It was dark and there were stairs inside leading to other doors. His father opened one of these and they went in. Mr and Mrs Strachan met them.

"Come on in. You must be Matt. Your Dad's told us all about you."

Matt clung to his mother, not sure what to say or do.

"Let's put the kettle on. You'll be wanting a drink," said Mrs Strachan.

His father showed them through to his room and tea was duly brought through. The three of them sat on the single bed.

"Well this is alright," his father said. "The three of us together again."

His mother didn't look as sure.

Later that evening, his parents had got him ready for bed and Matt had lain down on the camp bed by the window. He lay there, pulling the blankets up around his shoulders and closing his eyes as his father read him a story.

"I think he's asleep," he said.

"Good, because there's something that I need to talk to you about," replied his mother.

The two of them sat back on the bed.

"I know that you like it here and it does look really nice. Matt seems to like it. But ..."

"It's a great city; everyone has been really friendly."

"Will you stop, will you listen?"

"What is it?"

"I'm pregnant."

There was silence on the bed for a few minutes.

"That's great." He paused nervously. "I mean how long, how long have you known, how far are you on?"

"I'm nearly three months, I found out just after you left. I'm scared though. I just don't know how I'm going to manage with Matt and a baby with you away."

A baby, Matt thought as he lay under the covers, his eyes still closed. That was going to be different. It had indeed been a very unusual day.

CHAPTER FIVE - A MEETING OF MINDS
(November 2013)

Matt had left a message at the French department at the University. Not quite sure who he was trying to contact he'd left his details with the departmental secretary the following day. His description of the young woman he'd seen at the coffee stall hadn't rung any immediate bells but the secretary had said she would ask around. There had been no contact and a couple of weeks had gone by.

He found himself settling into a routine. EH15 was beginning to feel like home and the flat had begun to feel more like his. He had bought a rug and a lamp. Things that in the past, she would have bought. They were important to him now. They were his mark on his territory. Anna at the Centre had remarked one day that he was in danger of becoming a student again. That thought had also occurred to him early on as he sat in the flat with his few possessions. But things changed when the container had arrived from Bath. That was what her letter had been about. She had arranged for a removal company to collect all his books and research studies. They'd been delivered minus the bookcases that had previously housed them and he'd arranged them chronologically around the floor of his living room. He would need a trip to a certain Swedish Furniture Shop he thought and had checked that there was one in Edinburgh. How had the world stored books before the invention of the Allen key, he wondered? She'd also added in his music collection, including his records that he no longer had the means to play. The letter which he'd found waiting for him that first evening he returned from the Centre, had also included the invoice from the removal company. It was a gesture that summed up where their relationship had deteriorated to. Bath was fast becoming a distant memory.

Although work meant that he had not been back to the Espy for breakfast, he had been in on a couple of other occasions, although he hadn't seen Ponytail again. By contrast, he had seen the Wasp most evenings and was even on nodding terms with its owner. It fascinated him how groups of young people were a challenge for those who didn't know them and yet the majority were doing nothing more than being young. He wondered whether anyone had ever asked them what they wanted and made a note to himself, to engage them in conversation one evening to see what facilities there were for them in Portobello.

It was a Friday and the end of his first month. His sister had texted him. Had he sent a card to their parents? *Yes*, he had replied. Why did she always think he might he forget?

It was also Alison's birthday and he and his new colleagues were going out for a drink after work. He'd also put himself in charge of the team collection and had gone into town at lunchtime to buy a card and some flowers. He was walking back to the Centre past the University Visitor Centre. He immediately thought of the times that he, that they, had been a visitor, something he no longer was. Suddenly his thoughts were brought back to the present. Through the glass door he could see a young woman making a purchase. It was her. Should he wait? She hadn't responded to his message. What would he say? His mind raced.

Inside, Aurélie completed her purchase: a hoodie for Nadine, her friend back home. It would be her birthday and she had promised to send something of Edinburgh and the University. Putting her purse away and her bag over her shoulder, she headed out. There was a man looking at her. He was an older man she thought. He was hesitating, looking as though he wanted to say something.

"Can I help you?" she said, approaching him.

"I'm sorry," stumbled Matt, "I was wondering. Do you work at the French Department over there," he said, pointing towards the square. "I think I may have left a message for you a couple of weeks ago. I think I saw you the day that you were at the Coffee Bar, you know. I think when that young guy tried to rob you ..."

"Excuse me?" Aurélie replied. "When what guy tried to rob me? Are you sure you've got the right person?"

Matt explained that he worked in the attic office further down the square. That he'd been stood at the window one morning. That he'd seen a commotion.

Things were becoming clearer for Aurélie. Of course, it must have been the morning that she had bumped into Gavin. Literally. She explained what had actually happened.

Matt immediately felt embarrassed. Blushing, he apologised profusely. "I'm really sorry. You must think me a right eejit!"

"Oh, don't worry. I'm flattered you wanted to help me." Aurélie said in her now mixed franco-scottish accent. "I must get back to work."

"Yes, you're right." Matt replied. The two of them walked back towards the square each making some inept comment about coffee and the way it brings people together - sometimes more closely than its consumers could have predicted. There was probably another PhD thesis in there, Matt speculated, although the number of potential PhD subjects was becoming more than any sane person would ever have time to complete.

The afternoon passed by. Matt presented Alison with the card and flowers. Alison said they shouldn't have bothered. Dougie whispered to Matt that there would have been trouble if they hadn't. At the end of the afternoon the team had wandered up to the High Street. Out of season, Edinburgh's citizens were venturing back into the tourist areas of the city like returning ants to the centre of a disturbed nest. For a few weeks before the Christmas shoppers and Hogmanay revellers arrived, the Royal Mile once again became the Canongate, the High Street and the Lawnmarket and overheard accents were less likely to be Spanish or American. The team found its way to the Jolly Judge, a bar down a side close near the castle. The bar had an underground feel to it but with a sense of warmth and belonging. Helen had stayed for one drink and a couple of Alison's friends had joined them. The late afternoon after-work drink, Matt thought, was at risk of turning into an early evening session as he observed many of the bar's drinkers making their excuses and heading home to the city's outlying suburbs and their families that would be waiting for them. The first of the weekend's revellers had started to replace them, prompting Alison and her friends to decide to head off for a birthday meal leaving Dougie and Matt. After a while Dougie left as well and Matt found himself contemplating a nearly empty glass and wondering how the rest of the weekend was going to develop.

Across the now less crowded bar his gaze and his thoughts about what he was going to do with the weekend, came into focus. Someone was smiling back at him. The same young woman that he had met earlier that afternoon. She beckoned him over. Matt stood and began to cross the bar when he noticed that she was with the young man that he had earlier accused of robbing her.

"Come and join us," Aurélie said. "Gavin, this is Matt who I was telling you about."

Matt immediately thought about what she had been saying about him. About how his misunderstanding might not have appeared as funny in the re-telling as it had done earlier that afternoon when the two of them had worked out the unlikely chain of circumstances. "I probably ought to apologise," began Matt.

"Ahh, dinnae worry mate, stranger things have happened to me," said Gavin. "I once had a set to with the polis on the way to a fancy dress party. Ah had ma mask under my arm an' they thought I was hidin' something. Ah told um it was ma mask fi the party but they had me up aside the car while they searched me. Ah got an apology. Ah can laugh aboot it noo, but it wasnae funny at the time. Know what ah mean, ken?"

Matt decided he didn't know what Gavin meant and, thinking that he knew his own name wasn't Ken, wasn't sure he fully understood him. It emerged later that Gavin was from Dunfermline and Matt remembered an encounter with the

Fife accent some years earlier when he had been invited by a friend to stay with his family in what the locals called 'the kingdom'. He had spent a weekend realising that whilst English may be a common language throughout the British Isles that, by itself, did not guarantee that its users could always communicate with each other.

Aurélie explained that she'd invited Gavin for a drink and to pay him for cleaning his jacket.

"I don't suppose either of you would like a cup of coffee, would you?" Matt offered.

They laughed.

He suggested another round instead. Gavin said he'd just take a half pint of lager as he was going mountain biking the next day and would need to get away.

When Gavin left, Matt looked at his watch. It was eight o'clock. It was good not to have an agenda once in a while. She'd always had a plan for them: a lifetime plan, a career plan, a retirement plan, a plan for this year, for this week, for tonight. Although the job and his move to Edinburgh had been hastily planned, today, right now, he had no plan.

Aurélie interrupted his gaze. "You looked as though you were miles away," she said.

"I was," he replied. "Just realising that I'm somewhere I've always wanted to be and I'm not sure how I got here, or what I'm actually doing here."

"I sometimes wonder that myself," Aurélie said. She told him about how she had come to Edinburgh as a student much to her family's consternation. But instead of settling back in France as they had hoped, she was back in Edinburgh to her own surprise.

Their conversation continued in the pizza restaurant on the corner of Victoria Street. It was something that neither of them had planned, yet both found strangely exciting. By the time that they sampled the desert menu, they had found that they had a number of things in common. They both enjoyed skiing, though Aurélie admitted that she had never skied in Scotland and certainly not on anything like the dry matting that the city's Hillend Ski Centre offered. Both of them liked the build up to big rugby games, but neither had ever been to a game let alone somewhere like the Stade de France or Murrayfield. They'd also both been at the previous year's Fringe and reckoned that they'd probably seen some of the same shows.

"A 'Sliding Doors' moment," Matt said referring to the film of that name. "You know the one where Gwyneth Paltrow trips getting on to a tube train and then a series of coincidences draw her and John Hannah together. It's been a bit like that this evening. If I hadn't looked out of the window and seen you with Gavin."

Aurélie thought that she might have seen the film, but thought that she understood what Matt was alluding to anyway. "Yes, I know. Crazy isn't it. If I hadn't been late because I had been talking to my mother the night before."

They both laughed.

"They could re-make the film on the trams on Princes Street," she suggested. "You could be the man."

Matt didn't respond.

It was after 11 o'clock when they finally left the restaurant. It had been a good evening. They looked at the night time traffic outside, the taxis, the late buses. It had been a long day.

As they separated Matt said: "I was actually thinking of going skiing at Hillend on Sunday. Call me, if you fancy it," knowing full well that they hadn't exchanged mobile numbers.

Aurélie had already taken a couple of steps to cross the George IV Bridge towards her bus stop, whilst Matt turned towards the High Street, reflecting on the impromptu evening and immediately cautioning himself not to get too far ahead.

"I'll need a number or an e-mail address if I'm going to do that - or are you on Facebook?" Aurélie called, crossing back over the bridge, her phone in hand.

....

He'd forgotten to reset the alarm on his phone. Its demanding clamour for attention brought him to the reality of his weekend too early. He reached above his head, his fingers finding its familiar outline on the shelf. His eyes slowly focused on its shape. He cancelled its incessant tone and checked for messages. There were none. It was still early he thought and it had been a late night. He turned over and pretended that the morning had not yet begun.

It was nearly ten o'clock when he finally surfaced and killed the electronic cacophony that his phone had continued to emit periodically for the last hour or so. What perverse pleasure did those who programmed these devices to make such noises get from it, he wondered. He went through the flat opening the curtains. The sun was up. The day was already underway with the sounds of a Saturday morning. To his relief too early for the Wasp though. Outside he could hear the noise of families on the nearby esplanade but from where he was he couldn't see them. It had begun to frustrate him that in spite of living so close to the sea he could not actually see it from his top floor flat.

After breakfast he started to tidy up and make a shopping list. Living and shopping for the moment had to come to an end. He would need to explore Portobello and find out what it could offer him. He recalled that he used to enjoy shopping. He had been part of the new man generation of the 1980s that could do housework and go to the football. However, he had never quite grasped the ritual of the Saturday morning shopping trip. Supermarket battle grounds, often involving whole families, which became open laboratories of human interaction and behaviour presented real opportunities for academic research. Another PhD? Why did so many people, often related to each other, herd themselves together and put themselves through such misery? Armed with his own shopping list he headed off in search of battle.

It was a bright still morning and he took time to take in his surroundings. Bath Street was actually a lot quieter than he had thought it would be. It was really only a single lane road that linked Portobello's High Street with its beach. Nevertheless, it had clearly been a main thoroughfare at one time judging by the grand edifice of the former cinema that was now a bingo hall. Most of the buildings were one or two storeys made of either blonde or red sandstone. There had clearly been a number of local shops at one time but most of these were now boarded up or had been turned in to residential flats, including those on the ground level below his own. Above the entrance door of his block, or close, had been carved, rather pretentiously, Windsor Mansions along with the year that it had presumably been built, 1896. How many people had lived in these mansions since then he wondered? Before he had chance to speculate too much though, a familiar noise distracted him. The Wasp was back.

This time the rider was alone as he slewed his machine to a halt beside the communal rubbish and recycling bins that provided the focal point for him and his accomplices to congregate later in the evening. Matt wandered over and exchanged a casual nod of recognition with the machine's owner. "Morning," he said.

A grunt emerged from inside the owner's helmet.

Matt interpreted it as a greeting. Contact had been established. He smiled and walked on up Bath Street towards the centre of Porty as locals seemed to refer to it. The High Street was busy with people shopping or going about their business. In the distance the unmistakable deep throated roar of a diesel engine of a London bound train gathered speed past the depot at Craigentinny. It was a reminder to him of his escape route if things didn't work out. Standing for a moment he checked his phone. Still no messages. It looked as though it was going to be skiing for one, he thought.

The Co-op was calming down from what had obviously been a busy morning. The strain was showing on the faces of the two checkout assistants on duty. Their lunch break couldn't come soon enough by the look of it, he noticed. He had soon filled his trolley, working his way through his list, quietly impressed by the range on offer. Not quite that of Bath itself, but hey, he thought, this was Bath Street Portobello, EH15. Not a slightly pretentious former Georgian Spa town in the south of England.

Heading for the door with his hands straining under the weight of the shopping bags he had filled, his phone buzzed. Why now, he thought. Impossible to safely put his bags down and not see their contents spew out onto the car park, he resolved to keep walking home. It was only about five minutes before he was letting himself into the close, in which time his fingers were nearly cut through and his anticipation about what secret the phone held was similarly pronounced. Reaching the flat he dumped the shopping on the landing and tapped in his password on his phone. Eventually it loaded the message: "Please contact this number about your outstanding PPI claim as a matter of urgency." As a matter of bloody urgency? It would be bloody and it would be urgent if he ever confronted those who dabbled in this modern day digital highway robbery!

Mrs McNiven, his neighbour, poked her head out of her door. "Are you alright dear. You did seem to be making a lot of noise."

"No, I'm very sorry Mrs McNiven. I've been having a lot of nuisance calls and I was hoping it might be someone else, but it wasn't. Anyway I'm glad I've caught you. There's something I've been meaning to ask you. Would you mind if I gave you a spare key for my flat. I'm not expecting to get locked out or anything, but I'd just like to know that if I did I'd not be sleeping out here on the landing, if you understand."

"Yes dear. Not at all. We'd be happy to do that."

Matt said he'd drop one in later then and after another brief discussion about her husband's obsession with tv quiz shows, Mrs McNiven retreated indoors. Matt let himself into his own flat. After putting his shopping away and getting a quick lunch he decided to explore the Esplanade and to follow it further round. He turned left at The Espy towards Leith. It was a glorious autumnal afternoon, with strong sunshine but the hint of a chill in the air. Dog walkers, cyclists and joggers mingled with families taking the opportunity that the sea front afforded before the winter chill of the coming months set in. Matt's attention was gradually drawn by a grey and pink track suited figure jogging towards him, a familiar ponytail bobbing from side to side. Its owner slowed as she approached him. Matt moved to the side to let her past, but instead she paused, hands on thighs as she gathered her breath.

"Hi, how's the job going," Ponytail gasped.

"Not bad. Settling in, getting to know people and all that," Matt replied. "Haven't really had the chance for long coffee mornings in The Espy though."

"No, don't suppose you have.

"How's your run, do you get far?" enquired Matt.

"Yes, I like to get round as far as Joppa if I can, maybe even Musselburgh," she said pointing in the direction she was heading. "Anyway must get on. See you around some time. By the way, what's your film knowledge like? There's a film quiz night at the Espy every Monday. You ought to come along."

"Might just do that," Matt replied, but she was already jogging on, her ponytail already set into its familiar swagger.

How ridiculous, he thought as he continued on his own way. He didn't even know her name. He couldn't keep thinking of her as just Ponytail.

Matt walked on past the amusement arcades, stretching the last custom of the year from those who were still out. He bought an ice cream smiling at the absurdity of it, and checked his phone once more. There was still no message.

He'd walked further than he'd planned and it was nearly dark when he returned to the flat. It was noticeable how much sooner it was getting dark compared to what he had been used to further south. He pulled his phone out of his jacket pocket. There was no little green light indicating a new message. The in box remained stubbornly empty.

Saturday evening blurred into Sunday morning and his interest in going skiing had waned. Skiing on the plastic matting at Hillend was not for the feint hearted. It wasn't co-incidence that the term 'Hillend thumb' had been coined in local Accident & Emergency hospitals to describe the injury sustained by skiers falling and trapping their thumbs in the plastic matting. Matt had ventured out as far as the Co-op again for a Sunday paper and resisting the embrace of the Butternut Squash, the café halfway along Bath Street, had settled down in the flat with a coffee and a couple of slices of

Selkirk Bannock, a fruit bread produced in the south of Scotland that he had a penchant for.

By the time he'd got through the Review section of the paper and the magazine, it was early afternoon. He finally made a decision not to go skiing. Instead, feeling the need for exercise nevertheless, he settled for a jog along the esplanade in the opposite direction to that in which he had walked the day before. There were noticeably fewer people around as he passed the Sailing Club. The autumnal sunshine of Saturday had given way to an early winter feel. The sky over the Forth loomed large and grey. The clouds were massing and provided a threatening backdrop to the end of the weekend. He plugged into his IPod, tuned into Dvorak's Cello Concerto, a piece that he found particularly stimulating, and headed along the coast towards Joppa. By the time he got there it had begun to rain. Turning to make his way back, head down into the wind that had built since he had set out, Matt doubted his weekend's decision making: it was neither what he had expected nor hoped.

Matt made sure that he was home quickly the following day. After the disappointment of the weekend, the prospect of the Quiz night at The Espy was a compensation he now looked forward to. The place was full as he entered and after ordering a pint of Deuchars, he stood at the bar looking round the various groups, trying to spot a familiar hairstyle. He was beginning to think that he had been let down again when there was a tap on his shoulder.

"Hi, you made it then," said Ponytail. "Why don't you come and join us," she continued, pointing at a group of three other women and one man.

"Thanks, I will," Matt replied, gathering up his beer and following her over.

Ponytail quickly introduced Matt to her friends, so quickly that he'd forgotten the women's names by the time he actually sat down. "And you are?" said Rob, the only man in the group.

"Sorry, my name's Matt. I've recently moved in just round the corner. I work near the University in town."

Ponytail explained that their team name was 'The Directors' and that they usually won. Matt produced one of his new business cards and dealt it on to the table. "There you go," he said. "My credentials for joining your team." He pointed to the reference to him being the Centre's Director.

Ponytail picked the card up and studied it with keen interest. "Well Mr Director. Let's see how good you really are," she said, slipping the card into her bag.

The quiz got underway at about 9.30. There was a keen rivalry between the seven teams with free drinks vouchers at stake. After two or three rounds it was clear that it was going to be between 'The Directors' and the 'Porty Pinups', a team of twenty-somethings with a seemingly insatiable film knowledge. At about 11.00, the quiz was heading into the final round. Matt was beginning to feel the need to get to bed. It was declared a tie between the two teams. Rob wanted a recount but they settled on a tie break. The question was, who starred alongside Gwyneth Paltrow in the 1998 British film Sliding Doors. Led by Rob, there was a determined view amongst 'The Directors' that it was Hugh Grant. Matt disagreed. He was confident that it was John

Hannah. As the newcomer though he didn't feel that it was his place to push his view. In the event the 'Porty Pinups' shared Matt's belief and took the tiebreak and the quiz.

The Espy started to empty as the quiz ended, Matt's team mates amongst them. Rob, shook his hand and suggested that he gets to make it each week, apologising for doubting his knowledge of John Hannah films.

"Don't get me started on that," Matt replied, "or I'll start reciting that poem he does at Simon Callow's funeral in Four Weddings."

Rob laughed.

"You mean 'Stop the clocks'," said Ponytail.

"Come on then Catriona MacLeod," Rob said. "I'll get you up the road, or Dylan will be wondering what's happened to you and as for Bobby, he'll think that his mother has abandoned him."

"Abandoned him? Chance would be a fine thing!" replied Catriona.

Outside, the cold of the dark November night was not one for standing around in as Rob and Catriona headed up Bath Street and Matt let himself into his close. Catriona, he thought. Ponytail was Catriona. Not quite the name that he had imagined though.

CHAPTER SIX - THE DEN
(Early Spring 1971)

Matt had become used to the idea of a baby. There had been much talk of it when his Dad had returned from Edinburgh and his grandparents had come for Christmas. They'd told him that he was going to get a little baby brother, or even a baby sister. He decided that that would be alright but as he didn't really know many girls, he hoped it would be a baby brother.

Hattonbridge School only had two classrooms at that time. To both children and teachers, the one where children started was known as the infants' class, whilst the other one which included those children in their last year in primary was known as the top class. Matt was in the infants class. He had come to enjoy school and had an appetite for the knowledge that it gave him.

From time to time, one or two of the children were allowed to stay inside at lunchtime to help prepare the classroom for the afternoon. The desks still had ink pots set into wooden surrounds and even though they weren't used regularly, on the day that Matt had been given the privilege of staying in, it was his job to fill them up tor the afternoon's handwriting lesson. He had meant to do this, but as he started to pour the ink carefully into the first pot his mind wandered. Instead of concentrating on the desk his eyes had wandered down to the rough wooden floor that regularly gave children splinters during exercise classes, or music and movement as they were called. He had often seen the grain of the wood as a patchwork of miniature hills and dales, like those that surrounded the village. What would happen he thought if he dripped just a little ink on to the floor? Where would it run to? Would it reach the next desk, or further? One drip had little effect. In fact he could hardly see it. It merely stained the wood. Another made not a lot of difference either. Soon he had tipped most of a potfull drip after drip and now the ink was starting to run, starting to fan out before joining up again as the grooves formed tributaries of larger river systems. He imagined the Hatton, joining the Yore and in turn the Ouse at York and finally the Humber. He imagined it all flowing out to the North Sea and beyond. South to Ghana perhaps, or, north to Edinburgh; north to his father.

At first, Mrs Simpson had been unsure of what to do or say and had stared at him aghast. She hadn't uttered a sound, standing in silence watching the catastrophe of her afternoon developing in front of her. Matt looked up. He gulped, wondering what was going to happen next. After what seemed like an eternity to both of them, Mrs Simpson calmly but deliberately made it very clear that he would never be trusted again and that he would have to go outside at play time no matter the weather. As punishment went it had its compensations. He would have more time to explore the fields and hedgerows that adjoined the playground. Playtimes were a mystery to him. He did not relish the prospect of some of the more boisterous playground games, such as British Bulldog, a game where a line of children attempted to ensnare and capture other children as they tried to run from one side of the playground to the other. Instead Matt had always yearned to go beyond the school playground walls to the fields and woods of Hattondale beyond. Outside school time the Dale was already his wider playground and provided the landscape for his imagination. Being confined to the playground was a frustration that, at times, he found hard to bear.

Across the field from the school was a cottage and outbuildings belonging to the village joiner, Mr Calvert. The day after the incident with the ink, Matt and his friend Andrew were sitting on the playground wall swinging their legs. Behind them a game of Bulldog was underway and the raucous noise of those involved, egged on by others watching, had distracted the teacher who was supervising the break time. Each swing moved them closer to the edge until together they dropped from the wall, into the field and out of sight of the teacher. Being early spring, the dew was still on the ground and very quickly their feet became wet. Reaching the building they tried the door and found it unlocked.

It was dark inside and there was a warm inviting smell of wood and machinery. Clearly Mr Calvert used the building to store some of his old tools and off-cuts and there was sawdust on the floor. Matt and Andrew crept inside, their hearts racing with both nervous excitement and trepidation. The noise from the game of Bulldog suddenly got louder in the distance. Another one of their friends had been captured in the playground; by contrast they were being lured further inside as their eyes grew accustomed to the dark.

On the far wall they found a bench and pulled themselves up onto it. It was an old pew that the village joiner must have replaced from a church at some point. They sat together swinging their legs and gazing towards the dirty window next to the door.

"It'll be alright us being here, won't it?" asked Matt. "I mean, Mr Calvert's not really using it is he?

Aye, it'll be fine," replied Andrew. "My Dad says that Calvert has got lots of buildings in the village. Barns, houses, sheds, he's got lots. He can't be in them all, all the time can he? We can have this one for us den. He won't mind. Anyway I asked him."

Their legs swung in time, each trying to both copy the other and go faster.

"Where is your Dad anyway?" Andrew interrupted. "There's just thee and tha Mum at your house in't there?

"My Dad's in Edinburgh," Matt replied proudly, trying not to suggest that this made him feel sad. "Me and Mum went there to see him before Christmas."

"Where's what did you call it, Ednasborough - when it's at home anyway?" Andrew asked. "Is it like Scarborough or Middlesbrough, or Riponborough or Yorkborough or Leedsborough?" he added, quickly running out of places that ended in borough that he could think of.

"No, it's in Scotland," Matt answered. "He's gone to university. It's like a school for grown ups."

"Why's he done that then? Is he, like thick or summat? My Dad says, you don't need to go to school any roads. Tha knows more from t'village and t'Dale than tha does from books, he allas says," Andrew replied. Their conversation subsided and their leg swinging correspondingly slowed down almost to a stop.

"My Mum's going to have a baby," Matt said eventually, breaking the silence of the barn.

Before Andrew could respond, the sound of the playground bell cut into their space from the other side of the field outside. The game of Bulldog was over and the other children were noisily making their way back inside the school. "Bloody hell fire," Matt said, using an expression that he knew his parents didn't like him using. "We better run for it. We're going to be for it."

The two boys left the barn quickly, forgetting to close the door behind them and ran back across the field. Reaching the wall at the playground, they struggled to find an easy way back up as it was higher on the field side than it was from the school side. Andrew, who was slightly taller, clambered up, finding a larger stone jutting out of the wall and just out of Matt's reach. Once on top of the wall he turned and reached down to Matt. "Here, give me your hand, I'll pull thee up." Matt reached up and between them they clambered over the wall. Falling into the playground they looked at themselves. Both had marks on their jumpers and their shorts; their shoes were wet from the dew of the field and Matt's right knee was scraped from climbing the wall. They both ran inside and straight into the toilets which were just inside the door. They each stood in a separate cubicle, their hearts pounding, each uncertain about what to do next.

Back in the classroom Mrs Simpson was taking the afternoon's register. It didn't take her long to work out that two of her class were missing. "Has anyone seen Matthew and Andrew?" she asked.

"No, Miss," came the almost universal reply from the rest of the class.

"Wait here, children," she said. "I need to go and speak to Miss Cussons." Miss Cussons was the head teacher and a friend of Matt's mother. They had both started work in the Dale at about the same time and, as women, were proud of themselves for finding good and respected jobs in post-war Britain.

Within minutes, Mrs Simpson and Miss Cussons were scouring the playground for the two missing boys. There was no sign of them. Mrs Simpson started knocking on doors of neighbouring houses whilst Miss Cussons went inside to call the village policeman Sergeant Woodward. Meanwhile, inside the toilets the two boys had started to calm down, their breathing gradually returning to normal. Quietly they tidied themselves up and slipped out of the toilets and through to their classroom.

"You two are going to get it," said one of their classmates.

"Don't say anything. Say we were in the cupboard," said Andrew pointing at a large old wardrobe that stood at the back of the classroom and contained exercise books and other stationery, as well as the cleaner's mop and bucket.

"Children," began Mrs Simpson re-entering the classroom. "Now we need you to be very calm and sit quietly for a little longer whilst Miss Cussons and I ..." Her voice suddenly stopped. The children had begun to giggle. Some of them were pointing at Matt and Andrew who were sat ram rod still in their places, almost holding their breath and looking as though they were about to burst. "Matthew, Andrew. Where were you earlier when I was taking the register? You weren't at your desks then. Where were you?"

"Please miss, they were in the cupboard. They were in the cupboard!" spoke up one of their friends. "They were in there!"

"Were you, were you in the cupboard? Mrs Simpson asked.

"It was Matthew's idea," began Andrew. "He said there was a story that said that children could go through a wardrobe to another place and like we thought we could try it and then like we couldn't get out and you didn't hear us knocking. We were scared Miss, it was really dark."

"Stop! That's enough Andrew. Matthew what have you got to say for yourself?" asked Mrs Simpson.

"We didn't mean to. Didn't want to make you cross Miss, it was just a joke," replied Matt.

"Did you find a way through to another place?" began another of the children.

"That's quite enough children. Now I do want you to sit quietly again. I need to go and see Miss Cussons." With that Mrs SImpson left the class who all began to eagerly ask the two boys where they had been.

We went to Edinborough to see Matthew's Dad," announced Andrew beaming from ear to ear. "It took us all of playtime and a bit longer, but we're back now."

Later that afternoon, the two boys were walking home together, a contented smile shared between them. "Why did you say, we'd been to Edinburgh to see my Dad?" pondered Matt.

"Well we had, hadn't we. He just wasn't there," Andrew replied. "I think we should call our den 'Edinborough' and then you can go there whenever tha wants."

"That'd be brilliant," said Matt.

Andrew pushed Matt on up the Green. "Come on, let's go and get us bikes and go to t'Dale. Bags I'm the Lone Ranger!"

Back at the school, Miss Cussons and Mrs Simpson were meeting with Sergeant Woodward. "I simply don't believe them. I just don't think they could have been in the cupboard when I was taking the register. The other children would have given the game away. I'm sure of it."

"But if they weren't there, where could they have been?" asked Miss Cussons.

"I may well have an idea about that," cut in Sergeant Woodward. "I had a nosey round at t'other side of yon field," he said, pointing beyond the school playground. "See Calvert's barn over there. The door was open and when I had a look inside there were some footprints on the dusty floor. If I'm not mistaken, I'd say they were little boys' footprints."

"I'll have a word with Matthew's mother," said Miss Cussons. "I know his father is away at the moment and I know it can't be easy for her with a new baby on the way."

"I'll see Calvert and keep an eye on t'barn," said Sergeant Woodward.

CHAPTER SEVEN - THE MARKET
(Early December 2013)

It had been a few weeks since Matt hadn't gone skiing with Aurélie. He'd settled into the Centre and its business and had submitted a couple of prospective research possibilities. He and Helen had led a workshop at a conference in Glasgow on measuring outcomes for children, whilst he and Dougie had had a number of meetings at Victoria Quay, the home of the Scottish Government administration, about the forthcoming legislation that was set to change the way that children were supported in Scotland.

"The best place for children to grow up, that's what they want," Dougie had said as they had left. "And it's up to the likes of us to prove it? I'm glad I've got an easy job!"

"Give me funding for the next 100 years and I might just be able to prove it, Pauline used to say," Matt had responded, recalling someone that he had once worked for. He also remembered how often in his career he had found that those responsible for implementing new initiatives such as the forthcoming legislation were relatively inexperienced in the areas that they led on. One week they could be responsible for reviewing the role of libraries in the care and support of older people, the next they could be managing a project on pre-school care. They rarely had time to become experts.

It didn't make the work of the Centre and places like it easy when such people changed roles so regularly, he had reflected to Helen one Friday afternoon. Over a coffee at the end of a busy week they were reviewing the Centre's work.

Matt stared through the office window. Even though it was still only mid-afternoon the light was already fading and the trees in the square outside were already silhouetted against the buildings opposite. Only the last few stubborn leaves were clinging on. Winter was definitely just round the corner. "The problem is that new policies are never given time to bed in, before another new idea is tried out."

"I know," Helen had replied. "I honestly thought it was improving in recent years and that we were getting a consensus on some of these things. But with the referendum coming up, I'm not so sure."

"I suppose that it's at times like these that we need to remind ourselves about who our real customers are," Matt said.

"Exactly, it's Scotland's children that we're here for and we shouldn't forget that, no matter who's in charge over at Holyrood or down at Westminster." The two of them exchanged glances: at least they weren't working to the coalition government down south with two political interests to try and reconcile. It certainly was a challenging time to provide the unbiased and balanced leadership that the Centre had developed an enviable reputation for.

Matt recalled a similar situation that he had worked with in England.

"We were forever having meetings in Whitehall. All they ever seemed to want to know was what would happen if they did this or did that. They never let it happen though before they were on to the next big idea. Contact Point was a good example. Dreamt up by the last Labour lot. On paper a great idea in theory. Every child's name accessible through one computer look-up. If the child wasn't known to any of the main agencies then it wouldn't show anything, but if it was then the teacher or the health visitor, or whoever had a good reason to check, would know who to speak to. It sort of got over the whole problem that enquiry after enquiry highlights, whereby all the information was known before a tragedy happened; just that no one had joined all the dots."

"I remember reading about it, but we never had it up here," Helen said.

"No, and that was probably no bad thing the way things worked out."

"So why didn't it work?" Helen asked.

"Because no one ever gave it time," Matt replied. "It was one of the first things the incoming government vowed to get rid of in 2010, even before they got elected. No reason really. The crazy thing though was that unlike many government IT systems - it worked. But they scrapped it anyway, even destroying the software!"

"You sound passionate about it!"

"No, not really, not about Contact Point anyway. I just think that we need to give some of these ideas more time. Contact Point cost a fortune for the pilots and all the software development costs. I often think, the way it was scrapped was like building those Aircraft Carriers that they're putting together over at Rosyth, then when they've completed their sea trials and we know they work, they're taken out into the North Sea and scuttled!"

Helen laughed. "I know the point that you're making. It's a good one as well. Let's see which way the referendum goes next year. Who knows what'll happen then?"

The two of them continued to go over the Centre's work, though as the time was heading towards five o'clock, both were fast losing interest.

"You doing anything this weekend," enquired Helen.

"Thought I'd make an early foray into the Christmas market on Princes Street. Never know, might actually start my Christmas shopping before Christmas this year," Matt replied. She had been the one who had done that sort of thing in previous years. Actually, she was rather good at it, he recognised; kept lists of what they'd bought for everyone in previous years; made sure that everything was bought, wrapped and posted where necessary by the beginning of December. Well, this year was his chance to show that he too could be organised.

"Go you!" Helen said. "Princes Street can be such fun at this time of year. We normally go down in a couple of week's time. The children used to like going on the big wheel. Tell you what; I'll walk down with you rather than getting the bus. I could do with the exercise."

Helen lived in Canonmills on the edge of Edinburgh's new town, the fashionable area to the north of the city's main shopping centre. Although many of the Georgian terraces and flats were now offices, the majority, particularly those further down the hill, were still occupied as family homes. Helen had invited some of the Institute's staff round for pre-Christmas drinks in a couple of week's time which Matt was looking forward to.

After Portobello, the new town and its adjoining suburbs such as Stockbridge, was an area that he'd always wanted to live in. It was an area that in previous years they had often spent time hypothetically flat hunting between shows at the Fringe, although he had been less hypothetical than she had.

She had never quite shared his passion for Edinburgh and was only really happy to be in the city during August when she thought it felt like London. "London heads north to Edinburgh in the same way that Paris empties and heads for the coast every summer", she used to say.

Helen and Matt walked up to the High Street continuing to speculate about the likely outcome of the referendum, now less than a year away. The tone of some of the commentary was already beginning to get ratcheted up in the media and amongst their friends and colleagues.

The numbers of people on the streets were noticeably larger as they reached the top of the Mound. It was a place that never slept. They looked down on Princes Street and the scene below. The lights of the stalls and the fairground with the big wheel and the sky tower, were enchanting. Once again Edinburgh had managed to create a wow factor. They made their way down the Playfair Steps at the side of the National Gallery and the lights of the Christmas market on the edge of the gardens shone out across the trains heading in to Waverley Station. 2014 was going to be an interesting year they concluded.

They parted at the front of the Gallery on Princes Street. Helen wished him well with his shopping and headed off for a bus and home. Matt paused and took in the sights, sounds and smells. The market had a German theme and there were stalls selling various wurst. It was incredible how the smells emanating from such places had the ability to stimulate a sense of hunger, he thought. He settled on a Currywurst and had an extra squirt of ketchup for good measure. There had been a Christmas market in Bath where they had lived but that had been much more about local produce, an extension of the farmers' market concept that had first been developed there. Although they had been available, Currywurst was not really an option in Bath, not if you wanted to maintain your Tofu and Falafel credentials anyway. He laughed at the thought and bit into his wurst, ketchup oozing from the corners of his mouth.

Matt made his way through the crowds of early evening shoppers and revellers in the direction of the Scott monument which was almost lost amongst the hubbub of everything else. He remembered that time as a child when he had first seen it. How he had thought it was an old man sitting very still and how within his family, it had been known as the 'white man in his church' long after his father had left University. How times have changed he thought as he gazed up at it, simultaneously devouring the last piece of sausage. One thing that hadn't changed in all those years though was the presence of a piper at the Waverley Bridge entrance to the gardens, although he doubted that it was the same one. The unmistakable lilt of Highland Cathedral, one of his favourite pieces, drifted through the cool air and was just audible over the top of the noise from the throngs of market shoppers and those just out for a Friday night.

He had begun to browse the stalls and also to realise that many of them were selling exactly the same items, mostly novelty Christmas tree decorations. He smiled as he pictured in his mind a large factory somewhere above the Arctic Circle hand crafting them especially for the occasion. But then he also thought of a factory, or more likely factories, in China churning them out in their tens of thousands for this and every other fake German Christmas market throughout the world. Nevertheless, he bought a selection, making a mental note that that would mean he would now need to buy a Christmas tree!

....

What was it with German Christmas markets anyway, he thought? Why Germany? What gave them the monopoly on how Christmas should look? Before he could speculate on the answer though, a familiar voice suddenly cut across his thoughts.

"How was the skiing?"

"I'm sorry, what?" Matt jumped.

"The skiing. You were going skiing. A few weeks ago," Aurélie began.

"Oh yes, of course, I'm sorry. I was miles away, thinking about the ..."

".... you looked to be," Aurélie replied.

There was a young man by Aurélie's side who Matt judged to be about her age. The evening gloom helped him to hide the instant feel of despondency that the expression on his face betrayed.

"Matt, this is my cousin Stefan. He's come over for the Christmas market and to see a bit of Edinburgh. It's his first time here," she said, before turning to the young man and continuing in French. "Voici Matt. Je t'ai raconté sur lui avant."

Matt looked puzzled, the French language had never been his forte in spite of him having visited the country many times.

Aurélie apologised and said that she'd just told her cousin that this was the man that she'd told him about.

"All good things, I hope," he replied, wiping the remains of his Currywurst from his hands on the paper serviette that he'd been given. "Wow. I mean, good to see you." He held out his hand as his facial expression changed.

Stefan shook it limply.

"What do you think of Edinburgh then? I guess Aurélie must have told you a lot about it."

Stefan smiled. "Excuse moi. Mon anglais. It is not good."

"Don't worry," Matt replied. "It's probably better than my French though!"

"I'm really sorry about the other week," Aurélie began, as they walked through the stalls. "It was my mother. She phoned me to say that my grandmother was sick. I needed to talk to her a lot. She was very sad. It was difficult. And I lost your number. Was the skiing good?"

"Yes, not bad," Matt lied. "Not as good as snow obviously, but it keeps you going. Heh, do you fancy going on that?" he said, pointing at the big wheel that stood next to the Scott monument. "It would be a good way to see the city, if you've never been here before."

Aurélie agreed and the three of them joined the queue. Aurélie sat next to Stefan with Matt sitting opposite. She translated the audio commentary about Edinburgh's history that accompanied the wheel's rotations. He didn't hear either. Deep inside him a feeling was awakening that he hadn't felt for some time. But it was not realistic, surely? After all she was undoubtedly some years younger than he was. But how many? Would it matter? The big wheel's gyrations ended all too soon for him.

The three of them strolled on, stopping at one of the bars. Aurélie and Stefan went skating on the outdoor ice rink whilst Matt watched. He made an excuse about having a sore foot. He didn't want to say that whilst skiing was his passion, skating terrified him, something illogical he knew, but then when was life ever logical? Another PhD? It was another opportunity though for his passion to be aroused and he found himself again contemplating Aurélie's beauty and appeal.

In spite of having only just eaten the wurst, Matt suggested heading to the food stands. They each chose something different from the eclectic mix on offer and stood together eating in the cooling night air. The atmosphere though was warm with the crowds themselves raising the temperature a few degrees. Their conversation turned to what else Aurélie should show Stefan on his few days in the city. They'd done one of the many open top bus tours earlier in the day, one with a French commentary; been to Holyrood and the Parliament building; walked the length of the Royal Mile and up to the castle. Arthur's Seat had been in mist most of the day so that hadn't held its usual attractions.

"Not a lot you've got left to do then!" Matt said. ... although I suppose that there are always the Pandas at the zoo if you like that sort of thing."

They laughed though Aurélie had to translate for Stefan what it was that Matt was suggesting.

"... and then there's always the beach. Not quite the Côte d'Azur I'll admit but a 'plage' I think you call it nonetheless. I'd be happy to show you it. Come down to Portobello. Have some lunch. There are a couple of really nice beachside bars."

"In December, you're suggesting we go to a beach in Scotland! You must be mad," Aurélie said. Stefan grasped what Matt was suggesting but failed to see the attraction of a beachside bar in winter.

"No, what's mad is this," Matt said pointing at all the extravagance of the market around about them. "This is mad. All these people out here on a cold evening in December in Scotland. But looking at them, do they look mad? No, I don't think so."

They laughed again agreeing that Edinburgh was a slightly mad sort of place with so much going on throughout the year.

It was almost unfair on other cities not only in Scotland but also in the rest of the United Kingdom. They were always playing catch up with the Athens of the North.

"Go on then," Aurélie finally conceded. "Beach it is. How do we get there?"

"There's a good bus service," Matt replied.

"No, I have my car. We'll drive over," she said.

Hubert was a blue Renault Clio. Bringing it over from France had given Aurélie independence and freedom to explore Scotland. Together, they had been as far as Loch Lomond in the west and south into the Borders. She prided herself on her sense of geography and reckoned that she could find her way through Duddingston to Portobello. After all she'd driven from Grenoble across France to Zeebrugge in Belgium and then from Hull to Scotland. Surely Edinburgh's southern fringes would, by contrast, be relatively simple, though she promised to put EH15 into her satnav to be on the safe side. They agreed 12.30 for lunch the following day. Arrangements duly made, they had another drink, talked skiing, the Euro, Greece and football. Matt felt content.

Saturday was mild and fine for early December and Hubert made it to Portobello with ease. They lunched in the Butternut Squash on Bath Street and afterwards they walked down to the sea front. In the clear afternoon the views even impressed two sceptical French people who hadn't been entirely convinced about being at the seaside in the middle of winter.

The water was gently lapping the shore and there were a number of ships and smaller vessels moored out in the Forth. Matt explained the view that was laid out in front of them. To the right they could see round to the power station chimneys at Cockenzie, awaiting demolition, whilst in the other, they looked over at a headland that ran down into the water in Fife. Between these extremes, the profile of the two prominent breast like shapes of the Lomond Hills framed the town of Kirkcaldy. To the east, out to sea and just out of sight, Matt explained, was the Bass Rock, a large volcanic lump which was smothered in bird droppings giving the impression that it was covered in snow. Aurélie grimaced whilst providing a literal translation for her cousin, who nevertheless laughed at her explanation. Matt also pointed out two other volcanic plugs at North Berwick and Tranent, and said that it was a shame that the afternoon's light was already fading as the views from these vantage points would have been a good trip out.

"Peut-être une autre excursion pour vous deux?" said Stefan.

"Peut-être," answered Aurélie.

Matt smiled warmly, understanding the suggestion. He invited them up to his flat for coffee. Aurélie looked at Stefan who nodded and a few minutes later they were looking out on the comings and goings on the street below from the vantage point of his living room window.

Matt opened a packet of ground coffee and took down the cafetière from the top shelf of the cupboard where it had stood since the day that he had moved in. It was good to have a reason not to resort to instant, he thought. They congregated in the kitchen whilst he made the coffee.

Aurélie noticed the Christmas tree decorations lying on the kitchen table. "Did you get these at the market?" she asked. "Are you planning on being here for Noël? - I mean Christmas."

"Yes, I'd bought them last night before I bumped into the two of you. I'm heading down to York to my parents' house. My sister and her husband and their daughter will be there as well. Mum and Dad's house is big enough for us all so it should be ok, though I'll be coming back up here before Hogmanay. I've never done an Edinburgh new year and I'm really looking forward to it. New Year, new opportunities, you know."

Aurélie nodded, cradling the coffee cup, whilst Stefan stared out of the window.

"How about you?" Matt asked, not wanting to get ahead of himself, but at the same time picturing an attractive festive season.

"Heading back to the Alps," she began.

Matt's mental picture suddenly lost some of its allure.

"... though I'd like to be back here for the new year as well. I've heard so much about it, it would be good to be part of, I think." She explained that Christmas wasn't really a big thing in her part of France but that she wanted to take the opportunity of the holiday to go home to offer support to her mother and to see her grandmother.

His mental picture regained some of its appeal.

They continued to chat about plans for the holidays and what else Stefan must see in the rest of his time in Scotland. It was dark by the time Aurélie decided that they must go as her mother would be calling.

Matt walked them out to Hubert. Stefan got into the passenger seat. By the light of the streetlight, he looked at the young woman stood before him and who had started to beguile him.

"Thank you for a lovely afternoon," Aurélie said. She leant forward and kissed him on the cheek. "Perhaps we will see each other at new year? I don't know anyone else who is going to be here. All my friends will be away. I'll maybe give you a call."

"That would be good," he replied.

She got into the car and drove up Bath Street. Matt watched them until they had blurred into the other vehicles and lights at the far end of the street. It was a cold evening, the cool December air settling on Portobello. Matt didn't notice. He had an inner warmth that had been missing from his life for some time. He bounded back up the stairs to his flat. Mrs McNiven was just closing the outer door to her flat.

"I'm glad I caught you," Matt said. "I'll be away for Christmas, but it looks like I'll be back for Hogmanay. Would you mind keeping an eye on things for me?"

"Not at all dear. We'll be here. We won't be going anywhere. Our daughter is coming to us for her Christmas dinner. It's himself you see. He doesn't like going out at this time of year."

Matt thanked her very much and let himself into his own flat. Closing it behind him, for a moment he leant back against the door and smiled. At long last things were looking up.

CHAPTER EIGHT - GROWING UP
(Late spring 1971)

His maternal grandparents lived in Ripon about twenty miles away. Matt's grandfather owned a haulage business that distributed coal to outlying villages in the Dales. In fact it was his grandfather who had first introduced him to the word pantechnicon, the word that Matt enjoyed reciting in his head so much. One of the company's green lorries with the family firm's name emblazoned in gold lettering on the cab doors would come through Hattonbridge every Tuesday and as well as dropping off coal for them, the driver would often have a box of treats for them from his grandmother.

By early 1971 these boxes included items for the impending arrival of the new addition to the family. His mother was 'nesting' as his other grandmother had put it, when, not to be outdone, she had travelled over to see them and to bring yet more items for the new baby. As the house was slowly filling up and the harshness of the winter had given way to spring, Matt was spending more and more time outside both by himself and with Andrew.

"I wish I could really go to Edinburgh to be with Dad," he kept telling his best friend.

His father was struggling to get time off from his studies before the baby was born and had implored Matt and his mother to visit him again in Edinburgh.

"Impossible. You, in your condition," his mother had told her. "But we could always take Mathew, if you like. You could have some time to yourself; get some peace and quiet for a few days." As a result it was agreed that his grandparents would take Matt to Edinburgh during the Easter holidays.

They drove up, staying in a Guest House not far from the Strachan's flat. It was a glorious few days of warm spring sunshine and the four of them thoroughly enjoyed themselves. They visited the zoo, where Matt was absorbed with the animals which were very different from the cows and sheep that he was used to in Hattondale. They walked up to the Castle and took in the views across the city. At Matt's request they all went out to South Queensferry to see the Meccano Bridge, as he liked to call it. They got to the beach at Portobello, where they played on the sand, his grandfather even taking his shoes and socks off though keeping his suit on. For Matt, there was one person missing though: his mother. His family was incomplete without her.

They left Edinburgh on the Tuesday after Easter and drove down through the Borders stopping at Carter Bar for a picnic, posing for photographs with one foot in each country. They visited Hadrian's Wall, because Matt was doing a project on the Romans at school. It was late afternoon when they arrived back in Hattonbridge and even though Easter had been early at the beginning of April, it was mild for the time of year.

His mother was asleep in a deckchair in the garden when they drove up. Matt and his grandparents tiptoed past her, but before they could get inside she stirred. "Well hello, you travellers. How was Edinburgh?

Nearly unable to contain himself, Matt told her about the places they had visited and the things they had seen: the

Mecanno bridge, the beach, the zoo and the castle. But, he left out one detail.

"How was Dad?" interrupted his mother.

Matt hadn't wanted to say because he thought it might upset her. "He was ok, I think."

"Just ok, with his favourite son visiting him?"

"No, he was really good Mum, really good," Matt replied.

"And was he missing me?"

Matt paused. "I think so."

His mother smiled. "Don't you worry. I'm sure he's fine. Come on, let's go inside and put the kettle on." She struggled to get out of the chair, her pregnancy now visibly well advanced. Her father-in-law helped her to her feet.

Before Matt's grandparents left to make their way home across the Vale of York, they had made his mother promise that she would call them if she needed them. They could be over in an hour or so they had said. She reassured them that her own parents were on standby as well but thanked them anyway.

Her baby was due in less than a month and spring had definitely sprung as she put it. She'd be fine she had told herself. There was also Dr McAlpine and the staff at the practice in Leyburn where she worked. They were only twenty minutes up the road.

Matt returned to school after the holidays full of stories about Edinburgh. It was all Mrs Simpson could do to keep him quiet. Andrew was still listening to his tales a few weeks later. It was the last week of the month and they were in their Den after school still believing that it was their secret. They'd continued to use it in spite of Sergeant Woodward's best efforts to convince Calvert to improve his security. Sitting in the late afternoon gloom Matt had described the animals that he had seen at the zoo. "Bloody hell fire. What, real lions and penguins? Together? Don't they like eat each other?"

Matt had reassured him that they didn't; well not whilst he was there anyway.

Outside the wind was starting to rise. A door banged. The two boys looked at each other, suddenly not as self-assured. Carefully and quietly, they made their way outside, the sky now overcast and the first spots of rain beginning to fall. They separated at the end of the Green, to make their own way home.

Matt's mother had been worried about where he had been and quickly closed the door behind him. A coal fire was already alight in the hearth in the living room. As it turned dark the rain began to fall more heavily. His father had phoned at about 8 o'clock. Matt had lain in bed listening to his mother talking on the phone before falling asleep.

It was dark when he awoke. To begin with he wasn't sure what had woken him. There had been a noise but whether it had been in his dream, or for real, he wasn't sure. The rain was lashing against the window of his bedroom. Then he heard the noise again. He thought back to the Den that afternoon and how scared he and Andrew had felt. He pulled the bed clothes over his head and closed his eyes tight. He lay in the dark and listened. A few minutes later he heard it again, only this time it was louder and was followed by someone shouting his name. Suddenly he realised that it was his mother. She was calling him. He quickly got out of bed and reached for the light switch. Nothing happened. The room remained dark. He felt his way out and on to the landing. He called out to his mother.

She replied from downstairs. "Mathew. I need you to come down here now."

He fumbled his way down the stairs in the dark and into the living room where the glow of the fire's embers still illuminated the room. His mother was lying on the floor holding her stomach. She screamed again as he entered the room.

"What's wrong Mum?" he said. "Is it the baby?"

"Yes," she replied. "I think it's on its way. I need you to phone Dr McAlpine. Do you think you can do it?"

Matt went back into the hall and found the phone in the darkness. He picked up the phone and listened. There was no sound. He pressed the buttons again, trying to get a line. The phone did not respond. "It's not working Mum," he called.

"Shit," she replied, followed by another scream.

Matt had never heard his mother use such a word.

"Why now, why a bloody power cut now?"

Matt made his way back into the living room. He hugged his mother, not sure what to do.

"I'm going to need you to be a very brave boy," she said. "It's raining and cold outside, but I want you to be very grown up and go and fetch Andrew's Mum. I need her to help me. Do you think you can do that?"

He didn't think that he could, but said that he would. He went to the back door and found his gabardine coat and his wellingtons. "What shall I say Mum?" he called.

"Just tell her I need her. Tell her the baby is coming."

Matt opened the door and went round to the side of the house. Although it was dark, there was just enough light to get his sense of direction. As he turned the corner the rain struck him in the face, stinging his skin. He cried. He found his way to the road and walked along to the top of the Green, stepping in puddles along the way. He was very wet as he got to his friend's house. He knocked on the door. There was no response. The house and all the others on the Green were in darkness. The streetlights were out as well. He hit the door as hard as he could. It hurt. He slumped to the ground crying.

Suddenly, the door behind him opened. It was Andrew's father. "You wor right Dorothy. There is someone out here. It's Matthew from up t'road. What's tha doing out here son? Th'all catch thee death o' cold out there. Come on in, come on in son."

Matt almost crawled inside.

Like his own house everything was in darkness. Andrew's mother had found a torch and came downstairs. "Ee what's wrong Matthew? Where's your Mum? No, is it t'babee?" she suddenly exclaimed.

Matt was able to explain what had happened and that he'd left his mother on the living room floor.

"Jack, you look after the boy. I'm away up to his Mum's." With that she quickly put a coat on over her nightdress and found a pair of wellingtons herself.

It was 7 o'clock in the morning before they heard anything. Matt had spent the rest of the night on cushions from the sofa in Andrew's room. The two friends had not slept much with the noise of the storm and talking about the new baby.

Andrew's mother opened the front door and came into the house. "By eck it's parky out there. There's snow on t'tops as well. Who'd ha' thought it wor end o' April as well."

"Well?" beseeched her husband.

Matt stood still staring at his friend's mother as she took off her wet coat and boots. She'd changed into a jumper and some trousers of his mother's.

"You mean t'babee? Oh, they're fine. She'd nearly delivered it hersen by t'time I got there. But we finished things off good and proper. Beth from t'Farm's popped in at moment, until t'phones are back on and we can get hold o' Dr McAlpine." She stopped what she was doing and turned to Matt. "I suppose you'll be wanting to know whether you've got a brother or a sister?"

Matt nodded in anticipation.

"She's a bonny wee thing, make no mistake. Your Mum says that she and your Dad had talked about calling her Fiona if she wor a girl. After her favourite doll when she was a child."

Fiona, Matt thought. "Fee-O-Nar." He started to say the word over and over in his mind.

Later that morning, Andrew's mother took Matt and his friend back up to their house. Although it had stopped raining and the sun was coming out, a cold wind was blowing through the Dale. Matt looked up towards Skelton. There was indeed snow on the tops of the hills.

They went to the back door from where he had crept only a few hours earlier. Letting themselves in they could hear a baby crying.

"Go on. Go and see your sister," said Andrew's mother.

Matt ran upstairs to his mother's bedroom. The farmer's wife was arranging the pillows behind his mother who was cradling his sister. He went straight to her and put his arm round her shoulders. "Can I kiss her?" he asked.

"Of course you can," his mother replied.

Matt leant forward and kissed his baby sister on the forehead. "Hello Fee-O-Nar," he said.

CHAPTER NINE – FESTIVITIES
(Late December 2013)

In the end, Aurélie was looking forward to Christmas. She and Stefan took the new direct flight to Grenoble that had been launched for the winter schedule. It had been a welcome introduction for Aurélie, even though she knew that it would be full of people heading for a ski holiday. They would be going to the ski stations higher up in the Savoie mountains with the welcoming wooden chalets that they would have rented at excessive prices for their Christmas holidays. One drawback of the new service would no doubt be that her fellow passengers would be keen to start their holidays early with at least a few drinks on the plane. Why did the British always need alcohol to get themselves into the mood, she often wondered?

By the time that they arrived in Grenoble, Edinburgh was a distant thought. The flight hadn't been that bad after all and she and Stefan had talked most of the way. He had teased her about Matt.

She'd blushed and said that they were just good friends: "Nous sommes juste amis!" And anyway it was none of his business.

Aurélie's father had collected them from the airport and within the hour they were home. A family raclette dinner had been drawn out ending well after midnight after a round of local Génépi and Single Malt Whisky.

Matt had thrust the whisky in to Aurélie's hand that morning as she and Stefan had left for the airport. She hadn't been expecting him to be there and she'd told him it was a nice surprise as she kissed him on the cheek and hoped he'd have a nice Christmas. He'd watched the bus turn along Princes Street, before turning round and heading into the station. There was a smile on his face as he boarded the train and headed south.

He was looking forward to a few days at his parents' house near York before his sister and family arrived on Christmas Eve. "It'll be just the three of us again. Just like old times," his mother had reminisced when he had first suggested arriving before Christmas itself.

The family dog, Edgar, so called because of its ability to hoover up crumbs from around the dining table, bounded out to meet him as he got out of the taxi from the station.

"Good to have you home son," his mother greeted him at the door. "Such a shame you're by yourself though. It would have been nice if the two of you were still together. It'll feel like there's an empty chair at the table," she said.

"Mum, its over. Probably was for some time truth be known. You know that. I have explained."

"I know. I'm just saying," his mother replied.

It would be the first family Christmas since she and Matt had split up and he already knew that his mother would want to underline how much she was missed. She had always got on well with his mother sharing things like the Christmas cooking. That would be another change this year. Fiona's husband, Graham, had offered to take charge of the festive menu. Matt had not put up any resistance when his sister had suggested it. Indeed, he had positively welcomed it. The prospect of a family Christmas was not something that he looked forward to anyway, so soon after the two of them had split up. Not having to argue about the cooking was a bonus, although the clearing up would probably be down to him and Edgar he deduced.

It was a surprisingly pleasant week. Just the three of them. He and his father, along with Edgar, had enjoyed a couple of bracing walks on the North York Moors. They'd been up to Osmotherley and up Black Hambleton, the highest point for miles around. They'd looked out across the Vale of York towards Yoredale, his father reminiscing about times gone by and the area that he had once covered in his work for the Estate. They were good days and ones he wouldn't change, he said looking north towards the industrial dereliction of Teesside and the career that he had been destined for until circumstances had intervened. They had carried on and visited the village that he had grown up in and from where he had left to go to Hattonbridge to his national service. In some ways it had been a more satisfying and rewarding period of national service than many young men of his generation had endured. It had given him a career and a family, two things that many who had undertaken more futile activities as part of their two years service had not enjoyed.

Matt had driven his parents' Volvo home that evening in the darkening gloom, his father complaining of not always seeing too well at that time of day. Matt suspected it was more to do with the latent tear that had sat in the corner of his eye for most of the afternoon.

Fi and Graham, together with their ten year old daughter Ella, had arrived on Christmas Eve as planned. They were full of the usual horror stories of driving away from London at that time of year: the M25, the M1, the Catthorpe interchange with the M6, the M18, whether to take the A1 or keep up the M1 to Leeds, then the A64 and the York bypass. It was the same every year. Matt knew that it would be the topic of conversation for at least that evening, if not the next few days. Anticipation of the reverse journey would also start in advance of the return trip, meaning that in some instances there might only be a few traffic free hours of conversation in between. It was why these days he preferred to throw himself on to the mercy of the railways.

His mother had prepared the meal for their arrival and over dinner on Christmas Eve there was a suggestion that they should drive up to Hattondale on Boxing Day. Christmas Day was the usual sort of day: late breakfast, delayed present opening, worrying about making sure dinner would be ready on time, clearing away, some falling asleep in front of the television whilst others ventured out for a walk around the village, and then everyone waiting for someone to ask the question: 'is anyone hungry?'

By contrast, Boxing Day was more enlivening, although it turned into a bit of an expedition by the time that they had all got organised and fitted into the two cars. Matt travelled with his father and mother along with an expectant Edgar. The weather was again pleasantly mild for the time of year. They drove to the top of the Dale and stood admiring the view all the way to Cross Fell to the north, Buckden Pike to the south and the expanse of the North York Moors in the distance to the east, from where Matt and his father had stood looking in the opposite direction only a few days earlier. Matt's father earnestly repeated to Ella what he had recently told Matt; how he had worked these fells and dales for the Yoredale Estate before she was born. Ella played with Edgar, trying not to disappoint her grandfather. For a moment the family could have been on top of the world.

Matt's phone buzzed. *'Joyeux Noël'*, read the message. He smiled.

"Anyone we know?" enquired his sister, putting her arm through his and trying to peer over his shoulder.

"No, just a friend, just someone I've met in Edinburgh," Matt replied, shielding his response from prying eyes. "There," he said, as he pressed Send, thinking that his own season's greetings were about to be delivered halfway across Europe.

"A friend in Edinburgh?"

"I am allowed one you know. A friend that is!"

The siblings had always baited each other about their relationships and seemed to know when something was more than just a friendship.

"I'm pleased for you Matt. I thought that it was sad that you left Bath in the way that you did. I always thought that the two of you would get married one day. You know I did. But hey if you needed to move on I understand. I'm just glad that you're not by yourself up there."

"No I'm fine. It's been a shock to the system that I'll give you. But the job and it being in Edinburgh just prompted me to stop pretending any more. We'd become very different people. We were sharing a house but we had separate lives. Because we both worked at the same place it was also very difficult, as our friends had started to take sides."

"I understand," his sister said.

They rounded the others up and together the six of them drove back down the Dale to the village past the small two bedroomed house that had been the family's first home and where Fi had been born. They parked at the top of the Green. All six walked down past the old school towards the church; four of them remembering how the village used to look; two of them thinking of when they had first arrived in it.

There was a display of decorated Christmas trees in the church which Matt's mother had wanted to see, each of the trees having been decorated by a different village group. The church was in semi-darkness when they entered with only the lights from the displays illuminating the old building. The family had started to examine each of the exhibits intently checking the names of those who had contributed to the displays. As they made their way down the nave there was a rustling from the vestry and an old lady emerged clutching a mug of tea. "Oh, I'm sorry," she said. "I didn't think anyone was here, so I'd just taken the opportunity to go and make a cup of tea to keep myself warm. We'll be closing soon though. Do take a good look, I won't rush you. Have you come far?"

Matt and his sister stopped short. The same thought had occurred to both of them. "Miss Cussons?" said his sister, marginally before Matt had chance to proffer the same enquiry.

"Yes dear, do I know you?" replied the former school teacher.

"We were at school here in the village back in the 1970s when you were the head teacher. This is Matt and I'm Fiona. You'll remember our mother and father as well," Matt's sister said, beckoning to her parents to come back and join in the impromptu reunion.

Before long the family were deep in reminiscences about life in the village and how things had changed. Who had moved away; who was left; the closure of Taylor's shop; the disappearance of many of the trades from the village such as Calverts the joiners; and of course the school itself being closed. Miss Cussons had retired before that had happened, she'd said, but it was something that she missed nevertheless as she'd continued to go back to help the children with their reading. But now, the few children that there were in the village had to get a bus to Leyburn, even the little ones.

Outside the church Graham and Ella were playing with Edgar in the encroaching darkness, the light from the Christmas trees in the church casting a glow across the gravestones. Matt emerged from the church and stood in the porch staring towards the former school and the buildings at the other side of the field, beyond buildings whose silhouette he could just make out in the gathering gloom. As he watched Ella and Edgar and reflected on his own childhood he suddenly realised how far away Edinburgh actually was. At that moment it could have been as far away as Ghana had seemed to him as a small child.

The journey home was quieter as everyone reflected on their personal memories. Driving through Ripon they passed the site where Matt's grandfather's haulage business and garage had once stood. It had been sold some years ago before being closed by its new owners. In its place a supermarket had been built which, on Boxing Day, was in darkness and eerily quiet, its customers at home overstocked, over-fed and over-excited.

....

Three days later, Fi drove Matt to the station in York. He promised to stay in touch and get down to London to see them sometime soon. He'd been away from Edinburgh for two weeks and wanted to get back for Hogmanay, although he still wasn't sure how he was going to celebrate it. Since sending the text to Aurélie on Boxing Day he hadn't heard anything. He wasn't even sure if she would be back in time, or whether it had been a throwaway remark that he should have just ignored. If nothing else, he thought, there was always the Espy, which he was certain was advertising something for Hogmanay itself.

Bath Street was cold when he got back to Portobello later that afternoon. There was a wind blowing in from the Forth. Matt let himself into the close and stopped to collect his mail from the box in the hall. Most of it was, as usual, takeaway menus and free papers. As well as an untimely credit card statement, he identified what he presumed to be a couple of late Christmas cards. He carried them upstairs resolving to speak to the close's other residents about putting the junk mail straight into the bins outside. It was a fire hazard if nothing else where it was, particularly as it was evident that no one ever read any of it. There was a chill in the flat when he opened the door and he quickly drew the curtains and turned the heating on. Sorting the mail, most of which was still heading for the recycling, one of the envelopes caught his attention. The address, including the EH15 postcode were in a distinctive French style of handwriting.

Matt eagerly opened it. It was a 'Bonne Année' card from Aurélie. It had been posted before Christmas. Of course, he remembered, the French don't send Christmas cards. He had wondered. She wished him well, said that she was having a good break, that her family had welcomed her, but had asked her when she was moving back. Her last sentence caught him by surprise though. He'd momentarily forgotten. She'd definitely be back in Edinburgh on the 31st and would he like to do Hogmanay on Princes Street with her. Was he up for The Pet Shop Boys?

He smiled.

With the next few days to suddenly look forward to and the flat feeling markedly warmer, Matt decided to spend the evening going through some of the boxes that remained stacked in the hall after their delivery from Bath two months earlier. Until now he had stubbornly and defiantly ignored them. He put a frozen meal in the oven and sat down in the living room. The first box had contained surprisingly few things of real interest and most of it went into either the recycling, or a box he assigned for the charity shop. However, the second box was decidedly more interesting. It was an accumulation of items from his childhood that he had long since stored away and forgotten about. There was a collection of coins he had once treasured and some toys that he assumed he had had a particular attachment to. At the bottom of the box, preserved under the weight of the rest of his childhood, was the scrapbook that his mother had bought him for his father's postcards from Edinburgh all those years ago.

He didn't remember getting them all. His father had sent most of them during his first year at University. They were mostly of steam engines as he had expected, but there were also some of famous Scottish landmarks including Edinburgh castle and the Forth Bridge. Some had begun to become unstuck and as he turned the pages of the scrapbook, the ageing glue gave up its grip and some of the postcards fell from their resting places. Matt began to turn them over. They revealed his father's unmistakable handwriting, which he was able to read for the first time in over forty years. It was neat and had clearly been written in a way that he would, as a young child, have been able to read. Most of the comments were of things that his father had seen whilst in the city, one even saying that he had seen the Queen. But what Matt noticed above all, was that his father had invariably ended them all with 'my love to you both'. He stood up and went to the window. He pulled back the curtains. It was dark outside apart from the street lights along Bath Street. A young couple were hurrying towards the High Street.

'Love' was not an emotion he had ever really associated with his father and yet here was evidence of him openly expressing it all those years before. Parents were often enigmas, he thought, when it came to raising their children. If only they were more confident in expressing their love for one another, the effect on their children would be life changing. He carefully put the cards back into the scrapbook once again closing in the sentiments that had lain hidden between its covers for so many years.

Matt woke early the following morning; probably too early bearing in mind it was Hogmanay. By mid-morning he found that he was staring at his phone again. He put it in the hall but later brought it back into the living room. Aurélie's card had not said when she would be arriving back in Edinburgh. It had also not suggested when or where they could meet. He tried picking up a couple of reports for work to read but very quickly the words began to blur and he realised that he'd read the same paragraph at least four times without taking it in.

Around 12 o'clock the phone suddenly buzzed. A text from Aurélie. He shrieked as he picked up the machine that he'd been cursing all morning. The message read *'Back in Edinburgh. See you at The Jolly Judge at 17h.'*

He was ready by 3.00, having showered and shaved and was on a bus into the city centre by 4.00. He stared out of the upstairs windows, a sense of nervous teenage anticipation overcoming him in a way that he had not experienced for many years. The traffic was lighter with most people having finished early for the day and already home. By contrast, others were beginning to gather in the city centre, anticipating the night ahead. There was a sense of excitement and optimism in the air which Matt shared. He was the young man again in the city at the start of a new year. Passers by were already wishing each other Happy New Year even though there were still over six hours of the old one left.

He made his way to the Jolly Judge where they had first got to know each other. He nervously looked around the already crowded bar. There was no sign of her. He managed to get to the bar itself and bought a pint and lingered. A couple from Germany engaged him in conversation and asked him if it was his first time at an Edinburgh Hogmanay as well. He admitted that it was but took pride in telling them that he did live in the city though.

Time went on. He was on his second pint and it was going up to 7.00 when a familiar voice interrupted him.

"Bonsoir. Been waiting long?"

"No, just got here," Matt lied.

Aurélie leant forward offering him the side of her head for two air kisses. "You look well. How was Christmas?" she asked.

It hadn't been too bad, he suggested, although he was more interested in hearing about the Alps and whether she had managed to go skiing. He remembered her grandmother and hoped that she was much better. Their drinks in the Jolly Judge continued until after 9 o'clock when they decided to find something to eat. By the time of the final hour, they'd tried to get down The Mound to see, or at least hear, The Pet Shop Boys in the gardens, which, they had quickly realised, was a forlorn hope in the circumstances. Instead, they'd walked down the High Street as far as the World's End; been interviewed by Japanese television; and been kissed and hugged by any number of complete strangers. It was a crazy time of the year.

The great thing was though, Matt thought, as he looked at Aurélie's arm tucked through his own, was that nobody cared if there was an apparent age difference between the two them. More important was that it was Edinburgh; and it was

New Year. "A hundred thousand, they're saying," the barman had said in The Jolly Judge before they had left.

As the cacophony and light show of the fireworks at midnight got underway, heralding in the New Year itself, they had found themselves at the foot of Calton Hill with a vantage point that took in the whole of the city centre. It was exhilarating. It was extraordinary. It was Hogmanay in Edinburgh as they had both imagined it would be. By the time they had later conga'd their way up the High Street and joined in an impromptu cèilidh on Teviot Square, the New Year was well seen in. It had all been a delicious blur.

Precisely how they had ended up at Aurélie's flat Matt wasn't sure. After the cèilidh they had become involved with a group of Australians for a short while. It had involved a rugby ball and some beer with the ball being kicked towards the can. If you knocked the can over, the beer was yours. The Aussies had moved on and Matt and Aurélie had ambled further across The Meadows sharing a can that she had claimed. Although fuelled by a cocktail of heady excess, beer and whisky, the night air had started to remind both of them that it was the first of January and not a summer's evening. It was also four o'clock in the morning. Aurélie offered him her sofa acknowledging that a walk to Portobello at that hour of the morning was not the best of ideas. The sofa was short and hard but she kissed him good night and thanked him for a great evening.

Some hours later he had woken to the smell of fresh coffee. Aurélie had brought it through to him already dressed. They'd been talking for some time before realising that neither of them had any real plans for the next few days. Aurélie said that she was sure that Hubert could probably find his way over to Portobello if Matt was likely to be in. He said that he was sure that he would.

Their conversation though was cut short by a phone call from France. Aurélie started by wishing the caller, who Matt presumed to be her mother, 'Bonne Année'. However, unable to understand what was being said he nevertheless understood that not all was well. Aurélie, put her hand over the mouthpiece and said "It's my grandmother," and then a short while later "I'll call you." Matt let himself out of the flat.

The Meadows on New Years Day was awash with those still finding their way home from the night before and those who weren't yet quite ready to do so. There were also joggers, pram pushers, cyclists and dog walkers venturing out for the first time in the New Year. Matt stood for a moment trying to take it in whilst picturing in his mind's eye that first day he had come to Edinburgh as a young boy and they had got off the bus at the other side of the Meadows on the way to the Strachans' flat.

He could not remember the last time that he had felt so relaxed and happy. It had taken him back to days that they had spent together when they had first moved to Bath. It was a good feeling and he smiled to himself as he watched Edinburgh's masses enjoying their Ne'er Day. Something sat uneasily with him though. Aurélie fascinated him and they had clearly enjoyed each other's company the previous evening and over recent weeks. But, what about the age difference? What would others, people like Helen or his sister, Fiona, think? More importantly what did Aurélie think? He recalled putting his arm around her shoulders once or twice as they had walked around the city the night before. She hadn't pulled away and yet he had felt uneasy. She'd put her arm through his. More importantly, she had also just kissed him on the cheek when he had left her flat rather than air kissing him as she had done the night before when they had first met in the bar and, what was more, she had said she would bring Hubert over to the seaside again. He let out an ecstatic "yes!" as he reached the old hospital buildings, much to the surprise of a young couple pushing a pram. "Sorry, if I startled you," he said smiling down at the infant who smiled back.

He headed for Princes Street in search of a bus to Portobello. He passed a shop open near the foot of Chambers Street and in spite of the croissant that Aurélie had offered him; a cold Steak Slice had never tasted so good. He found himself eating it whilst smiling broadly at total strangers, as he made his way down North Bridge above an untypically quiet Waverley Station.

As he sat on the bus heading towards Portobello he began to think of the New Year ahead. Helen had been right he thought, the new Act and the referendum were going to be pivotal in Scotland in ways in which they could not yet predict. The promises that were increasingly being made about independence seemed to Matt to be largely untested and yet, by contrast, there was no voice of opposition. The 'No' campaign was a strange political alliance of so-called unionists including those from both the left and the right and those who were just naturally opposed to independence for their own personal reasons. Their problem, Matt perceived, was that they had no mouthpiece, nothing or no-one to rally around. It was going to be a long year if the 'Yes' contingent was going to have it all its own way.

One thing Matt did acknowledge though, was that Holyrood had been good for children. With or without independence, devolution had given Scotland its voice. It had helped it to find its feet and to forge its own brand of social democracy for which it had a long tradition, but which at times felt as though it was marginalised within the rest of the United Kingdom. Since devolution, Scotland had achieved some courageous and challenging things for children, including the new Children's Bill. For a change it hadn't just tartanised what had been previously introduced for England and Wales. Matt felt proud to be working in Scotland and looked forward to influencing the final outcome.

CHAPTER TEN - ONE HOT SUMMER
(Summer 1974)

June 1974 was warm in Edinburgh. The temperature was over 70 degrees Fahrenheit for much of the month including the day of Matt's father's graduation. He had completed his ordinary degree the year before but had stayed on and produced his dissertation to turn it into an Honours degree. It was a momentous year in the broader country as well and there had already been one general election which had returned a minority Labour government at Westminster in London. In Scotland, the Scottish National Party had returned seven MPs to parliament and had received nearly a quarter of the vote. Graduating in Edinburgh that summer left Matt's father excited and keen to get on with his life and to support his young family.

They had managed to visit him on a few occasions, whilst he had taken every opportunity to travel south to be a father to both Matt and his new daughter, Fiona. However, although their mother had managed to return to work on a part time basis, money had been extremely limited and both sets of grandparents had helped out as often as they could. The Estate had remained supportive and had held a job open for him to return to. July and the opportunity to start earning again could not come soon enough.

As well as the three of them, Matt's grandparents had travelled to Edinburgh for his graduation and they had paid for them all to stay at the Guest House where they had first stayed with Matt shortly before Fiona was born. It was a hectic morning on the day of the graduation itself and everyone was becoming fraught. Matt had quietly got on with breakfast whilst others became more and more frantic. He finished his own plateful and then quietly cleaned up those of his mother and his grandmother. It was only when he had dripped tomato sauce from the baked beans on his white shirt that anyone else noticed. He was quickly taken back to the bedroom by his mother who attempted to clean it off.

"You could have kept it clean," she said. "At least until later." She sponged it down but the stain stubbornly refused to move. "You're just going to have to go as you are."

Matt looked at himself in the mirror and thought that it would have looked a lot less conspicuous if his mother had left it alone.

The day was warm and they headed for the bus into the centre of Edinburgh. The bus was busy and they had to stand, Matt's grandmother holding onto his sister whilst his mother supported her pushchair. Matt and his grandfather stood near the back. By the time they arrived in the middle of town they were even hotter as was the mood amongst the adults. They met Matt's father on Chambers Street. He was already wearing his academic robes which may have been appropriate for the occasion but not for the weather. Matt's grandmother insisted on photographs on the steps of the museum. It was going to be a long day, Matt thought, already bored.

The graduation ceremony itself was a long and formal affair and although they were not consulted it had been decided that it would be too long for Matt and Fiona to sit through. Consequently it had been arranged that Mr and Mrs

McCallum, the couple that Matt's father had stayed with most recently, would take the children up to the castle, before they would all meet for lunch in a hotel on Princes Street. Although the castle was one of his favourite places in the city and whilst he knew the McCallums, it wasn't entirely what he had been expecting. He had been there when his father had first moved away to university; he had supported his mother when she had missed him; he had been there when his sister had been born; and now aged nine, he had very much wanted to be there at the end. Why else had his mother asked Miss Cussons if he could have the time off school, he thought, as they walked around the castle. He tried hard not to appear too ungrateful when Mr McCallum took him to see Mons Meg, the Canon that was fired at one o'clock every day. But it was hard.

They met up with his parents and grandparents at the top of The Mound. The four of them were smiling and laughing and thanked the McCallums for looking after the children. Matt stood back and grudgingly offered his own thanks after his father encouraged him to do so. Lunch was similarly a contrast between the four adults' excitement and the children's indifference, although Fiona had soon started to feed off their infectious enthusiasm.

After lunch they walked in the gardens, bought ice creams and enjoyed the warmth and the sunshine. They were approaching the Scott Monument when Matt's father encouraged him forward and said "Come on. Why don't you and I go to the top? Do you remember that first time when you thought it was a real person?"

The two of them bought their tickets and climbed the 287 steps to the top. They walked round the viewing balcony looking down on Princes Street and the others far below. "I'm sorry you didn't get to come today. Perhaps I should have got you a ticket as well. I just thought ..."

"I just wanted to be there Dad. I know it's your degree, but it's been hard for Mum and me as well you know."

"I know. I realise that now. I suppose that I haven't realised how much you have grown up since I've been here. You were only just starting school and now you're nearly ten. I'm sorry." His father put his arm around his son's shoulders and for a moment they stood in silence, broken only by the noises of the city around them.

"Dad, I wish we could live here," Matt said eventually, looking up at his father. "I really like it here."

"Maybe one day. One day when you're a bit older. We'll see," said his father. "Come on, let's go down and join the others."

A week later Matt and his mother and sister stood on Northallerton station looking expectantly towards Darlington. They had come home with his grandparents after the graduation whilst his father had stayed on to sort a few things out and pack up. His father's train appeared on the horizon. Holding Fiona, his mother stepped forward when he got off the train. They hugged. Matt stood back thinking back to the day that his father had departed from the same station. It seemed like a lifetime ago.

His father seemed to talk all the way back to Hattonbridge in the car, or so it seemed to Matt. How things were going to be different now he was home; the things that they would do together as a family; the jobs that he would be able to do around the house; the things that he could help with. Matt gazed out of the window of the car. For the last four years he had been the man of the house, or so he thought. He had fetched the coal in and laid the fire each morning. He had put the rubbish out for the dustbin men on Fridays. The cottage that Matt had known as home all his life was also very quickly going to feel too small for the four of them, particularly as his mother had said that he would have to share his bedroom with his sister. It was going to take some getting used to having his father home.

School broke up for the summer a week later and his friends were talking of their holidays: most heading for Yorkshire's east coast, with a few making for Blackpool. One or two from the Pennine View estate were going abroad. Although they'd said where they were going, it meant nothing to Matt. His family weren't going to be able to have a proper holiday this year as his father needed to get back to work. He'd have to make do with a few days with his grandparents in Ripon, although his aunt had promised to take him to the Test Match in Leeds at the end of July where England were playing Pakistan. Matt enjoyed playing cricket in the school playground and he was looking forward to a day out in Leeds, particularly with his aunt who always spoiled him. It would also make up for England not being in that summer's Football World Cup, although he had found himself supporting Scotland instead. At least they were there he had thought.

But for much of the summer and the school holidays, Matt and Andrew spent their time in the Dale itself, venturing further and further up towards Skelton as their confidence grew. A feature of the Dales are the stone barns found high up the hillsides set alongside the limestone walls. They were an inevitable attraction to the two boys who moved their Den into one of these barns for the summer. It was their escape. They could look out over the fields and the summer flowers below. The scent and the warm sunshine of the summer were intoxicating. It felt to them as though they could stay there all the holidays and no one would miss them.

They talked of many things over the summer, including what lay ahead for them; what they were going to do with the rest of their lives. Andrew was keen to follow his Dad, driving some of the machines that worked on the farms in the Dale and with the Estate. His Dad sometimes took him with him in the cab. He knew how to drive a tractor, or so he tried to convince Matt.

"Don't believe you," he said. "You're not old enough any road."

"Tha doesn't have to be any age to drive one on t'fields. That's why my Dad sez."

There was an uneasy silence between the two friends, broken only by the noise of the gentle breeze and the bleating of the lambs in the fields around.

"What's tha wanna do when tha grows up?" said Andrew eventually.

"I don't really know I suppose. Just summat, but maybe not round here." Matt gazed down the Dale towards the village. "Hattondale is beautiful though. I just think I wanna be somewhere else."

They scampered back down the hillside, laughing and tumbling through the grass, narrowly avoiding the cow pats, until they reached a stretch of the River Hatton where they had built a dam out of stones and mud. The two boys waded into the river and started adding to their construction, joined in their mutual endeavour. After a few minutes, Matt stopped and looked up, gazing across the fields.

"What's wrong with thee?" his friend said.

"Don't know really," Matt replied. "I just don't want this to stop." He wiped away a single tear that rolled slowly down his cheek with his grubby hand leaving a dirty streak across his face.

School resumed in early September and the boys' time in the Dale was limited to after school and weekends when they would still escape as often as they could. Their dam had been breached on more than one occasion and it was an increasing challenge for them to keep revisiting it to reinforce it. Eventually its attraction waned as the leaves on the trees began to show the first tinges of bronze and late summer turned into early autumn.

At home, Matt's father had recognised that the cottage was no longer big enough for his growing family and as he had settled back into his job he had put in a request to the estate for a larger property. It was expected that one further down the Green towards the Hattonbridge Inn would soon become available and they had started packing up even though a move had not yet been confirmed. Matt was not happy with the prospect of the move as even though he was now sharing his bedroom with his sister, it would deprive him of the view up the Dale from his window. Although the house was bigger, being in the village it also had a smaller garden.

"Yes," his father had conceded. "You're right, but think of it this way. You'll be nearer the stop for the school bus when you start at the High School next year."

Matt thought of it, but couldn't reconcile it. It was just another indication that the world as he knew it was set to change yet again and he didn't seem to have any control over it. "If we've got to move, why can't we all move to Edinburgh, like you said?" he'd asked.

His father had replied that none of them wanted to leave the Dale really, did they? It was where his and his Mum's jobs were and his grandparents were just down the road, and also it was where his friends were. "Andrew wouldn't want you to move, would he?" his father said.

Matt was confused. His father was right. He didn't want to leave the Dale. It had been his playground all through the school holidays and he hadn't wanted it to come to an end. But the trips at the start of the summer to Edinburgh and Leeds had shown him, even as a nine year old, that there was a world beyond the Dale, one that was full of opportunity and excitement.

School was closed for the day on October 10th as it was used as a Polling Station for the second General Election of the year. There were posters up in some of the windows around the Green for the local candidates, although it was a relatively foregone conclusion which party would win the seat. Matt found himself taken in by both the theatre of the election and the way that it was being played out. It underlined for him that the Dale and the area were very different places from those that were regularly being seen on the television. He developed an interest in geography almost as a consequence and his fascination for reciting peculiar words in his head was rewarded with the names of some of the constituencies that were being contested. Where exactly were Huyton and Sidcup anyway? It wasn't only geography that had begun to take hold of him. The fervour of some of the debates that were being played out sowed the first seeds for him of what he would later know as social justice. Even to a nine year old some things were clearly important.

CHAPTER ELEVEN - A NEW YEAR
(January / February 2014)

It was early afternoon when he got back to Portobello. There were a number of people gathered by the Espy and on the beach. Some were in fancy dress and, mad as it looked, ready for a bracing Ne'er Day dip in the Forth. He declined the opportunity, wished them well and with a slightly incredulous smile on his face headed inside. The need for sleep was fast creeping up on him as he unlocked the street door and climbed the stairs to his flat. He passed Mrs McNiven on the landing and wished her a Happy New Year. Closing the door behind him though, the sense of anticipation with which he had left the previous evening quickly drained away.

Sitting down he put the television on. Kirk Douglas and Richard Harris were re-enacting The Heroes of Telemark for the umpteenth time. It was either that or the Sound of Music on New Year's Day. Why the second world war, whether set to music or not, was appropriate viewing for the optimistic start to a new year Matt had never understood, but he settled down in front of the Norwegian snowy landscape nevertheless.

The credits were rolling some time later when his work phone buzzed and jolted him from his slumber. He was puzzled as to who would be texting him on his work phone at this time of year. Rubbing his eyes, he entered his password and waited for the message to load.

'*Hi, how U doing. Happy NY. I'm having a party tonight. Do U want to come.*' There was no name and he didn't recognise the number. Only business contacts and colleagues had that number and he thought of Alison, Dougie, Anna and Helen. It was unlikely to be Helen. He couldn't imagine her using abbreviations and besides, apart from Alison, he had their numbers stored in his phone.

It was another few minutes before the phone buzzed again. It was the same number. *'Sorry, brain fade. Its Catriona. Phone me for directions.'* It took him a short while to work out how she had his number. Then he remembered. He'd given her his business card at the Film Quiz at the Espy. A short while later he was showered and changed and with a bottle of wine he was saving for an occasion in his hand, he was making his way over the High Street towards the address that Catriona had given him when he had called her back. Lee Crescent was a terrace of two storey family houses, not quite Bath's Royal Crescent but well presented nonetheless.

Just as Matt had identified the house he was looking for, a familiar sound materialised from behind him. The Wasp overtook him slewing to a halt a few yards further on. Its rider dismounted and parked his machine by the side of the road. He made his way to the door that Matt had just spotted and let himself in. Matt followed him.

"Thanks for getting that Dylan," Catriona said, coming to the door as he opened it, the noise of music emerging into the street. Catriona took a carrier bag from her son and went to close the door. "Sorry, didn't see you there," she said to the waiting Matt. "Come in. Sorry about the texts earlier. Come on in. Matt, this is Dylan my son. Dylan, this is Matt, a friend from The Espy."

"I know," said Dylan. "Hi."

Catriona showed Matt through to the lounge where a number of people were already gathered. "Rob, you remember Matt from the Espy," she said, reintroducing Matt to her quiz team partner. "I'll just take these bits through to the kitchen."

"Yes, no problem," replied Rob. "How's your John Hannah poetry doing then Matt?"

"Not bad!" answered Matt. "I must try and get there again on a Monday. It was good fun."

The evening was a relaxed affair, just chatting. Probably what he needed, he felt, given the time that he had finally gone to sleep on Aurélie's sofa the night before. He even found himself talking to the Wasp's owner, or rather Dylan as he had discovered. Dylan was studying music production at college and was involved in the local music scene. Not quite the social irritant that Matt had first encountered when he had moved into Bath Street four months earlier. The Wasp itself, it transpired, was a seventeenth birthday present from his father, Nick, who was an engineer in oil and gas and worked in America. Before he had chance to ask if Nick lived with them when he was home in the UK, Catriona pulled Matt away.

"Come and meet my best friend," said Catriona taking Matt by the arm and pushing him through to the kitchen at the back of the house. "Kate, this is Matt." He recognised her as one of the other mums from the Espy when he had first breakfasted there. Kate was some years younger than Catriona, he noted.

Before long Matt realised that Kate was prodding him for information. Oddly he found himself happy to give it. Yes, he was single. No he didn't have a significant other, nor did he have children. Yes, he knew Edinburgh and he called it home; and not just somewhere to stay; but Yorkshire had a pull on him as well.

Instead of responding with information about herself though, Kate started to tell Matt all about Catriona. She was from the west coast, somewhere near Skye, though Kate wasn't quite sure where. She'd moved to Aberdeen to go to college; lived with her cousin apparently. College hadn't worked out though and she'd met Nick. Nick was from the north-east of England and was in oil and gas. Dylan was born a year later. Life had been good to them as Nick's career had developed. A nice house, comfortable life style, everything that working in the oil industry could provide. What it had also given Nick though was the opportunity to travel and with the travel an opportunity for other relationships. Their own had become strained and Catriona had gradually come to complain of feeling like a married single parent.

They'd separated and after the sale of their house just outside Aberdeen, Catriona had moved to Edinburgh with Dylan where she subsequently discovered that she was pregnant with Bobby. Nick had stood by his responsibilities though and he did continue to support his children. It was too late to save their marriage though and they'd divorced shortly after. Eventually Nick had settled in Houston with his second wife, an American woman ten years his junior. Catriona had reverted to her maiden name after the divorce. It had all been just over six years ago. "Living the American dream had always been Nick's ambition according to Catriona," Kate told Matt.

Of course he had, Matt thought, reflecting on the names of his children. It also explained why Ponytail was that little bit older than the other mums in The Espy.

It was a good party. Matt relaxed, feeling himself more at home in the city than he had ever done before. It was going to be an exciting year, he reflected to himself. The new children's legislation going through the parliament at Holyrood for which the Centre had a role to play; the independence referendum to come in September; and, by contrast, the Tour de France starting in Yorkshire and heading for Hattonbridge. He smiled contentedly as he poured himself a glass of red wine.

The evening wore on with the usual party mix of chat, music, drink and food, although the latter became more and more ignored as time went by. Matt and Rob eschewed the virtues of cold sausage rolls to each other, wondering on the proportion that were eaten at this time of year, against the percentage that ended up in the bin. Probably more of the latter, they both agreed over a glass of a particularly smokey Single Malt that seemed endlessly more appealing than the pastry and sausagemeat concoctions that stared back at them from the table.

Dylan joined them and Matt began to see more and more of the man inside the boy. She had always said that she wanted children and by now they could have had a son of Dylan's age. By contrast, he thought, Nick did have a son and yet there were thousands of miles between them. As a father he had to be content with doling out periodic largesse in the form of mopeds and the like, to the grief of his ex-wife's friends and neighbours.

Towards midnight Matt realised that he had probably only had two or three hours sleep in the last 24 and he began to find himself drifting into that wonderful semi-comatose state, brought on by alcohol and a warm environment. Catriona noticed him. "Hey, come on you, enough of that. This is supposed to be a party. Come on, let's have a dance."

Reluctantly Matt raised himself to his feet and stood in the middle of the floor, gently swaying to the music, occasionally lifting one foot. By contrast, Catriona was alive, dancing around his totem like pose, her ponytail once again mesmerising him. "I'm sorry," he said at one point as her trajectory brought them close together. "I don't think I've got a lot left in me I'm afraid."

The music on the CD player ended. "Come on then," said Catriona, "I'll walk you home."

"Walk me home? I'm not that far gone!" replied Matt. "And anyway what about the others?" he said, looking round and quickly realising that there were in fact only a few others left.

"Oh, Dylan'll look after things here, I fancy a walk," said Catriona collecting her coat at the front door.

The sobering effect of the cold night air hit them both as they ventured outside. Catriona instinctively put her arm through Matt's. They staggered along the Crescent supporting each other and speculating about the house lights that were still on in the street and what was going on behind their curtains.

They began to giggle like a pair of adolescent teenagers as their explanations became more and more preposterous.

Portobello High Street was a sea of light as they crossed it, even though it was the early hours of the morning. There were others around and various loud and drunken New Year's greetings were exchanged. Walking down Bath Street Catriona began to question Matt more closely about himself and his work. What exactly was CECS? Excellence in what? What were Children's Services anyway? Matt had to think hard. It was difficult trying to explain such things without resorting to jargon at the best of times but in the early hours of the morning and with the influence of a few glasses of wine and a Single Malt or two, it was a significant challenge. "Maybe another day," he said.

"No, I want to know now," Catriona replied, teasing him and prodding him until he giggled.

It was a still night when they got to the end of Bath Street and they carried on the few yards beyond Matt's door to the esplanade where they gazed out over the Forth. Lights on the northern shore in Fife twinkled in the distance.

"Quite magical," said Catriona. "What's your New Year's resolution then?" she asked.

"Not sure I believe in that sort of thing," he replied. "Been let down too many times I'm afraid."

"Oh, go on. You must have one. We all do really. Even if it's only a dream, we all still have them. Seven years ago I had one and it certainly didn't include Portobello." She laughed. "Do you know what? Now I probably wouldn't have it any other way. This place has been good to me. Just one thing missing though. Just one thing."

"And what's that then?" Matt asked.

"Can't you guess?" she said leaning forward, embracing him and kissing him on the lips.

....

Hubert did not make it to Portobello as promised. Her text had been brief. Her grandmother was not well again and she was on the phone to her mother all the time. Matt was not sure whether this was some sort of code. He was getting used to her grandmother's ailments. Was it co-incidence that they seemed to get worse when he and Aurélie had made a tentative arrangement?

With no further distractions, he had used the rest of the long New Year's break to look forward to the coming year. It was the day before he was due back at work and he was checking his diary to remind himself what awaited him on his return. Standing by his flat window he found himself nearly blinded by the trajectory of the mid-afternoon low winter sun, which was descending quickly to the horizon at the far end of Bath Street. One feature of the year's new legislation for children continued to challenge him. It was also beginning to get coverage in the press. It was an idea that every child or young person growing up in Scotland would have a champion or a guardian angel, as some were choosing to call it, although in reality they were to be known as 'named persons'. The libertarian perspective was that this was a bridge too far, an invasion of family life, whilst the alternative view of those who supported it, was that it was about protecting children, about giving them a safety net. For some the debate was an indication of the government's interventionist standpoint. Matt saw parallels with the independence debate itself, although the irony for him was that the positions were reversed. On the one hand, the unionists were effectively arguing that Scotland needed a 'named person' in the form of the government at Westminster in London to look after its safety and to protect it from itself and the wider world. On the other, the nationalists, striving for independence, were suggesting that the Scottish family was strong enough to look after itself and no longer needed the British guardian angel.

CECS was closely involved with consultation around the Act and early in the New Year Matt and Helen were invited to a meeting at Victoria Quay, the monolithic building in Leith to the north of the city that housed the government's administration. It had been built on the site of the former docks which Matt had first seen when visiting his father at University. In their heyday, the docks had been an important part of Edinburgh's economy and had emphasised the city's historical and commercial links with those northern European countries that the government had been keen to emulate when it had first come to power.

Afterwards Matt and Helen had made their way to the nearby Ocean Terminal, for a debrief over a coffee rather than making their way back to the University. Ocean Terminal was a ubiquitous complex of shops and entertainment opportunities that had been developed on the dock site to provide for Scotland's civil servants as well as those living in the glass and steel apartments overlooking the waterfront. The café was empty apart from two staff who were engaged in conversation about their respective New Years. Matt and

Helen sat by the window. Outside, silhouetted against the setting sun was the former Royal Yacht Britannia. Another irony, Matt noted, as he contemplated this former symbol of British power and empire, captured now as a museum piece so close to the centre of emerging nationalist power.

Helen was going over what they had learnt and was talking about how they would respond to the planned consultation when it was launched, but Matt found his attention distracted. A group of people had come in to the café and had sat a few tables behind Helen. They were placing their order with one of the members of staff who had broken off from recounting her Hogmanay highlights.

"Un grand café filtre pour moi, s'il vous plaît," said a familiar French voice. "Oh, I'm sorry, I forget, I mean, a large coffee please." Other voices placed their own orders, of which at least one other was French. Matt paused, not sure what to do. He stared at Britannia, its shape now only a grey outline against the ever darkening sky as the sun had disappeared from view.

Helen interrupted him. "Matt, are you with us?"

"My apologies, I was miles away," he lied. "That ship out there has had me thinking. A bit of a relic, like myself."

"Speak for yourself," Helen retorted. "Now, are we going to get this consultation planned?"

They continued their deliberations over Helen's laptop for the next twenty minutes or so with Matt keeping his voice deliberately low, to Helen's obvious mild irritation. As they stood up to leave Matt glanced over, desperate to see who

Aurélie was with. He quickly caught sight of the group at the table. There were four of them. Aurélie had her back to Matt but was sitting next to a young man who Matt quickly concluded was about her own age. There were two other young women sitting opposite them. All four were laughing at something that the young man had said. Matt left the café with Helen and the two of them caught the bus back to the city. Helen got off half way as they reached the new town, but before she did she told him that she and her husband, Simon, were having a dinner party at the weekend and would he like to come. Apparently they always had some friends round once Hogmanay was out of the way. It served to bring the New Year's celebrations to a more sedate conclusion. Matt replied that he'd love to.

As Helen stood up to get off the bus, she turned to Matt. "Oh and do bring someone if you like. It will be four or five couples; though don't worry if you want to come by yourself. We'll fit you in."

"Thanks," Matt said. "That sounds really nice," lying for the second time in as many hours to his boss.

Matt caught the bus to Portobello from outside Jenners. It was beginning to rain but he didn't notice as he stood contemplating his options. A week or two earlier, he hadn't known anyone socially within the city, but now he was faced with Hobson's choice! The rain dripped on his collar and ran down inside his jacket. He gave an involuntary shiver as the bus came round the corner from Princes Street.

Thirty minutes later he was walking down Bath Street past the Co-op, the rain whipping up the street from the estuary, challenging his supposedly storm proof umbrella as well as North Face's advanced technology. An unlit car was coming out of the car park as he stepped across the short access road. Matt hadn't seen it. A short blast on the car's horn brought him up sharp. "Put your bloody lights on then," he began, but didn't finish. The driver was beckoning him to get in.

The car's interior was warm but damp and condensation was in danger of winning the battle with its heater. "Missed you," said Catriona, reaching over and giving Matt a quick peck on the cheek as he got in out of the rain. "You need to pay more attention. I could have run you down and then where would we be. No more nights like the other week!"

"You need to look where you're going," Matt replied, aware that he was dripping over the car's seats.

"Come on, I'll drive you down the road," said Catriona.

"Thanks. That would be good. It's a nice night for ducks out there and not a lot else."

They drove slowly along the street until they reached the communal bins opposite Matt's flat. There was no sign of the Wasp or Dylan. Catriona pulled the car over and turned the ignition off. "Did you know they once filmed an episode of that tv programme about the Edinburgh detective here?"

"You mean Rebus?" said Matt.

"Yes, that's the one. They disguised the Espy, made it look all boarded up. The baddy was meant to be holed up inside."

"Amazing what they can do for films. I must look out for it. It's bound to turn up on one of those strange tv channels you can get these days that shows repeats from twenty years ago. Listen, do you want to come in?" Matt asked.

"I'd love to, but I'd better not. Dylan's looking after Bobby and he's meant to be going out later if this weather lets him," Catriona replied. The rain was turning lumpy as it lashed against the windscreen. Snow was not far away.

"Oh well, never mind, maybe next time," said Matt.

"That would be good, maybe at the weekend. How about Saturday?" replied Catriona.

"Yes, why not," he said. "Why don't you come round for something to eat? I'm good at cooking - honest! Oh, actually, I've just remembered. I've just been asked by my boss if I'd like to go to hers for dinner on Saturday. But she did say, I could bring someone if I wanted to. Would you like to? I know that sounds a bit crass, but I'm sure you'd be more than welcome."

"Why not? Sounds a laugh," said Catriona. "I'll drive you as well if you want. Let me know what time you want me to pick you up."

Matt leant over and proffered a kiss. He was too wet for anything else. He got out of the car and hurried across to his close. He turned and watched as Catriona drove away, her tracks clearly visible in the developing slush.

Later that evening, as he was loading the washing machine with his wet clothes, his phone rang. It was Aurélie. Not who he had expected particularly after having seen her earlier at Ocean Terminal. Slightly taken aback he asked her how the rest of her new year had gone and enquired after her grandmother and her family back home. She said that her grandmother was much improved and that her family were well. She'd missed the festival of the three kings that her village celebrated on January 5th but New Year's Eve in Edinburgh had more than made up for it.

Matt was beginning to think that it was going to be a 'letting him down gently' sort of conversation, when without any build up Aurélie suddenly said, "so, do you fancy showing me Scotland's so-called skiing this weekend? I'm busy Saturday afternoon, but we could go Sunday if you wanted. Hubert needs to see more of the sights of Scotland."

Before he'd had chance to think too far ahead, Matt found himself committed to going skiing to Glenshee with Aurélie that coming Sunday.

CHAPTER TWELVE - A WINTER CHILL
(Winter 1978 - 1979)

Matt's father had been right. The move to the house in the village was closer to the school bus stop. Although he missed the freedom of living on the edge of the Dale, on cold, wet and dark mornings he was grateful for the shorter walk. By that autumn he was starting his third year at Yoredale High School. Moving up from the small village primary had been a chastening experience for him. Initially, he had been daunted by the numbers of young people around him and the scale of the buildings that the school site was spread over. He didn't find the more formal studying and homework, that secondary school required, easy and subjects that he had once enjoyed became increasingly challenging. He was not going to be the scientist that he had once aspired to be.

Third year, he had quickly discovered, was also something of a forgotten year. The black hole within the school's function through which an individual child's interest, and consequently their prospects, could be lost. They were neither the new pupils, nor the ones that teachers devoted time and attention to, to help them through their exams. Others around about him fell away that autumn. Their homework was rarely completed; they were regular candidates for detention; and their sullen behaviour was an increasing challenge for those charged with imparting knowledge and wisdom to them.

Matt found himself caught in the middle. On the one hand he wanted to conform and to meet his parents' expectations. On the other, he found himself increasingly drawn to those who saw school and education as a mere distraction. His friend

Andrew had already become one of this group and the two of them had spent little time together that summer. They no longer sat together on the bus, with Andrew preferring to sit at the back and to fool about with others from neighbouring villages that Matt did not even know.

It was a confusing time for a thirteen year old boy. Not only was he wrestling with the uncertainties that being an adolescent threw at him, but there were also things going on beyond the broader Dale that puzzled him. His developing interest in the political as well as the natural landscape was also intensified that autumn. Strikes were a constant feature of every early evening news bulletin that his father insisted on watching when he got in from work and it was reported that the government was apparently under threat.

"I don't know where it's going to end," Matt's father said one evening in November after it had been announced that the government had narrowly won a vote of confidence over its pay policy. He found it difficult to reconcile his own position. His own non-conformist background gave him a natural left leaning political position. Working for the estate and those that it represented though, put him in contact with a number of interests that held an entirely different political view. He respected the right to challenge injustice and indeed the right to oppose it, a right that been upheld in an earlier generation meaning that his national service had not been served in the military. Yet he also wanted to see order upheld and saw that much of the unrest that accompanied the industrial strife that was affecting the country as, at best, unhelpful and, at worst, dangerous. Others that Matt knew were less equivocal. His aunt who took him to sporting fixtures was clear that there was a need for a new government. On a trip to Elland Road in

Leeds to watch a football match she had told him at length that it would only be a few years before he was able to vote and he should think carefully about what that meant. What was more, she had said, it didn't mean that he had to vote the same way as his parents did. Matt was sure that he already knew that but kept silent in the car.

A week or so later, he was on the bus on the way to school. He was gazing out of the window at the tops of the hills on either side of the Dale. Although the sun was out, there had been a dusting of snow overnight and the landscape had a Christmas feel to it, something that was now only a few weeks away.

"Hi. Anyone sitting here?"

Matt turned, his concentration distracted. "No," he said, looking around and seeing that the seat next to him was not the only empty one on the bus.

A girl with blonde hair tied back in a ponytail sat down next to him.

Matt shuffled himself into an upright position in his seat feeling instantly both uncomfortable and yet excited, a feeling that he did not recognise. He looked at the back of the seat in front of him, then tried hard to look at the floor but couldn't because of his bag. "Urm. Hi," he muttered back.

"Is the bus always as cold as this?" she asked.

"Ur, yes. There's never any heating on.

"It was the same at my old school. They always give us the rubbish buses."

As if to emphasise it, the driver crashed the gears and the bus lurched as he found a low one.

"I'm Lyndsey, by the way. We've just moved here from down south. My Mum and Dad wanted me to start before Christmas to get to know the new school. How about you?"

"I'm Matt, though my Mum and Dad still call me Matthew."

When he got off the bus twenty minutes later he had a smile on his face that he couldn't understand but which stayed with him for most of the day. Lyndsey had told him that she was also in third year and he'd seen her for a couple of classes as well. They'd exchanged a casual 'Hi' from opposite sides of the room.

Later that afternoon as they were walking up the green, Andrew had even asked him "Who was that bird that tha was sat with?"

Matt had said that she was someone new who was just starting at the school and he didn't really know much else. He'd lied. He knew a lot more. He knew what her parents were called; where they had moved from; what their pet Labrador was called; and that she liked horse riding and skiing.

Christmas and New Year came and went. Matt and his family had gone to Ripon to spend Christmas Day with his grandparents. Heavy snow a few days later though had meant that his father's parents had not been able to get over to Hattonbridge for New Year. On New Year's Eve he'd stayed up to watch the television which was showing a programme from Scotland. He found it very strange and it seemed to be from a different time from the one that he remembered from Edinburgh. Nevertheless he was grateful for being allowed to stay up, long after his sister Fiona had gone to bed. Like most of the village, they'd all gone sledging in the field behind the school on New Year's Day.

Back at school in January 1979, he felt somewhat older. He was going to be fourteen in three months time. It felt more grown up. It was like being a real teenager. One evening in the first week back, Lyndsey made a point of sitting next to him on the bus on the way home. He felt that feeling again. They discussed the holidays and the Morecambe and Wise Christmas television special, each recounting the jokes in turn.

"Did you see the poster outside the canteen?" she asked as she stood up to get off. "The one about the ski trip."

Matt admitted that he hadn't.

"You should go. I'm going to ask Dad tonight," she said. "It's to Austria."

Later that evening, Matt carefully introduced the subject into the conversation around the tea table, pausing to take account of the latest news about the country's worsening industrial position. Tactically, he talked of wanting to take German 'O' Level and emphasised that they were studying mountains in geography that year. In reality, he hadn't a clue as to what skiing involved or whether he'd like it. His Mum suggested that he found out more information and then they'd see, though he later overheard her talking to his father as they were doing the washing up that perhaps they could ask her parents if they'd help pay for the trip.

"Yes!" he said quietly to himself, tiptoeing up the stairs.

As it turned out, the winter was the coldest and snowiest across the country for fifteen years. There were days during January and February when the roads were impassable in the Dale and the school bus couldn't get through. Like other children in the village Matt was out playing in the snow rather than taking the opportunity to catch up on his homework. There was always plenty of time to do that later he'd explained to his mother one particularly cold and bright day when the roads had not been cleared and the bus was not running. He wanted to get out and get involved in a large snowball fight on the village green.

The winter was also harsh in other ways. The industrial unrest that had started in the autumn in opposition to the government's pay policy spread quickly to all sectors of the workforce. There were stories in the press and on television of rubbish not being collected, food not being distributed and of dead bodies not being buried. Although much of this had largely passed Hattondale by, Matt's family had not been immune. Both sets of grandparents were affected: his granddad on Teesside was having trouble getting work, whilst the family business in Ripon was threatened by a lack of fuel deliveries for their lorries.

His grandparents had been good to their word though and had paid for Matt to go skiing. It was the week before Easter and along with Lyndsey, twenty other children and three teachers, he headed off on his first foreign holiday. The group were taken by coach to Gatwick airport south of London and then a flight out to Munich, from where another coach took them up into the Austrian Alps.

Matt had looked out for Lyndsey at the school before they had set off, but she was with a group of girls. He'd tried to keep a seat for her on the coach but in the end one of the teachers had sat next to him. The journey to London had been disappointing. It was not what he had been anticipated.

Once in Austria the group were split up in to those who had skied before and those that hadn't. Matt was in the latter, along with eleven others. For the first two days they spent a lot of time falling over in the slush of the nursery slopes, not making much progress. Collectively they agreed that they would have stood a better chance of learning to ski on the slopes of the Dale that Easter than in the mild sunny uplands of continental Europe. To make matters worse Lyndsey and those who had skied before headed up the chairlift each day to the higher slopes with deeper better quality snow. At the end of the afternoon, they would ski back to the village executing perfect parallel turns as they passed the beginners' group. Matt looked on in awe and envy and, though he didn't know it at the time, in love.

In the evenings there were various activities mostly involving some form of competition. Teams were invariably boys versus girls. It was a shrewd way, Matt thought years later, of keeping the two genders apart. At the same time, it was also probably easier to keep an eye on them all. As it was, Matt found himself looking across rooms at Lyndsey rather than sitting or standing next to her. In fact by the end of the week he realised that he'd hardly said a word to her all trip.

Nevertheless, by the end of the week they had all made some progress and on the last day some, including Matt, were taken up the chairlift. Skiing off the top for the first time, admittedly a little nervously, he could have been in heaven. The view was extraordinary like nothing he'd ever seen before. The sky was blue for as far as he could see and the sun glinted on the snow and on the jagged mountain tops. The air was cold and yet the sun felt warm on his face. As the group edged slowly down the mountain their confidence, and in turn their ability, grew. They were skiers. They were champions.

On the final afternoon after skiing the group were allowed to go in to the village to buy gifts for their families. Matt bought a cuckoo clock for his sister and chocolates for his parents and grandparents. Some of the group were managing to buy small bottles of schnapps which they later smuggled through customs ingeniously concealed about their bodies.

When they started back at school in the summer term a number of things had become clear. Third year had changed Matt's outlook on many things. Some subjects no longer held his interest, whilst others were more enthralling. Friendships, he discovered, were apparently not for ever. People had changed and moved on. It was even possible to be friends with girls, although his relationship with Lyndsey had left him bewildered and confused. One thing was certain though: in skiing, he'd found an activity that excited him, that set his nerves racing and thrilled him. He was in love with it and with the mountains and the space that they defined.

CHAPTER THIRTEEN - LOW WINTER SUN
(Late January / February 2014)

From the Centre's office the view of the square was very different from the one that he had first encountered. Without their leaves the trees stood silhouetted in the afternoon sun, their twisted shapes standing like gnarled characters in some gothic fantasy. No one seemed to use the garden much at this time of year. The students hurried past without a second glance and the coffee kiosk was invariably closed. January in Edinburgh was definitely not a time for lingering, except that that was exactly what he was doing faced by his dilemma that weekend.

It had been a quick week since he and Helen had been at Victoria Quay. Alison had teased him about having no-one to go to Helen's dinner party with and had offered to go with him herself. Matt had responded that he may yet take her up on her offer, but had not shared his unenviable position with her. He was in the office by 8.00 o'clock on the Friday morning. Before the others arrived he logged on to his computer and checked the mountain weather forecast for the coming weekend. It did not look promising. Good, he thought. If skiing was going to be off, the decision might be made for him, although he'd still have to find a way of breaking that to Aurélie. Later in the morning, as Helen headed off to work from home she confirmed times for the following evening; told him he didn't need to bring anything apart from himself; and, as she was going out of the door, suggested that he put Alison out of her misery.

"Of course," he replied. "Sorry, I should have said. I will be bringing someone. Catriona. She's a friend that I've met in Portobello."

"That's great. Look forward to meeting her. You know where we are. We'll see the two of you about half seven then." And with that, Helen left, leaving Matt staring out of the window, once more pondering his weekend. Normally, they were a welcome break to the stress of work, but this time it was going to be the other way round. As he gazed at the square he looked forward to Monday.

Alison was not difficult to resolve. She'd only been teasing him and she guessed that Helen didn't want too many colleagues around her dining table at one sitting anyway. After Alison left, Matt found himself alone in the office. He reached for his mobile. Three attempts at composing a text to Aurélie later, he put his phone down and logged back on to his computer instead. He was putting off the inevitable. Just after five o'clock Joe, the Institute's janitor, popped his head round the door.

"You going to be much longer?" he asked. "Just, that I'm trying to lock up early tonight. It's my daughter's birthday party."

"Yes, not too long. I'll be away by half five if that's ok. How old is she?" asked Matt.

"She'll be six. Thinks she's a real grown up. Got ten of her friends coming for tea. My wife's doing it all, but I've got the pleasure of clearing it all away," Joe said.

Matt sat back and thought of the innocence of childhood. Of his own time as a six year old when he and Andrew had made their den in Calvert's workshop. 5.30 came and he was on the bus back to Portobello. He had still not contacted Aurélie.

Later that evening he was dozing in front of The Graham Norton show on television. It was the usual mix of American film star, comedian and music, none of whom he had really heard of. But it served its purpose, allowing him to vegetate the end of the week. The music finished and Graham Norton was introducing the red chair sequence where a member of the public recounted a story laced with innuendo and in return was upended. Matt was semi-comatose and contemplating turning it off and going to bed when his phone rang.

Expecting it to be Aurélie, he instinctively answered. "Doesn't look like skiing then". There was silence at the other end of the phone. "Hello?" he enquired. He looked at his phone. There was no number displayed. Straining to listen, he could make out a feint laboured breathing noise. Someone was crying. "Look, can I help? Who is this?" The sobbing got louder but then stopped. Matt was awake and thinking, the soporific value of Graham Norton had completely worn off. "I don't know who you are and I don't know how you got my number, but if you don't talk to me, I won't know what's going on," he said.

"It's me Matt," said a voice at the other end of the phone.

"What the hell?" He paused.

"Now who's not talking?" the voice said, stuttering through held back tears.

147

"I'm sorry, but I wasn't expecting you. I mean you were the last person that I was expecting," he replied.

"Obviously. I just need to talk to someone and I really need to talk to you."

"But why now?" Matt answered. "We haven't spoken in months!"

"I know. I've been trying to phone you all day. Pushed your number a few dozen times but couldn't press 'Call'. Sorry. Listen, it's probably too late to talk just now. I'll call you back tomorrow."

"No wait, now's fine," he said. "And anyway, I'm awake now."

There was no reply. The line had gone dead. Without the displayed number Matt could not return the call.

He didn't sleep much, his mind constantly questioning what she wanted. Saturday dawned as a dreich and dismal day. The forecast was abysmal. He decided to phone Aurélie without delay and at least get that part of his weekend sorted out. There was no reply. He tried again about half an hour later. Still nothing. He texted her: '*Weather not good for skiing tomo. Phone me. Let's re-arrange.*'

By mid-afternoon, there was still no reply from Aurélie. He'd been to the Co-op to do his shopping and called at the Butternut Squash on the way back for his lunch. A familiar face greeted him from behind the counter. "What can I get you," said Dylan.

"Huh? Sorry." Matt looked startled. "What are you doing here?"

"Mum told me I had to get a job."

Well done her, he thought.

"It's my first day. On a trial for the next two Saturdays."

"Well good on you. Good luck. I'll have a small Americano and a piece of that Flapjack, please." he said, pointing at the cake display.

"I'm babysitting Bobby tonight," Dylan answered, whilst making Matt's order. "You and Mum are going somewhere, she said."

"Yes, that's right. It's really good of you. It's my boss's dinner party. Your Mum said she'd go with me." Matt put his coffee down on a table by the window, setting his phone prominently next to it. Who would call first, he thought.

The cup was long since empty when Dylan approached Matt. "You wanting anything else?" he enquired. "It's just that the manager says we're going to be closing soon."

Matt gathered himself, breaking his concentrated stare, picked up his phone, apologised for having taken so long and gathered up his shopping. "Can you tell your Mum I'll be ready about half six."

"Aye, ok," Dylan replied.

Matt made his way home and climbed the stairs to his flat. So, Aurélie hadn't called after all. But then again, neither had she. He worried about both of them, but for very different reasons. He took a shower and readied himself over the next hour or so, aware of his phone, waiting for the flashing light of a text message or the ringtone of a voice call. Neither interrupted his preparations.

At half past six he looked out of his curtains and saw Catriona's car parked by the bins where her son had once bothered him. Picking up the bottle of Châteauneuf that he had bought earlier, he made his way downstairs. They air kissed as he got into the car. There was no embrace. Matt was aware that he was perfunctory as they drove into the city. He checked that she knew her way to Canonmills and asked after Bobby. Catriona concentrated on the driving.

They found the flat relatively easily. It was on the third floor. The close and stairs were clearly well maintained. Some of the other flats had pot plants outside their doors and bikes were propped up on the landings, one with a wicker shopping basket on its front. A black cat greeted them as they reached the third floor landing.

"Hello there you," said Catriona, bending down to stroke it, her own ponytail falling loosely over one shoulder as she did. The cat purred.

Matt pictured her the first day he'd seen her in The Espy. He leaned forward. "I'm sorry for being a bit of a grump tonight. A couple of things going round in my head." He put his arm tentatively towards her shoulder.

"Don't worry," she said patting his hand. "Dylan told me you'd been staring out of the café window all afternoon. You can tell me later. Come on we've got a dinner to go to."

Helen answered the door and welcomed them in, Matt introducing Catriona as she did. The flat was much larger than

Matt's, the hall itself being the size of his own living room. Helen showed them through to the living room where two other couples were in conversation with Helen's husband, Simon. She introduced them, making it clear that Matt had taken over her old job, but not the whole organisation. Matt was careful to call Catriona his friend without over-personalizing the connection. The conversation was light hearted and congenial.

The fourth couple arrived just after eight o'clock apologising about the babysitter being late and then having difficulty getting parked. Helen ushered everyone through to the dining room and served up the soup. "So, you must be Matt," said one of the latecomers who had sat next to him. "I'm sorry we haven't been introduced. I'm Geoff. Used to work with Helen at the Centre until just before you started. I've moved on now though. Started my own consultancy. Doing a couple of case reviews at the moment."

Matt was aware of Geoff Newlove and had seen his name on some reports. In fact Dougie had suggested to him shortly after he'd started that Geoff had assumed that he would get Helen's job one day. Matt turned to Catriona who had started a conversation with Simon. Catriona was explaining how she and Matt had met. They were talking about the esplanade in Portobello. Simon was remembering it from years gone by as he had been born and had grown up in the city.

"It was a great place to go as a child. My parents used to take us there during the summer to play on the beach. Good days they were. Used to take Helen until a few years ago. What's the pub on the corner called? Used to be the Utopia I think," he said.

"It's The Espy now," Catriona replied.

Matt stared past them and through the window beyond. The night sky outside was particularly dark and unforgiving.

It was later in the evening, after Helen had brought through the cheese, that Geoff turned again to Matt. "Do you have family of your own Matt? Helen said you'd moved up from down south. By yourself?" he said, looking at Catriona.

"Yes, that's right," Matt replied.

"Must have been a wrench moving all this way north. Where was it you moved from?"

"Bath. I had a research job down there. But this was an exciting opportunity when I saw it. Couldn't resist it really."

"Yes, but it must still have been a long way. Where are you from?" asked Geoff.

"Good question. I was born in North Yorkshire, but I suppose I've always thought of Edinburgh as home." Matt explained about his father being at university and the times that he had spent visiting the capital as a child. Others around the table joined in and quizzed Matt further about his connection with the city. At first it was light hearted and Matt was keen to emphasise his love of the place.

It was when Geoff asked if he'd had a happy childhood that Matt felt unease. That was something he'd never discussed with anyone but her and he was certainly not about to disclose his feelings to someone like Geoff, someone who clearly had his own agenda.

Helen stepped in to Matt's relief. She reminded people of the research that she had done the previous year on the nature of childhood in Scotland as a whole. It would be interesting to see what investment a future independent Scotland would make in children, she suggested, if the referendum went in that direction. Before long the discussion had moved on to that bigger question. In turn, Matt's discomfort lessened, although he was aware that Geoff kept looking at him, and also at Catriona, in a way that suggested he still had unanswered questions.

It was around 10 o'clock and the coffee was on the go when Matt's phone buzzed. He had completely forgotten about it. After spending most of the day staring at it he had become oblivious to it, put it out of his mind. The unresolved dilemma of what he was going to do the following day had escaped him. He looked discretely at the screen. It was Aurélie. Were they still going skiing the following day? At this time of the evening? Why couldn't she have got in touch earlier, he thought?

Matt had re-checked the on-line forecast for Sunday before Catriona had called for him. It was depressing for any prospect of skiing: *'An extensive area of rain followed by showers will spread from the west with snow on higher ground. It will be very cold with strong to gale force winds'*. Not exactly the best way of introducing someone who was used to the blue skies and perfect powder snow of the Alps, to skiing in Scotland. Matt excused himself and went to the bathroom to check an internet ski blog: *'Needed the piste fences at Glenshee today as the visibility was bad for the majority of the day. Had to wring my gloves out after the morning! It was worth it though. The forecast for Sunday is*

bad enough that I'm not even contemplating heading out.'
Good, he thought! The first time he had ever welcomed the
prospect of bad weather when he had the chance to go
skiing. He texted back: *'Not looking good for skiing. Weather
bad. Peut etre un autre jour?'* Pleased with his little bit of
French he returned to the rest of the group confident that
things were resolved.

Matt and Catriona finally left Helen's just before midnight.
They walked to the car. The night was cold and the wind was
beginning to get up. Matt walked closely alongside her and
she didn't move away. His arm naturally fell around her
shoulder and he pulled her in close.

"That's good," she said, happy to share his warmth. "So that
was Excellence in Children's Services then, was it? A bit of an
odd bunch but I dare say no odder than the oil and gas lot
that Nick and I used to mix with. Though your lot aren't a
patch on them when it comes to drinking!"

Catriona paused as they got to the car, searching in her
handbag for the keys. "What was that odious Geoff wanting
you to say. I didn't understand him."

"I don't know. I really don't know." Matt replied. He stopped
and looked back towards Helen's flat, a picture forming in his
mind of the Strachan's flat that his father had lived in as a
student. Aurélie and skiing as well as the fact that he still
didn't know what she had wanted were completely absent
from his thoughts. "What I don't think I'd realised until
tonight is how much I obviously enjoyed being a child in this
city. It feels like I've come home after all these years. It's
where I live. It's where I love. Does that sound silly?"

Catriona put her arm through his, pulling him gently towards the car. "Come on let's get you home you blabbering old fool, before you have me crying for you! And I won't be providing an excellent children's service unless I get home and look after my two."

....

Helen's dinner party had left Matt thinking. The previous five months had seen him settle into a job and a routine and importantly, or so he thought, into living in Edinburgh. Yet, he knew he wasn't content and Geoff Newlove's probing, unwelcome as it had been, had only served to highlight this. And that in spite of him having growing relationships with two women. Two women who had enticed and enthralled him and in a city that had beguiled and beseeched him.

He was also still frustrated by her phone call and not knowing what it was that she had wanted. He had tried calling a couple of their mutual friends in the hope that someone might have a new contact number for her, or might know what it was that she wanted. But it appeared that she had cut off contact with most of their friends. The Monday Quiz night at The Espy had been a distraction and Matt was now an established member of 'The Directors'. Coffee afterwards at his flat with Catriona was also occasionally part of his and their routine. There had been no word from Aurélie since they hadn't gone skiing on the Sunday after the dinner party.

The referendum, or 'indieref' as it was inevitably being shortened to, was beginning to take centre stage and opinions from both sides of the argument were being more regularly shared in the media. As he journeyed in to work each day on the number 26, Matt observed that small blue posters with the one word 'Yes' were starting to appear more regularly in the flat windows past Meadowbank and through the east of the city. These signs were, he pondered, either a statement of certainty and of a belief and conviction, or alternatively, an outbreak of hysteria and lemming-like behaviour that may yet drive the country over the cliff. Time would tell, he thought.

By contrast, and 'indieref' aside, Matt found his time increasingly taken up with the passage of the Children and Young People's Bill through parliament. Various pressure groups were hard at work campaigning for a range of interests. One of these would see the age at which those young people who had been through the local authority care system continue to receive support up to 26. To Matt, this seemed eminently sensible as by contrast with England, it had always perplexed him as to why Scotland was so keen to push children towards adulthood so young. The age of criminal responsibility had traditionally been 8 and the transition to being an adult for many things was 16. It just seemed to him to be plain absurd, particularly given the significance that politicians were keen to give to the United Nations Convention on the Rights of the Child which enshrined the status of childhood until 18. It was therefore encouraging that the increased confidence and self-belief that devolution had brought could challenge such long established principles within the wider community. Would independence perhaps allow them to go a stage further and as a new young country fully enshrine that principle, he wondered? Again, time would tell.

In the mean time, the season was beginning to change. Although only February, days were lengthening and there was a renewed sense of optimism at the Centre. As he looked down from his office, Matt noticed that the coffee stall had re-opened though it still lacked the level of custom that he had first observed.

One afternoon Matt was gazing out when Alison came into the room making him jump. "Penny for them?" she asked.

"Oh sorry, I didn't hear you. I was just thinking how I don't need a calendar working here, what with the changes to the square and the trees out there," he replied.

"Yes, it's always fascinated me as well. I used to have this office when I first started here, but then Helen was appointed and it became the Director's office," Alison said. "By the way, I forgot to say earlier, there was someone in yesterday looking for you. A young French woman I think. Lorelei, perhaps?"

"Aurélie?"

"Yes, that sounds like it. Said to tell you that she's around at lunchtimes this week if you want to give her a call."

He left it for the rest of the day, although it did keep playing on his mind as he tried to put together a briefing on the named person provisions of the Bill in response to some of the more florid suggestions that were emerging in the media. Since he had first met her, it seemed that Aurélie had a way of coming into and out of his life in a way that he couldn't control. Perhaps it would be better if he didn't see her again. At least that way he wouldn't have expectations that wouldn't be met. But then again, she excited him, made him feel young, made him feel as though he was living for the moment, something that they had done when they had first moved to Bath.

At six o'clock Alison poked her head round the door. "I'm away. There's no Joe tonight and everyone downstairs has gone. Don't forget to lock up. You're the last one in the building."

Matt acknowledged her, not looking up from the screen. He listened to her footsteps going down the three flights of stairs and then the door buzzing and shutting behind her. The building was silent. He reached for his phone. Pondering it for a few minutes eventually he texted: '*Just got your msg. How about lunch tomorrow? My treat*.' He stared at the phone's small screen, his finger hovering over the send arrow. His hand twitched as his fore finger touched the glass.

An email from the Children's Commissioner's Office caught his attention on his monitor and he had started to respond when the phone in front of him buzzed. Aurélie never responded that quickly he thought. He continued to respond to the Commissioner. Eventually his curiosity won. Unlocking the phone he read the message. It was Aurélie. '*Hi. Are you in town now? Fancy a coffee?*'

They met half an hour later in a café on the Grass Market. Unusually there was no mention of Aurélie's grandmother or her ailments. Things were also distinctly cooler than when they had parted on New Year's Day. Nevertheless, conversation turned once again to skiing and, weather permitting, arrangements were made to head north that weekend.

CHAPTER FOURTEEN - ONE BIG SOCIETY
(Summer 1983)

He had become very fond of all of his grandparents. They had all been good to him over the years, whether taking him to visit his father in Edinburgh, supporting him with extras through school, such as the skiing trip, or just being there. As they'd grown older he'd also looked to support them as well, visiting whenever he could to do odd jobs for them. It had been a wrench therefore to have lost three of them during his last years at school. Just at the time that he had wanted to share his ideas and hopes with them, they were no longer there. He had been particularly fond of his paternal grandmother and had been upset at her funeral. It was the first one that he had ever attended and he didn't find it a helpful experience. He had taken himself up the hill that overlooked the village where she had lived, whilst the others had had the ubiquitous funeral tea. From the top, the view extended over industrial Teesside, much of which was changing significantly in the early 1980s.

Both of his grandfathers had died in fairly quick succession at the start of his final year at school. The family haulage business had been sold a year or so before, something that in spite of his increasing ill health, his grandfather had never really come to terms with.

Matt had nevertheless enjoyed his last year at Yoredale High and had focussed on ensuring that he had sufficient 'A' Levels to get him into higher education should he decide to do that. One thing he had decided though, was that unlike many of his friends who were, he felt, coerced into applying for university, he was not going there straight from school. There was a bigger world he wanted to explore first, one that politically was increasingly uneasy with itself.

Following, the slow death of the Labour administration in the late 1970s, a Conservative government had been elected with a large majority. Margaret Thatcher had come to power. It was a fascinating time to study government and politics. In fact, it was his teacher, Mrs Benton, who had encouraged him not go straight to university. She had suggested that, like others, he needed to get away from the Dale and its narrow social confines. His parents had taken some convincing. Why wouldn't he want to get a place at university secured? One big reason, Matt made clear to his parents, was that he hadn't a clue what he wanted to study, if anything.

It was late June when the exams had finished and the end of year staff and pupil dance had been held, that Matt found himself getting off the school bus for the last time. He stood on the Green as the other children made their way home. His sister, who was at the end of her first year at the High School by then, had gone straight home. It was a warm afternoon and there was a gentle breeze running through the leaves of the Chestnut trees. A couple of the village's older residents were preparing the Quoits courts for the evening's game. He smiled to himself as the reality of the moment crept over him. He could only look forward from here. There was no back. What's more, Mrs Benton was right, he realised. Forward for him lay elsewhere.

He'd already got a job for the summer at a shop in Leyburn. It was one of a number that were opening up throughout the Dales catering for the growing number of tourists and day trippers who visited the area. They often provided some questionable souvenirs as well as a small collection of outdoor clothing. Whilst those who shopped in such establishments generally went away with purchases that made them feel that they were part of the community, many local people had reservations about this influx, particularly as it was clogging up roads at weekends and bank holidays. Others, by contrast, welcomed them as they meant that shops were staying open bringing income into the Dale. Matt, himself, was sceptical. During his own lifetime there had certainly been a change in the character of the area. Old businesses were closing, of that there was no doubt and there were fewer opportunities to work on the land. Although his father's job was secure, it was the first year that the Estate hadn't taken on any young apprentices. In Hattonbridge itself, Calvert had recently died and with him his joinery business, whilst a pottery had opened where the decorators had traditionally been. But such changes were also reflected in what was going on across the country. Much of the traditional industry was struggling and the political and industrial unrest was continuing. There was talk of further closures in the coal mines and the protests that this would lead to. Nationally, some were talking openly of insurrection and were looking forward to a confrontation between the miners and the Conservative government.

It was a Tuesday in late July and Matt was sitting by the war memorial at the top of the market place in Leyburn eating his lunch listening to the new Top 40 on Radio 1. Paul Young was at number one for the second week with *'Wherever I lay my hat that's my home'*. Matt was singing along.

"Hi, Matt," a familiar voice said. "Budge up." Lyndsey sat down.

"Oh, hi," he jumped. "How's it going?"

"Not bad. I'm just in town to get a few things for starting next week."

"Next week? What are you doing?"

Lyndsey explained that she'd got a job volunteering at a homeless shelter in Leeds for the rest of the summer before she started university. Her older sister had done it the year before when she'd left school and had convinced her to give it a go. It was apparently hard work but rewarding and it had changed her sister's outlook on a number of things. They talked for the rest of Matt's lunch break and both relaxed in the warm sunshine. Lyndsey walked back to the shop with him and kissed him on the cheek at the door.

"Fancy meeting this weekend?" she asked.

"Yes, that would be good," Matt replied.

They arranged to meet up on the Friday evening. The rest of the week went slowly, as he looked forward to the weekend. They met at the Hattonbridge Inn. Lyndsey drove over in her mother's car, having passed her test at the start of the summer. Matt watched in envy at the ease and confidence with which she parked. They sat alone together in a corner of the lounge, laughing and talking of school, of things they would never do again and of people they would never meet again.

It was a warm evening and when they left the pub later on there was still daylight in the sky. They both looked at each other. Suddenly neither of them wanted to leave, nor the moment to end.

"Fancy a walk?" Matt suggested.

Lyndsey locked her car at the Inn, and the two of them strolled slowly up the Green.

Tentatively, Matt put his arm around Lyndsey's shoulder. She didn't move away. They stood for a moment in the fading light before walking hand in hand as far as the bottom end of the Dale and Matt's old house.

"I don't know about you," she said looking round the Dale, "but I'm going to miss this place."

"I know," Matt replied.

They kissed and held each other close. It was his first.

Eventually Lyndsey said that she'd have to go and slowly, reluctantly, they walked back down the Green past the Primary School, enjoying the remaining warmth and smells of the summer night. They paused at her car in a now deserted pub car park for one last embrace.

"Why don't you come and see me in Leeds in a couple of week's time?"

"I'd love to," he replied.

Kissing him goodnight, she got into her car and promised to call him once she was settled. Matt watched her drive off and listened until the noise of the car had faded away. He walked back up the Green towards his house. It was after midnight, but by the grin on his face he wasn't at all tired.

His parents and his sister were going on holiday. They'd rented a cottage in Wales for two weeks, leaving Matt at home by himself. Suddenly, he wasn't bothered. Whereas at the outset with the prospect of working whilst they were away, he'd felt left out, he now had something to look forward to. Lyndsey was true to her word and wrote to him a week later. The letter was waiting for him when he got in from work. She'd arrived safely and was living in lodgings that the shelter had arranged. She'd be there for two months and it would be great if he wanted to go down and see her. He wrote back that evening, saying that he would go for the day on the Saturday; his parents and sister weren't due back till the Sunday.

Two buses to Northallerton and a change of train in York meant that it was early afternoon before he got to Leeds. The return journey was not going to be any easier which meant that he was either only going to have a couple of hours with Lyndsey, or, if he dared get the later train, he would have to walk the last few miles because he would have missed the last bus. He wouldn't mind. They walked from the station to where she was staying and then to the hostel. She introduced him to the others who were working there. Matt had never been to such a place or even really knew that they existed. Lyndsey showed him round. It was a sad place. There were a few residents playing pool. Some were young men not much older than him. Lyndsey had described some of the circumstances of the residents. Some had been in care and had left without any real support. Others had been in

Detention Centres. Few of them had contact with their own families.

Later they walked back into the centre of the city. It was a still warm evening though Matt didn't feel it. By contrast, the hostel had been cold. Matt admired her for what she was doing and told her so. It also left him thinking about what he could do. Although he hugged her when they got to the station for the later train, it was not the sort of embrace that he had imagined that they would have had that day. As he got on the train, she asked him to come and see her again. He said that he would.

It was a difficult journey back as he reflected on the day. The headlines in the newspaper that he'd picked up in Leeds didn't help as they announced closures in the steel industry in South Yorkshire with the prospect of more redundancies to follow. The contrast to the evening that they had spent in Hattonbridge only two weeks earlier, could not have been starker. As expected he had missed the last bus back to the village and having to walk the last few miles meant that it was actually Sunday morning when he let himself in to the house. He didn't sleep well that night as his mind, hampered by his renewed admiration and love for the young woman that he had left behind in Leeds, wrestled with what he wanted to do with the rest of his life. The words of Paul Young's number one played on a loop in his head.

It seemed that he'd only been in bed a few hours when his alarm woke him to remind him to get up before the holidaymakers arrived home. They were too full of their holiday to notice his own disposition and he didn't tell them about his trip to Leeds.

On the Monday he spent his lunch break in the library in Leyburn. They had some leaflets and information about volunteering positions. By the end of the day he'd used the shop's phone to contact a couple of places. He struggled to concentrate at work over the rest of the week as thoughts of what he had seen in Leeds lived with him. Arriving back from lunch one day about two weeks later there was a message for him to contact a Centre in Newcastle. They were looking for someone to work in a community project working with young people and would he like to come for a look round and an interview. With some apprehension, he made arrangements to visit the following week. On his way home that evening, he thought that at some point he'd have to tell his family what he was planning, but for now he'd keep it to himself.

In the event he decided to wait until after he'd been to Newcastle. Consequently, he found himself getting off a train alone in a strange city on a Tuesday morning in early October. How things had a habit of repeating themselves he thought. Unlike his father's arrival in Edinburgh though, someone was there to meet him. Alan, the Centre's Project Manager, collected him and drove him out to the housing estate where the project was based. It was only a couple of portakabins with a large play area. Funded by donations and grants, the project provided an opportunity for young people to meet and play after school, in the evenings and during the school holidays. Matt was impressed. It seemed more alive and full of hope than the Centre where Lyndsey was working in Leeds. By mid-afternoon he'd looked round and met some of the volunteer parents from the local community who, along with Alan and one other youth worker, helped to run the place. After an informal interview with Alan and the chair of the management committee, they'd offered him the position. They'd also arrange accommodation for him within the community.

It was after four o'clock when he finally left to catch the bus back into the centre of Newcastle. Suddenly, he realised the time. His parents would be expecting him home from the shop at five and here he was over 60 miles away! He found a phone box at the station and phoned home.

"Yes, Newcastle," he said. "I know I should have said, but I wanted it to be a surprise. I'll tell you about it later, but I've got a job!"

His mother was both angry and proud of him, although she didn't tell him the latter until a few weeks later.

He put the phone down and made his way on to the platform for the train to Northallerton. The station announcer cut into the thoughts that were running around in his head.

"The next train to depart from Platform Two will be the five o'clock departure for Edinburgh."

"Edinburgh," he thought. He'd forgotten all about that place. That would have to change.

CHAPTER FIFTEEN - MID WINTER BLUES
(March 2014)

Even though February had become March, Aurélie had still had to scrape frost from Hubert's windscreen before setting her satnav for EH15 and driving over to Portobello to collect Matt. It was a Sunday morning and there was little traffic as they headed round the city bypass. Mist was hanging along the water's edge as they crossed the Forth Road Bridge. Soon there would be a new bridge to join it. There'd been a competition to find a name for it. Dougie had wanted to enter "Salmond's Leap," indicating the massive leap of faith that was being taken in launching the referendum. At that hour of a cold Sunday morning in March, with the referendum just over six months away it seemed that both the expanse of water over which the bridge was emerging and the land over which the debate was taking place, would require something more than faith.

The motorway through Fife was quiet and they were past Perth and in Blairgowrie by half past eight. A quick breakfast stop at a petrol station in the town and they headed up Glenshee itself. It was a clear though dull morning and the cloud hung low over the summits as they made their way up to the ski slopes in a by then steady procession of traffic. Nevertheless, the prospects for the day looked good, Matt thought, as he glanced at Aurélie. They had booked equipment on line and after changing their clothes in the car park along with everyone else, they joined the queue at the Ski Hire. Forty five minutes and two queues later, one for lift passes and the other for the first chairlift, their skis swung into the air. Sunnyside was not aptly named that morning. At least the snow was thick and all the pistes were open. "Welcome to Scotland!" Matt exclaimed, his voice trailing into the distance as he turned his skis downhill and headed for the foot of the Cluny poma.

By late morning the cloud remained stubbornly low and the wind began to get stronger making navigation increasingly difficult. "Lunch, I think," Matt suggested after a particularly tricky descent of Glas Maol into Coire Fionn in near white out conditions. Aurélie agreed and they rode the parallel pomas out of the coire before traversing to the wooden hut that housed the Meall Odhar café.

"Not quite your alpine standards I'm afraid," Matt said, clicking off his skis. He'd warned her in advance about what to expect, but did point out that it was a vast improvement on what had been available when he had first skied these slopes as a student in the 1980s. Then it had all been Bridies, Sausage Rolls and Scotch Pies - 'different shaped pastry with essentially the same filling', one of his friends had once suggested. Now, there was a choice of hot meals and even fruit and vegetables, he noted. Scotland was moving with the times, independence or not!

Over lunch, they chatted about skiing: where they had skied; who they had skied with. Nothing too personal; nothing too intruding. Matt had imagined this day for the last three months ever since they had first sat in the pizza restaurant after Alison's birthday drinks. Yet now it was happening, it seemed to mean little. Perhaps it was the way that it had come about. There had been too many false starts, too many maybes.

The afternoon was at least a repeat of the morning and Matt suggested that they move over to the Cairnwell side. It was a forlorn hope. The snow was thinner in places and the wind was even stronger. There were some races taking place, which they paused to watch, the skiers emerging from the gloom, zombie like as they cut between the slalom poles. Standing at the top of Càrn Aosda, the wind was biting and whipped up the ice crystals into their faces. Matt had hoped to be able to show Aurélie the views from here that on a better day extended across the north-east of Scotland. He had often stood at this point on past trips and gazed into the distance, dreaming of journeys and destinations beyond the horizon. Today was not one of those days. Looking beyond the end of their skis was itself a fantasy!

After a hard pole to reach the head of Butcharts Gully, they decided that enough was probably enough and Matt suggested that they call it a day with a late "Chocolat Chaud et Gâteau" at the Cairnwell café. An hour later and their skis returned, they were heading back towards Blairgowrie. In spite of the weather, both of them glowed. "I really enjoyed that," Aurélie said. "Thanks for being my guide." She smiled at him.

"It was good. I'm glad you came," Matt replied. "And thanks for doing the driving."

Their conversation became more relaxed and Aurélie began to explain about her grandmother and about how her mother constantly worried and how she needed to discuss everything with her all of the time. It made making arrangements very difficult. She was sorry. Although he understood, there was one question that Matt kept rehearsing in his head, but seemed unable to ask: who had she been with at Ocean Terminal that day a few weeks earlier?

They stopped at a pub near Dunfermline. Over dinner and already reminiscing about the day, Aurélie announced that a friend of hers had a couple of spare tickets for the Scotland versus France Rugby international at Murrayfield the following Saturday. Although Rugby Union had never been his game, his mother's family having connections with Rugby League, Matt agreed to go with her.

When Aurélie dropped him off in Bath Street there wasn't a great deal of weekend left. She declined the offer of coffee and headed back across town. Matt thanked her and they air kissed as he got out of the car. At the end of it, it had been a good day after all, although not quite the ending to not quite the week, that he had imagined.

By the following evening the effects of a day's skiing were making themselves felt and he had to force himself to shower and change and walk the short distance to the Espy for the quiz. He was not going to be a great asset to the Directors tonight he admitted to Rob as he sat down. There was no sign of Catriona. "If it's only you and me tonight," he said, "I think we're in trouble!"

"Speak for yourself!" Rob replied. "And anyway Catriona called earlier to say that she and the others might be a bit late. She said she'd tried calling on you yesterday to let you know but it didn't look as though you were in. I guess that's because you were away skiing."

The first round was horror films of the 1960s.

"Guess this'll be over to you then," Rob said. "The 60's are pre-history as far as I'm concerned!"

"Yeah, right, I don't think!" Matt frowned, feeling instantly both old and tired.

As the round was drawing to a close, the door opened and Catriona and her friends entered. "Sorry," she said as they squeezed between tables, her trademark ponytail swaying rhythmically as she did. Sitting next to Matt, she whispered that they'd been at a pampering evening organised by the school's parents committee to raise funds and that they'd already had two or three glasses of prosecco.

Looks like they were not going to be winning any prizes tonight, Matt thought.

As each round went by, it became even clearer that the Director's luck was out. They tried in vain to answer a round on theme tunes from musicals, an area that would normally have been a speciality for Catriona's friends. At the interval, Rob announced that he was going to call it a night and Matt said that he thought that he would get an early night as well, his skiing exertions catching up with him. The three women announced that they were staying for another round.

Matt began to walk the short way back up Bath Street to his flat feeling that it had been a bit of a wasted evening. He stood opposite his front door in the shadow of the communal bins. It had been 24 hours since Aurélie had dropped him off in the same place and he found himself smiling as memories of the adrenaline filled day re-emerged in his mind's eye. She was an enigma to him. She was every young female French skier that he had ever seen; that he had ever followed down an alpine piste; that he had ever sought to impress in the bars and clubs of the mountain resorts; and had ever fantasised about having a relationship with. Up until now they had always been as inaccessible and as unreachable as the summits that looked down on the ski slopes themselves. Yet Aurélie was real. She had been with him only yesterday, had driven him to Glenshee, had shared a day with him. He closed his eyes momentarily. But for all that, she was non-committal, unreliable, undependable. In fact, he realised, all the things that someone of Aurélie's age living away from home should be. And there lay the problem. They had different expectations of Edinburgh and what it could give them. The Portobello night air was providing him with clarity.

As he began to think about going inside, the door of The Espy down the street to his left opened and the noise of chatter and light spilled out. The familiar voice of the quiz organiser was reading out the results seemingly taking pride in announcing that the Directors had this week come last. Not so much last, Matt thought, as capitulated. His gaze was caught by the light from the pub doorway and he watched as a familiar figure emerged and slowly but purposefully crossed the street. Approaching his door, it stopped and looked in the bag that it was carrying eventually finding its mobile phone. Fumbling to make it work in the dark, its fingers pressed at the screen. Matt's own phone in his pocket vibrated, the sound still being off from being in the quiz.

"Are you nae answering?" Catriona said, addressing the phone as though it was in part responsible for not delivering what she expected. "You're nae in then?"

Matt observed her difficulties from his position across the street and pondered his own. He looked at his own phone's screen: two missed calls. One from Catriona and one from? Matt held his breath as his phone updated itself and displayed its secrets. Unknown number? Unknown bloody number at this time of night! It wasn't likely to be PPI that was for certain. But was it her?

Catriona had started to walk away, muttering under her breath something that Matt couldn't make out. He crossed the road behind her and caught up with her. "What the ..!" she exclaimed. "You! You bastard. Don't creep up on me like that. I could have landed you one. Anyway, where the hell did you spring from, I was trying to phone you."

"I know," Matt replied. "I was just down at the beach, thinking."

"At this time of night? You're mad!"

"I know," he replied, putting his arm around her shoulders. "Come on, I'll walk you home," he said, conscious that whilst her phone was zipped up in her bag his own was vibrating again in his pocket. Someone else was keen to get hold of him.

They reached Lee Crescent without saying very much. Matt was thinking of other things, whilst the cocktail of the earlier Prosecco, the Pinot Grigio in the Espy and now the cool night air, coupled with the shock that Matt had delivered, had quietened Catriona. When they reached the house she invited him in and was surprised when he said no. He made an excuse about having an early meeting to get to in the morning.

As he turned away he checked his phone. There were now seven missed calls but no listed number. Whoever it was, really did want to talk to him. He hurried homewards eager to be available next time they tried. He was passing the art deco building of the bingo hall, when she rang again. "Hello," he said. "Who is this, is it you?"

"Yes, Matt. It's me," she replied.

"What do you want?"

"I need to talk. I mean, we need to talk."

"At this time of night? Can't it wait? I mean, I'm not even home," Matt half protested.

"It's up to you," she said.

Matt continued towards his flat quickening his pace, keen to get inside and also to keep her talking hoping that she wouldn't hang up again. He was breathless as he finally let himself into his flat, stumbling out of his shoes and jacket. "Well?" he asked.

"I lost it, Matt," she slowly said, emphasising the 'it' as she did.

There was silence. Matt expected her to continue, but she didn't. "You lost what?" he eventually enquired.

"It. It," she repeated. "Our bloody baby, Matt. I lost our baby."

Matt sat back on the sofa staring through the window up the length of Bath Street, the curtains undrawn.

"Well say something then," she said.

"I'm sorry. I'm not sure what there is to say. It's been too long. You. Me. How could I know?"

"You couldn't," she replied.

The phone call continued for nearly an hour. When she eventually hung up she did agree to phone him back in a few days, but still wouldn't give him her number. Matt stood by the living room window illuminated only by the dull orange glow of the streetlights outside. The cold of the night seeped into the otherwise unheated flat. He tried to take in the gravity of what he had just learnt. He had spent the last six months getting away, moving on, and starting a new life for himself here in Edinburgh. And yet for most of that time a new life had started amid the wreckage of his former one only to be cast aside without recognition, without ceremony, without care. How cruel life could be, he thought, as tears slowly edged down his cheek.

....

Unable to contemplate sleep, he checked his emails. There was one from his sister. Had he heard about Mum's fall? She'd been taken to hospital with a suspected broken hip. Could he get time off to get down? She was going to try and get up there tomorrow.

He slumped back on the sofa. It was turning into a long winter.

Matt got a taxi from York station to the hospital. He'd caught an early train out of Waverley leaving a voicemail on the

Centre's phone for Alison and Helen explaining his sudden absence. He'd managed to get some sleep on the journey in the relative quiet of the East Coast 225. At that time of the morning it was mainly smartly dressed and largely silent business passengers whose employers were paying inflated peak time prices. He'd paid his own. There was little noise other than the invasive sound of the tapping of laptop keyboards and tablet screens. Quite different, he observed, from travel later in the day when the excitement of those making journeys to go on holiday or to visit friends and relatives, pervaded the sanctity of the earlier commuters carriages.

The hospital in York is relatively modern having been opened in the late 1970s. It is in the north of the city not far from the former Rowntree's chocolate factory upon which much of the city's economy had been built. Fi had arrived shortly before him not waiting at the station to share a taxi. In spite of him texting her en route and suggesting that they met at the station, she had needed to get there as soon as possible. He had struggled to see what difference 20 minutes was going to make to their mother's care or situation. In fact by the time he arrived, Fi had taken charge, as she always did. She'd talked to the staff, determined how long their mother needed to remain in hospital, spoken to their father and agreed that she would be able to stay with him for a few days to help him organise things at home. She'd also tried to speak to social services about what support they could offer. Not a lot, Matt thought, in this post austerity world, although he'd let her find that out. By the time he sat with his mother, his lack of sleep in the preceding 24 hours was catching up with him.

"Why have you come?" his mother asked as he gazed through the window next to her bed, almost ignoring her presence.

"To see you. Why did you think?" he replied.

"It's a long way and you look tired."

Matt agreed. On both counts. As Fi came into the room and started to explain what she had organised and what was going to happen, Matt's mind's eye was picturing a different hospital. One where she and their baby were. The cries of hope of newborns replacing the assertions of his sister. How cruel a world, he reflected, as he looked at his mother and thought of his unborn child that he would never know.

Back at their parents' house later that afternoon, there was a strange quietness. Their father raked out the hearth and managed to get a fire going whilst Fi made the three of them some tea. Matt tried to play with Edgar but he seemed unusually morose. There was an odd mood in the house, so different from when they'd all been together for Christmas.

"How was your New Year, then?" his Dad asked.

Matt wasn't really up for small talk. Instead, he tried to get a conversation going about what their mother needed and indeed about how they were going to manage. But no matter what Matt said, Fi and his father continually changed the subject. He had always thought that they were alike in many ways whilst he himself had always felt closer to their mother, born of the time that the two of them had spent together when his father had been at university. Their relationship had been forever bonded the night that Fi had been born.

Edgar slept on the rug in front of the fire seemingly oblivious to the atmosphere around him.

There was no point in him hanging around he decided and after evening visiting to see his mother, Matt got a taxi to the station to catch the last train back to Edinburgh. It was just before midnight when he got back to Waverley. It was a day for reminiscences, he thought, as he stood in the cool and strangely quiet expanse of the normally bustling station concourse. He imagined his father arriving here all those years before having so recently left his wife and son back in the Yorkshire Dales. What would he have been thinking as he stepped off the train and into his future, Matt wondered? The emotions of the day were obviously catching up with him.

It was a late start the following morning when he met Helen on the stairs after he finally got to the Centre. She said that she'd not really expected him in and asked if he wouldn't be better off at home. But he was clear that more time by himself was not going to be necessarily helpful and that he needed to get his mind into some work. He immersed himself in a further consultation on the named person provisions in the forthcoming legislation. There was an increasing unease about this in certain parts of the media, although it didn't seem to be garnering wider public support in spite of threatened legal challenge. It was a fascinating political environment, Matt reflected over lunch with Dougie, and one that was increasingly uncertain. Normal loyalties and years of tradition certainly seemed to count for little in some of the current debates.

But it was something that Dougie said that both intrigued and unsettled him. "Why did you come to Scotland, Matt?"

It was an odd question he thought. Not, for example, why did you apply for the job, or why did you want to work at CECS? Coming after Geoff Newlove had quizzed him at Helen's dinner party about his motives for moving to the city, Matt thought long and hard before replying. "I suppose it was because I've always identified with Scotland," he said.

"Aye," Dougie replied. "Maybe. But Edinburgh is not Scotland. It's only one very small part. There's a much bigger country out there and one that has little in common with this place. I mean there is an argument to say that this city has more in common with London or the south-east of England than it does with places over in the west, or for that matter up north. So what was it about Scotland that you were looking for?"

"It's maybe a hard thing to describe, but I've always admired the sense of place in Scotland which I don't think you find down south."

"Aye you're right at that," Dougie said. "The thing is, Edinburgh is different from Glasgow, which is different from Perth, which is different from Wick and so on. But teyve all got one thing in common: they all know they're Scottish. I mean, if people from all those places met up in some town on the other side of the world, they'd quickly work out that they had being Scottish in common."

Matt nodded.

"Yet, it's funny," Dougie continued. "Having established that, the next question they'd ask each other would be *where do you stay* not *where do you live*. I've always found that a funny concept. *Staying* sounds more transitory than *living*, as though you don't expect to be there for very long, as though there'll be a reason to move on soon."

Their conversation drifted on, with both reflecting how the referendum was a good thing in prompting these sorts of discussions, even though not everyone was seeing eye-to-eye. The very prospect of independence had encouraged people to talk which was healthy. However, the two of them acknowledged that it remained to be seen how long unity and cohesion would continue once the referendum's outcome became clear.

When Aurélie phoned him that evening to make arrangements for the Rugby, Matt realised that it had only been three days since they had been skiing together. Yet time and distance seemed to have been stretched unfathomably over that short period. They agreed to meet outside Haymarket station at about three o'clock as kick off was not until five. When the call ended Matt realised that only a month or so earlier the mere prospect of being in Aurélie's company would have excited him and given him a renewed drive. Whether it was the conversation with Dougie at lunch time, or the unresolved issue that her phone call had left him with, or his mother's fall and his sister's insistence on taking charge, but that prospect did not grab him in the way that it once had.

And then there was Catriona. He'd forgotten about her. The one person who had shown him genuine affection since his move to Edinburgh and in amongst everything that had happened in the last few days, he'd completely overlooked her. Impulsively he reached for his phone, found her in his phonebook and pressed her number. After a few rings it went to voicemail.

"Damn," he thought, but left a message anyway saying he hoped she'd got over Monday.

Although five o'clock was primarily to cater for the television audience, there were still going to be well over 65,000 spectators making their way to the game. Along with the gathering gloom and the floodlights around Murrayfield stadium the sheer number of people created a cauldron like atmosphere. Their seats were in the West Stand just behind the try line. From there they could see the entire pitch. Below them on the touchline were a throng of television presenters and other journalists speculating about how the game was going to unfold. Aurélie was on the edge of her seat as though she was searching for someone amongst them.

The pre-match build up, Matt thought, seemed even more intense than usual and Flower of Scotland was sung with a particular passion and volume amidst a sea of lions rampant and saltires. Although the French got a penalty in the first two minutes and seemed to settle quickest, Scotland were leading 14 - 9 at the break. In spite of this, the home team seemed almost in awe of the occasion. At the interval Matt and Aurélie fought their way through the half-time crowds for a coffee to stave off the cold of the Edinburgh evening. As they returned to their seats Aurélie lingered awhile on the stairway gazing towards the edge of the pitch where a group of journalists were again gathered. She smiled.

In the second half, Scotland set about France with a renewed vigour and the game was very close. The intervention of the

New Zealand referee was ultimately the determining factor as with only two minutes to go he awarded a controversial penalty to the French. It proved too much for the Scots and France ran out eventual winners 19 - 17. As they left the stadium and joined the sea of supporters making their way back up Roseburn Street towards the city centre, Aurélie had a broad smile on her face. She had never looked as happy, Matt thought, as she locked arms with him. For the Scots, amongst whom he counted himself, there was a sense of so near and yet so far and he wondered how many of those around him would be left thinking that come September, whatever the result.

Aurélie was laughing and teasing him as they reached Haymarket. "A beautiful day don't you think?" she said. "What are you doing this evening? Let's make a night of it!"

Matt's initial thought was 'why not' thinking back to New Years Eve. He had certainly fallen for her Gallic guile and charm since they had first met and the prospect of spending another evening in her company should undoubtedly have been appealing. But something had changed he thought, as he looked at her, as they jostled to be served in a bar on Shandwick Place.

"My round, I think, as we lost," Matt said, struggling to be heard above the noise.

"Half of lager," she said. "I'll get the next one."

Standing at the bar he was momentarily unaware of the noise around him as he looked back at Aurélie. He saw a young confident beautiful woman, far from home and yet visibly excited and happy, her future still unfolding for her. He thought back to similar days when everything had seemed possible, when they had first got their jobs in Bath and later when they had first set up house together. He was oblivious to the cacophony around him as he began to realise how their lives and futures were never going to be joined. It wasn't just their ages or their cultures. It was their expectations. He was searching for something more finite, more tangible, some root he could finally put down; she was still looking into the distance, beyond the horizon. The game may have been very close at the finish, but their relationship was not. There was always going to be a greater distance between them.

They drank together though and Matt found himself relaxing as he came to terms with his realisation. Aurélie suggested getting something to eat and they started up Lothian Road. Her phone rang. She answered intently in French and Matt struggled to follow the conversation, although he gathered that it centred on the earlier game. As they entered the restaurant at Tollcross, Aurélie asked for a table for three.

"Three?" Matt enquired, as they sat down.

"Oui," Aurélie replied. "Jean-Louis is coming. He got us the tickets. You'll like him."

A few minutes later, a figure that Matt recognised entered the restaurant and embraced Aurélie. He recalled him as the young man that he had seen Aurélie with at Ocean Terminal just after New Year. He stood up as Aurélie introduced the two of them. She explained that Jean-Louis was a sports journalist working for a French sports website. He'd been covering the game earlier. In fact it wasn't the first time he'd recently been in Edinburgh reporting on rugby, Aurélie said. It was when he'd been over in January for the game between Edinburgh and Perpignan that he'd offered to get her a couple of tickets for the international.

Matt thanked him and took his seat. Things were becoming clearer for him now.

Over dinner it emerged that Aurélie and Jean-Louis had been at university together, both studying English. It also became clear to Matt that there was something between the two them, a chemistry that, until recently, he had imagined that they could share. Matt excused himself when the other two ordered coffee, left a contribution towards the bill and after congratulating the French on the result, thanked them both for a great evening.

He walked back towards Princes Street and caught a bus back to Portobello. As he made his way down Bath Street there was a smirr in the air, the sort of rain that seems inconsequential and yet can leave you just as drenched as a torrential downpour. He didn't seem to notice it though as the thoughts about what he had learned that evening focussed his mind. There were some other things though he needed to get clear.

One of them involved her. It was the following afternoon that she called. She was more relaxed than in her earlier calls and the two of them were able to talk more openly about their time together, something that they had not done for nearly a year. A year, Matt thought. Where had the time gone? She also talked about first finding out that she was pregnant. It had been after Matt had left. She'd wanted to tell him but hadn't wanted to contact him. He acknowledged that it must have been difficult for her but that he would have liked to have known. When they finished they hung up amicably. That was progress, he concluded.

At the Espy the next day the Directors played with a new sense of purpose, the previous week's debacle apparently being overlooked. Catriona appeared, initially at least, to be cross with him for walking away, but was soon teasing him about the rugby result when she heard that he'd been at the match. At the end of the evening, having won, they were in good spirits and Matt walked her up Bath Street saying that he really did need an early night.

Before they parted at the High Street Matt suggested that they might do something together one weekend. If she would like to, that was. It would depend if Dylan was working and could look after Bobby, she said, but if he could she'd love to. She asked him if he'd ever been to North Berwick. Matt admitted that he hadn't since he was a child. "Great," she said. "I'll race you to the top of the Law then! I'll call you or we can arrange it next week at The Espy." They kissed and parted. It was as though they were two young people again, planning a date. A contrast, he thought, to his feelings in Aurélie's company. Age mattered, he had learnt, and yet it was also relative to how one felt and also how others perceived it. He recalled one of the old farmers in the Hattonbridge Inn once saying that age was a sexually transmitted terminal disease that affects us all eventually and for which there is no known cure. As a young student at the time he had ignored it, but increasingly he understood it.

CHAPTER SIXTEEN - FOUR MORE YEARS
(1984 - 1988)

His year in Newcastle had not always been easy. Even though his lodgings had been taken care of by the project, living in a city on the small allowance that they had also paid him had been difficult. Nights out were limited and trips home few, although his parents had visited him every six weeks or so. The year had taught him a lot though, particularly about the social value of community and the impact of political decisions taken miles away. Margaret Thatcher's government had continued to polarise opinion with its policy of letting heavy industry decline throughout the country. In Tyneside this had seen the virtual ending of shipbuilding, which. along with the coal industry, had provided the economic backbone to the area for much of the previous hundred years. There were fewer opportunities for the young people of the estate where Matt was working and many were becoming increasingly disaffected.

The situation was set to deteriorate further when, in March 1984, the miners started their industrial action In South Yorkshire. Some of the men from the estate were employed in the nearby coalfield and Matt was struck by the effect on the children that he was working with, for even their attitudes were hardening. As the year went on it seemed to him that they were in danger of losing some of their innocence, or rather there was a risk that it was being taken away from them. This was most apparent at the Christmas party that he organised that year. There had been little enthusiasm for the traditional activities as for some families there was not much joy and, more importantly, even less income than they had been used to.

It was a conversation with Alan, the project manager, though, that was the catalyst for the next stage of Matt's life. He'd been home for the weekend and whilst driving him back to the station in Northallerton his father had questioned him about his career ambitions. Matt had confessed to Alan that he still wasn't sure what he wanted to do. In response Alan had been helpful; not lecturing or beseeching him like his father. Instead he suggested that if Matt really did want to make a difference to the lives of people like those he was working with, then he needed to try to influence policy and outcomes for them and to do that he would need to continue his own education.

Matt had come to respect Alan and listened carefully to what he had to say. Alan was from near Dunfermline in Fife, over the border in Scotland. Earlier in the year he had invited Matt to join him for a weekend up north. It was a former mining village whose mine had closed some years earlier. It had, Alan had told him, been for many years a prosperous community with little unemployment. That had changed in recent times and young people were finding it difficult to find jobs or training as they were frequently up against adults a few years older than themselves who had been made redundant when the mine had closed. In spite of this, during a night out in the village's working men's club, Matt had observed that the sense of community was still very much alive, even though he'd had to admit to Alan that he had struggled to understand much of what the locals had said to him.

"Aye, I ken. Imagine, what it was like for me with the Geordie accent when I first moved to Newcastle, then," Alan had responded.

As a result of Alan's advice, Matt decided to put his earlier reservations about further study to one side and to look at what opportunities were open to him. He remained sceptical about the value of a traditional university course and instead looked at Polytechnics. To some, they were a second class form of higher education, whilst to others they were socially less aloof and because of their focus on more vocational courses, often felt closer to the real world. This suited Matt and by October he was set to study politics and social sciences at a Polytechnic in the Midlands.

In August though, he first re-acquainted himself with Edinburgh. Whilst living in Newcastle he'd become involved with a group who were staging a show on the Edinburgh Fringe. A political satire it was loosely based on a TV game show where audience members were invited on stage and instead of competing to win prizes for themselves, had to decide what government money should be spent on. 'A different ending every night!' was the show's strap line. In return for a floor to sleep on, Matt had agreed to help with advertising the production.

For two weeks he had walked up and down the High Street during the day thrusting flyers into the hands of potential audience members. It was a largely thankless task, particularly because for most of the two weeks that he was there, it rained. He didn't really notice it though as it was the city that he was mainly there for.

On the Friday of the second week and the last day of the run, the sun had deigned to make an appearance lightening everyone's mood. The show had had reasonable reviews and those directly involved were pleased, even congratulating Matt on his ability to hook people in. He was patrolling the middle of the High Street near the Fringe Office and was chuckling to himself about his ability to talk complete nonsense about the history of Scotland to tourists. "Yes," he had said to one American couple. "Mary, Queen of Scots lives in the big house at the bottom of the hill. You might be lucky and catch her in if you're quick."

He'd watched the pair as they hurried away, a large grin across his face.

"Well, hello there Matt. What are you doing here?"

Matt turned, all thoughts of the Americans suddenly gone. "Lyndsey?"

The young woman that he'd last seen in Leeds nearly a year earlier stood before him. They'd promised to stay in touch and indeed had written to each other a couple of times. But time and distance had intervened and whilst she had started her university studies, he had become immersed in his work in Newcastle. Now they were stood looking at each other in a street in Edinburgh and yet there was no embrace, no kiss.

"Matt, this is Chris. Chris, Matt."

Matt reached out and shook the hand of the young man next to Lyndsey. Momentarily he thought that he recognised him.

"You'll remember Chris," Lyndsey said. "He worked at the hostel in Leeds as well. We've been going out for nearly a year. How about you? How was Newcastle, wasn't it?"

Matt explained that he'd spent most of the year there. Had thoroughly enjoyed it and that finally he'd decided to go on to higher education after all. They stood talking for some time, feeling easier in each other's company as time passed. Lyndsey and Chris took one of his flyers and said they'd see him at the show that evening.

He waited for them after the production ended, but there was no sign. Maybe he'd missed them he thought, as he joined the rest of the team in the bar around the corner from the venue. Although he occasionally looked across the bar each time the door opened to see if they'd found their way there, Matt joined with the others in toasting the show's success and by the end of the evening had forgotten his earlier brief encounter.

Matt left Edinburgh the following day and caught the train back to Northallerton. As it crossed the Royal Border Bridge at Berwick he gazed out of the window thinking of the times that his father made the same journey in years gone by. The irony of this was not lost on him when his mother met him at the station and drove him back to Hattonbridge.

He spent the rest of the summer visiting old haunts and old friends in the village and the Dale. For a week or two he also became a regular in the Hattonbridge Inn. His father even joined him on a couple of occasions introducing him to some of the farmers and others who worked on the estate. They were names that Matt had got used to as he had grown up but until then had never met. Apart from one that was.

Andrew Tait's father recalled the night that his sister was born. "I'll never forget that night. Tha were like a drowned rat! Now look at thee. Your Dad says you're starting Uni."

"No, Poly actually," Matt replied, frustrated by his father's apparent inability to convey this small but important distinction. "How's Andrew doing? I haven't seen him for some time." Andrew had left school at the first opportunity, passed his driving test and had followed his Dad as a contractor in driving machines in the Dale and beyond.

"He's away over at Warcop in Cumbria on t'harvest. Non stop at this time of year he is."

"Tell him I was asking for him. We must catch up sometime."

His father drove him to Poly at the start of October with the family estate car loaded up. He'd chosen to go self-catering and had been assigned a room in a small cluster of student accommodation. He found himself sharing with three others. The first year was a joint course with students studying to be social workers and Matt found the interplay between the two groups helpful. Nevertheless, his first year studies frustrated him as he sometimes felt that they were not moving fast enough. He became very aware that his time in Newcastle had given him a broader life experience than many of those coming straight from school and it often seemed to him that there was more than 12 months between them.

By the end of the year though, he had fallen into the routine of studying and was keen to get into the later stages of the course which seemed to be intellectually more challenging. He spent the holidays that summer in the city, moving out of the first year student accommodation and into a house with two of the others on his course. He got a job helping on a summer playscheme on one of the city's sprawling council estates. A year on from his time in Newcastle, not a lot had changed. Unemployment was rising and the clothing industry which the city had been built on was in recession. The Asian immigrants who had been attracted there to work in the now closed or struggling factories were themselves becoming increasingly disillusioned. Most of the children who took part in the playscheme were too young to understand what was happening though and it was a largely enjoyable month of activities.

After a brief holiday back in Hattonbridge, he began his second year with a renewed determination to succeed. His studies took him to new levels in subjects such as economics and politics. Although he had studied them at school, he finally recognised the opportunity for intellectual discourse that higher education provided. He found his own ideals being challenged, at the same time as he openly challenged those of others. With the social and political change underway throughout the country, it was an exciting and stimulating time to be studying politics.

He became increasingly involved with the Tenants Group that organised the playscheme and by his third year he was helping to run a weekly legal surgery whilst also volunteering at the Youth Club. Each week after they closed up, the volunteers would head to the pub on the estate. After one session, Matt found himself drinking with a couple of the other volunteers, one of whom was new.

"Hi, I don't think we've been properly introduced," he said, sitting down with his drink.

"No, I'm Jane. It was my first night."

Jane explained that she worked as a researcher at a Unit based in a university in a nearby town although she was volunteering at the Youth Club to get some broader experience.

Over the next few months Matt and Jane became close friends, finding that they had a similar outlook on many things, including a shared passion for skiing. That winter they joined a local ski club and signed up for their first taste of skiing in Scotland with a weekend trip to Glenshee. It involved an extremely long coach trip from the English Midlands and, although it was a sunny weekend with good snow, both Matt and Jane vowed never to do it again.

During the final few months of his degree he found himself spending more time working on the estate. It allowed him contact with what he saw as the real world in contrast to the febrile student atmosphere in the Poly with which he was increasingly disillusioned. He and Jane were also spending more and more time together, although only as best friends. Oddly he saw her as the big sister that he had never had, reminding him, when he needed it, to focus on his studies. In the end he completed his time as a student with both a 2:1 degree and a sense of satisfaction.

His own graduation was in the city's cathedral. Unlike his father's, it was a family affair with not only his mother and father but also his sister Fiona in attendance. There was no need to arrange for anyone to look after the children, he reminded his father over dinner afterwards. "I've never quite forgiven you for that," he said.

"I suppose we just thought that you'd find it all a bit too long and boring," his father replied.

"Perhaps the best thing to have done would have been to have asked. Never decide what's best for children. Remember, even if you don't like what they might say, they will still have a view that you should listen to."

In the end, encouraged by his mother, they had agreed to disagree. His parents and his sister headed home later that afternoon. Whilst waiting for a couple of friends to call round before going to the Graduation Ball in the evening, he caught the news on television. It reported that parliament had passed the government's legislation that would introduce something called the Community Charge, or Poll Tax as its opponents were referring to it. There was apparently talk of it being introduced in Scotland first and the news coverage, from a street in Edinburgh, was suggesting that this could provoke renewed calls for Scottish independence. Something for later, he thought, as he turned the television off and headed for the Ball.

CHAPTER SEVENTEEN - HOPE SPRINGS
(Late March/early April 2014)

As it transpired, there was a problem. It was nearly three weeks later and the last weekend in March before Dylan had a day off from the café and could look after Bobby during the day. He'd laughed apparently, teasing his mother about going on a date at her age!

Along with Arthur's Seat and the Castle Rock in Edinburgh itself, North Berwick Law is one of a number of ancient volcanic plugs that are a feature of the landscape of the Lothian region of Scotland. It also affords spectacular views of the whole of the Firth of Forth and the surrounding area. True to her word, Catriona got to the top first, although Matt declared from the start that it wasn't a race. They stood by the whale bone arch on the summit and gazed out across the Forth. There was still a coolness in the air and standing close to Catriona, Matt awkwardly put his arm around her shoulder. In spite of New Years Day and Helen's dinner party, it felt as though they were together for the first time. Catriona didn't pull away and for a while the noise of the wind was all that broke the silence.

"You know," Matt eventually said. "See the Bass Rock over there. As a child I used to think it was covered in snow and my Dad never let on that it wasn't." He pointed towards the rocky outcrop out in the Firth gleaming white in the spring sunshine, but so coloured because of the sheer number of birds and their droppings.

"I know," replied Catriona. "I used to tell Dylan the same when we first moved here. I used to bring the children out here a lot at that time. It reminded me of home in some ways."

"Home," Matt enquired, thinking back to New Year and what he'd heard about how Catriona had ended up in Edinburgh. "Where is home for you?"

"Good question," she began. "Anywhere I currently am I suppose. But if you mean where am I from, then it would be the north-west. A village called Lochcarron. Not far from Kyle of Lochalsh and Skye. But then I haven't lived there since I went to college in Aberdeen. Went there to do art. I was a good artist. Used to do paintings of west coast scenes and then sell them to tourists in the cafés in Kyle and Plockton. But I didn't get on with studying. I just wanted to paint."

"Do you still paint?" Matt asked as they sat down on a rock, enjoying the view and each other's company.

"Now and again. But I don't really have the time. Bobby makes sure of that." Catriona went on to explain how she'd first met Nick in Aberdeen. How it was at the time that oil was on the up. How it was about living the dream and how they had. She wasn't bitter and he had been fair in supporting his children. But it wasn't the same as if he had been there to be a father. Bobby in particular had never really known his father and he increasingly looked to Dylan for the things that she couldn't give him.

Matt pondered this for a moment recalling his first impressions of Dylan when he had only known him astride the Wasp. Funny to think of him now as a surrogate father figure. Childhood, as he knew, was so brief and the importance of attachment could never be under-estimated.

As Catriona explained more about her life, Matt began to realise how much he admired her. Although it was her appearance and in particular her ponytail that had first endeared her to him, it was her stoicism in the face of what life had thrown at her that now drew him towards her. His arm was now more firmly around her shoulders and he squeezed gently pulling her closer to him.

The sun was getting closer to the horizon when they finally got back down to the town. "No time for an ice cream then?" Matt said.

"No, I need to get back for Dylan. He's going out tonight," Catriona replied. "Heh, do you fancy going out for dinner when we get back?" she said as they got into the car. "We could take Bobby with us if you didn't mind."

Matt didn't mind.

They'd said that Bobby could choose where to go for dinner. As a result they'd ended up in Luca's ice cream café and restaurant in Musselburgh. Matt learnt that it was a place that Catriona and her two sons often went to to celebrate things. He felt privileged. He also learnt a little bit more about Catriona too: that growing up on the west coast she had developed a passion for singing from her grandmother, although often limited to the kirk on Sundays; that she was proud of being able to speak Gaelic, but that she was sorry that she didn't paint as much as she once did. He learnt that when she and the children had first moved to Edinburgh, she had worked in the café on Bath Street where Dylan was now employed. She and the then owner were best of friends and had allowed her to take Bobby with her to work. In fact they had talked about going into business together at one stage. Apart from the money that Nick gave her for Dylan and Bobby, she also had had money from her parents when they died. They had left her their house which she had subsequently turned into a holiday cottage to give her some extra income. What was important to her most though, along with running and her appearance, were her children.

For the first time since he had moved to Edinburgh, Matt found himself at ease as they sat together in Luca's. To the other diners they must have looked like a happy family group. Strange how things weren't always what they seemed, he thought as he gazed at Catriona and Bobby who were deep in conversation about what they were going to do in the Easter holidays. Catriona was telling Bobby about something that had happened to her when she was a young girl growing up in Lochcarron. He was enthralled. She'd lived in the village when they had been blasting to build the new road to Kyle of Lochalsh on the south side of the loch, to replace the need for the old ferry at Strome. There had been explosions every day and she had thought that the hills were all going to fall into the water. One day, one explosion had been particularly loud and she and her friend Shona had run up from the beach where they had been playing and had hidden further up the hillside in the deep bracken. They had been scared to go back down to the village. As the day went on they had become more and more frightened, telling each other ever more alarming stories of what was going to happen and that they were the only people left alive. Their parents and their neighbours had eventually started to look for them and it was getting dark before Catriona's father had come across them. He'd been both relieved to find them and very angry.

Bobby listened excitedly as Catriona recounted her childhood experience. It was obviously a story that he knew well but was one that clearly impressed him, judging by the way that he encouraged his mother to go into more and more detail. By contrast, Matt sat in awe, hearing the tale for the first time.

"You look shocked," Catriona said.

"Shocked? No, I was just taking it all in. It must have been scary though. For both you and your parents," he replied.

"I suppose so. But then it was part of growing up in the country. We were always outside. Always away from home. It was good. You must have known something similar living where you did."

"That's true. The Dale was certainly our playground. I don't think I could have ever grown up in the city."

"It's been a challenge I suppose," Catriona replied. "But I think I've done quite well," she said, looking fondly at Bobby who smiled back up at her. Their bond was obvious.

Bobby kept asking his Mum for more stories about her childhood, about the village where she had grown up and significantly, about his grandparents. Catriona was happy to oblige and their stay in the restaurant extended later than they had anticipated and it was after 10 o'clock when the three of them eventually left. It was raining as they drove back to Portobello and the road surface glistened in the car's headlights. Catriona and Matt chatted about the day and they were nearly back at Lee Crescent before they realised that Bobby was fast asleep on the back seat.

"Fine parents we make," Catriona remarked, as she coaxed her semi-comatose son out of the car.

Matt stood to one side, reflecting on what she had just said and not really sure whether to head off.

"You'll be coming in, I guess?" Catriona suggested. "Look, here are the keys. Can you get the door and lock the car whilst I get this young man inside?"

Matt opened the front door to their house and then went back to lock the car. When he let himself in Catriona was already upstairs with Bobby. He wandered into the front room where the New Year's party had been. It was oddly quiet compared to what he had remembered. It was also extremely neat, clean and well looked after.

"Can you pop the kettle on," Catriona called down. "I'll be down in a minute. Help yourself to a drink. There should be some wine by the fridge."

He walked through to the kitchen, almost tiptoeing as he went. For a house that had two males living in it, there was nothing out of place and clearly a place for everything. The kitchen surfaces were conspicuously crumb free, something that he had never been able to manage no matter where he had lived. Just off the kitchen was the den area where he and Rob had debated the merits of cold sausage rolls at Hogmanay. He filled the kettle and plugged it in before looking through the cupboards for wine glasses. Finding two, he helped himself to a glass of Pinot Noir from the opened bottle by the side of the fridge, poured a second and sat down.

"Oh, thanks for that," Catriona said as she walked into the room moments later, accompanied by the waft of something expensive. "I think we've deserved this," she said picking up the glass that Matt had poured. She'd let her hair cascade out of its customary restraint, and had refreshed her lipstick. She was not expecting Matt to leave imminently. "What sorts of music do you like then Matt?" she asked, walking over to the CD player and the well stocked tower next to it. She didn't look at him - or wait for a reply. "These are mine in here. Dylan's music is in the other room, though most of his are on his computer these days. Maybe I'm old fashioned but I like to be able to hold my music, to see it, to somehow touch it." She paused for breath. "Dylan's got some really weird stuff anyway. Music I don't understand. In fact I'm not even sure it is music half the time. Odd that, given that he was named after one of the greatest songwriters that's ever lived."

She carefully selected a particular disc from the well organised collection. "I like to have music with me when I'm on my own. I don't really have one type though. That I like that is. Of music I mean," she continued nervously. The disc loaded in the machine. The soft jazz sound of Jamie Cullum's 'Twentysomething' began. Catriona stood by the window gazing into the dark garden beyond.

An uneasy silence developed broken only by the sound from the CD player. The track ended. "I need more wine," Catriona said, starting over towards the work surface.

Matt jumped up from the sofa. "I'll get it." He got to the bottle first, slightly before her. "Let me pour it," he said turning towards her. She was at his back though and kissed his neck putting her glass on the surface as she did. Her hands reached around his waist. The bottle joined Catriona's glass on the surface as their lips met.

Their embrace was intense as their hands and bodies found the rhythm of the music. The two of them were clearly unaccustomed to such close intimacy though and neither seemed sure about taking the next step. Eventually as the music faded Matt reached for the wine bottle. "I'll pour us some more wine."

"Yes," Catriona replied. "But don't do it here. Let's take it upstairs."

They left the music to itself and made their way upstairs. Catriona's bedroom overlooked the street outside. She drew the curtains. A large metal bedstead, the feature of the room, stood on a stripped wooden floor along with three white rugs. It was, like the rest of the house, beautifully organised. She walked over to the dressing table, took a match from a box and lit two candles on it, as well as two on the mantelpiece of the old fireplace on the far side of the bed. "You can put those glasses and the bottle on there," she said, pointing at a large dresser in front of the window.

Matt did as she instructed. The smell of jasmine from the candles rose in the air, scenting the room. He turned. Catriona had removed her top and was lowering her trousers. He stood motionless, his senses aroused. Soon 'ponytail' stood naked before him. His own clothes joined hers on the floor making the room instantly untidy.

Their bodies met as they approached the bed. Catriona pulled at the white lace quilt dragging it too to the floor. They entwined, kissing and exploring each other's bodies, challenging the equilibrium of the room as they did. Their passion was unencumbered like teenagers discovering the joy of sex for the first time. Time was suddenly irrelevant as they intimately explored each other's bodies.

The key in the front door lock would normally have been sufficiently loud in the night time calm of the building to have alerted any one who wasn't asleep, but this night was different. Two people in the house were very much awake but oblivious to anything but each other. Footsteps on the stairs, especially ones with a drunken gait, would have also alarmed someone attuned for unusual nocturnal sounds. It was the knock on the bedroom door though that they both first heard.

"You awake Mum?" asked Dylan from the landing.

Their bodies still entwined, Catriona grabbed for the quilt on the floor and pulled it awkwardly and roughly back on to the bed. "Yes, hi. Sorry, Dylan. What do you want? Have you had a good night." She thought about lying, about saying she'd just been asleep and hadn't heard him come in, but looking at the shape of Matt's body under the quilt, thought better of it.

Matt pulled himself to the edge of the cover and peered at her. He mouthed 'what do you want me to do?'

Catriona put her finger to her lips.

"Just checking you're ok," replied Dylan from the landing. "Sounded like something was going on. I could hear it in the street. I guess you've had a good night then." He chuckled. "Night then, Mum. Night, Matt." Dylan's footsteps crossed the landing and into his own room. The door closed behind him as he turned on his music.

Matt and Catriona sat up, a giggle stifled between them. Matt suggested he should leave but Catriona wouldn't have any of it. Instead she walked over to where Matt had earlier placed the wine bottle. Naked, she poured them both a glass and returned to her bed. They sat up, cuddled together, drinking the wine and enjoying the calm of the night air. Gradually the candles began to fade one by one and the room was soon lit only by the glow of the streetlights from outside. In time, sleep, a deep satisfying sleep, crept over both of them.

The orange glow of the streetlights had been replaced by strands of daylight when Matt awoke. He took a moment to work out exactly where he was and he found himself smiling as the memories of the previous day and night filtered in to his consciousness. Catriona was right, there had been something missing, even if at times he'd been looking elsewhere for it. He turned over and looked at her sleeping form. How beautiful she was, he thought. Even in the morning, ruffled by a night's sleep, she still portrayed an elegance and sophistication that he had first encountered in The Espy.

Matt could hear noises from downstairs. Someone was up and moving about. There were cupboard doors opening and the kettle was boiling. Dylan must be up, he thought, marvelling at the capacity of the young to burn the candle at both ends. He lay in the calm, content with himself as Catriona's eyes opened and looked fondly up at him.

"Good morning," she said.

"Good morning to you too," he replied, kissing her on the forehead.

They both heard it simultaneously. The clanking of crockery on a tray being carried upstairs. "Shit, it's Mother's Day," said Catriona moments before the door opened.

"Good morning, Mum," said Bobby walking into the room. "Happy Mothers Day!"

Matt had stayed for breakfast. Catriona had insisted. She had felt it was best that Bobby didn't think that they had anything to hide. She'd thanked Bobby for thinking of her on Mothers Day but had quickly convinced him that it would be best if they all had something to eat together downstairs. Matt and Catriona had found it difficult to contain their giggles though and had found themselves behaving like youngsters laughing behind their parents backs, except that on this occasion the roles were reversed.

It was nearly 12 o'clock when Matt finally left to walk back to his own flat. Catriona had kissed him on the lips as they parted on the doorstep. A public display of affection for the benefit of the Sunday lunchtime bowls players making their way to the bowling green at the end of the street. It was a fine sunny day. There was warmth in the air and there was a real sense of spring. At the end of Bath Street he walked on to the esplanade itself and gazed out over the estuary. How different from some of the occasions he had stood there during the winter months when the weather was very much in control. Spring was a time when the human spirit was resurgent, when all things seemed possible and when only imagination stood in the way.

....

Spring was also reflected in the mood of at least half of the nation itself as the 'Yes' campaign was gaining confidence in the referendum debate. Judging by reports in the Sunday paper that he had bought on the way home, the First Minister was sounding ever more assured, whilst those seeking to stay part of the United Kingdom didn't appear to have an effective response. They had no natural leader, Matt felt. And yet, there was a lingering doubt for many people. One that would not go away. Memories of the financial crash of 2008 were still fresh in people's minds and many people in Edinburgh had suffered when the Royal Bank of Scotland, which was based in the city, had had to be bailed out by the government 400 miles to the south in London.

'What would have happened to an independent Scotland if that had occurred after separation from the rest of the UK?' was a question that bothered many people who Matt had spoken to. It wasn't that they didn't want independence, more that they doubted the country's ability to be independent. It had been a long time since Scotland had been truly independent and no one seemed certain about exactly what it would mean. Matt didn't yet know how he would vote, though he was proud to have one in what was being trailed as a once in a lifetime opportunity. Only time would tell whether it would be. Reflection over, he went inside, a contented smile on his face.

As he climbed the stairs to his flat though, there was no way he could have prepared himself for what happened next.

Mrs McNiven peered round her door. "Hello Mathew. Is that you?" she said.

"Aye, it is, Mrs McNiven. What can I do for you?" he said, the smile still etched in his face.

"Well," she said, stepping out on to the landing. "Yesterday, your buzzer was ringing all the time. Every hour or so. It was really annoying. Even he heard it and above his television as well."

"I'm sorry about that," Matt said.

"In the end, I pressed my own button and said that you weren't in. It was a woman. She was very polite. Had a nice English accent. Said that she needed to see you."

Matt stopped.

"She came back again last evening. She asked me to pass on a message. To say that she's staying at the big Hotel on the Grassmarket and needs to see you. I asked her her name, but she said you'd know."

"Thank you Mrs McNiven. That's very kind of you," Matt replied.

He let himself into his flat, went over to the window in the living room and, as was now his custom, gazed up Bath Street as he thought of what he would do next.

An hour later he was showered, changed and on a bus into the city. Up the Mound and across the High Street, he passed the pizza restaurant where he and Aurélie had eaten the previous autumn. Down Victoria Street he found himself on The Grassmarket standing outside the hotel. Only then did he pause. What was he going to say? What did she want, coming all this way to Edinburgh? And why now, why, given the last 24 hours this day of all days?

He wandered around the square a couple of times imagining what he was going to say. Eventually he entered the hotel and went to the desk. "Excuse me. I think you've got a Charlotte Hampson staying here," he said. "I wonder if you could give her a call for me. Tell her it's Matt."

"Certainly sir," said the Receptionist. She dialled the room and Matt heard her talking. "She says that she'll meet you in the bar, sir."

"Thank you," he said. He went to the bar and waited.

"Hello," a familiar voice eventually said, approaching him from behind. It was the second time that day he had been greeted in such a way and since his school days there was only one other person, his mother, who normally used his full name. Charlotte offered her cheek.

Matt extended his arm ushering her to sit down. "Can I get you a drink?" he said.

"A glass of red wine, please."

Matt ordered two glasses of wine and sat down. "Why have you come?" he asked.

"Straight to the point as usual," she said. "Good to know you've not changed."

Matt stifled a protest. They engaged some pleasantries. Matt bided his time and ordered two more drinks.

Eventually she said, "It was your sister, Fi. She Facebooked me to say that your Mum had not been well."

Bloody Facebook, Matt thought. He neither understood it, nor the need for it. But trust his sister to be able to find her so easily when he had been struggling, waiting for her to contact him for so long.

"It left me thinking. Thinking that perhaps I'd not been fair with you. I should have told you about the baby."

"It would have been nice."

She slowly told him of finding out that she was pregnant shortly after he'd left Bath. Of the grief that she had felt but also the burden. She'd not told anyone. Not even her daughter. The midwife had encouraged her to do so, but she hadn't felt able. And then it had happened. Just at the point that she had come to terms with being pregnant again, with the risks that it presented to her and the child, with the challenges that she would face, just then, it happened. There had been little warning, a few spots of blood and then the niggling pain. She'd guessed almost immediately though. She had sat in the bathroom in the house that they had once shared and stared at it. She'd cried. Both inside and out loud. The Health Centre had been responsive and the midwife had come straight round.

It was only afterwards though when the hurt set in, when the conflicting emotions of anger, remorse, loss and injustice hit hard, that she had wanted him. Wanted the physical contact of someone else. Someone to love her, someone to cuddle her, someone to tell her everything was going to be alright.

Matt sat, still, almost motionless, his wine untouched, unsure of what to do or say. In one moment he had wanted to reach out to her, to cuddle her, to give her what it was that she had wanted, but in the next he felt restrained, restrained by the surroundings, by time, by distance. They were not the couple that they had once been. He leant forward though, held out his hand, which she took. "That's awful. It must have been crap. Life really can be shit sometimes."

They sat in silence, both holding back tears.

A waiter came by and asked them if they needed more drinks. It broke their isolation, brought them back to the present. "No thanks," Matt said on their behalf.

Charlotte reached for her bag and took out an envelope. "I brought this for you," she said.

Matt took it and opened it slowly. He knew what it contained. He'd seen them before; passed round in offices that he had worked in; amongst friends and by his sister some years earlier. The grainy ultrasound image was clear. It was a human life form suspended in the limbo of its mother's womb. His gut churned. It was his child this time. He'd spent his entire career working for the benefit of children and yet had never experienced the sheer joy and pleasure of being a parent himself. Yet in his hand was a picture that brought only pain. The tears he had held back slipped slowly down his cheeks.

Charlotte leant forward. It was her turn. She held out her hand. Matt took it and their arms went around each other's shoulders.

They decided to leave the hotel and go for a walk. It was late afternoon but it was calm and clear and they walked up Johnston Terrace to the Castle Esplanade where they gazed down on the flat that they had once holidayed in. They reminisced about happier times, whilst both acknowledging that life had not always been easy as their aspirations had not always reflected the needs of the other. Strolling down the High Street they looked in the windows of the tourist shops. Easter eggs were on sale. They found a restaurant and had dinner together for the last time. It was nearly 10 o'clock when Matt walked Charlotte back to her hotel. They embraced on the steps, deciding that it was easier to part there. As he turned to leave, she gave him a business card. 'Charlotte Hampson, Independent Social Care Consultant', together with her phone number, email address and Facebook details. "I did it Matthew. I did it. I said I would. Stay in touch."

He said he would.

Matt caught the bus back to Portobello. It had been a long weekend and a strange Mother's Day. 'Oh shit', he thought. Mothers Day and he hadn't even contacted his own!

The following day in the office, Matt found it difficult to concentrate. The growing interest in the implications of the named person sections of the Bill meant that battle lines were becoming hardened. Matt had his own views but he was being asked daily it seemed, to provide a statement or evidence that would support one lobby group or another's point of view. Helen and he had decided to keep the Centre at arms length as far as possible and he was able to politely decline most of the requests that he received. This helpfully enabled him to avoid a number of emails that filled his In Box. Instead, he found himself staring out over the square contrasting his experiences of the previous weekend: the liberating feeling that he had experienced on Saturday evening with Catriona and the sense of completeness that they had each felt on Sunday morning; against the emptiness and grief that he and Charlotte had shared later that day. He took the picture out of his jacket pocket and looked closely at it.

He had to go through to Glasgow that evening for a meeting with a group of universities and it was a full week before he had chance to meet up with Catriona again. They stayed in touch; spoke a couple of times on the phone and texted each other every day. By the following Monday he was therefore eager to see her and he was one of the first into The Espy. He was already sitting at their usual table when Catriona and the others arrived together. Matt stood up and Catriona walked straight over to him. As they kissed, her friends shared a giggle at the bar.

"Aye aye, something to share?" asked Rob, a smile crossing his face, as he sat down with the tray of drinks.

"Might have," Catriona replied. But before she could say anything the first round of the quiz was underway.

Matt looked on, a warm glow inside.

During the interval, Catriona, sitting a little closer to Matt, confessed to the others that they had been out together the weekend before, had been to the top of North Berwick Law before taking Bobby with them for a meal in the evening. She left out the detail of the mother's day breakfast though.

"Good for the two of you," said Rob. "I'm pleased. I really am."

At the end of the evening they hadn't won, in fact none of them had really concentrated at all, a fact remarked on by the question setter when announcing the final scores. None of them really minded. It was the first Monday in April and it was a mild spring like evening as they left the pub together and parted outside. Rob and the others made their apologies, said that they would leave the lovebirds to it and headed off. Matt and Catriona took their time and strolled arm in arm up Bath Street.

"I've had an idea," she said as they approached the High Street. "The cottage. You know, the one I told you about. The one my parents left me. I've had a cancellation for the Easter weekend. Do you fancy going up with me? I always like to go up at the start of the season. Give the place a once over. I got a call over the weekend from Nick. He's coming over to the UK on business and has asked if he could see the boys. Bobby wasn't sure to begin with. He doesn't really know his father, but when Dylan said that he didn't mind, Bobby wants to go as well. There's talk of the three of them going to Centre Parcs or something. What do you say?"

"Sounds great. That's fantastic," Matt replied. "Why not!"

They kissed each other goodnight and Matt promised to call her the following day. He walked back down Bath Street, a definite spring in his step.

CHAPTER EIGHTEEN - A MAJOR ACT
(1988 - 1991)

Matt was back in Hattonbridge when he got the call. Apart from a few days at the Fringe catching up with his drama group from Newcastle, he'd spent most of the summer helping at the playscheme near the Poly. But when that had ended he'd returned home to the village. The leaves were beginning to turn brown on the Chestnut trees on the Green and he still had no job, as his father kept reminding him.

His mother called upstairs to him. "Matthew. Phone for you. From the University."

He'd almost fallen out of bed and scrambled downstairs to take the call, not pausing to put any clothes on. His sister Fi, who by then was in her last year at school studying for her 'A' Levels, was still eating her breakfast in the kitchen. She gave him a look of horror as he took the receiver from his mother.

"Yes. Hi. This is Matt."

"Hello Matt, this is Professor Baker." She was the Director of the Research Centre that Jane worked at. "It was good to meet you at the interview. We'd like to offer you the paid PhD opportunity with the Centre," she said.

Jane had told him about the position one evening that summer. It was a chance to both study for a PhD over three years and to join an increasingly influential Social Sciences Research Centre. He'd jumped at the opportunity, particularly as it would mean that his own research would be supervised by Pauline Baker herself, someone whose work on poverty and human need he had revered during his earlier studies.

He had accepted the post there and then. Putting the phone down and still naked, he'd let out a loud scream.

"You're disgusting!" exclaimed his sister.

A month later he was back in the Midlands town where the University was located. Although it had a long history as a technical college, it was one of a number of universities that had been created on greenfield sites around the country during the 1960s. The landscaped grounds, the concrete modernist architecture and the lake at the centre of the campus were in stark contrast to the rarefied atmosphere of the more austere buildings of older more traditional universities. They were exciting places to study and work though and many had developed a reputation for challenging conventional wisdom, whilst others some saw them as hotbeds of political insurrection.

The Centre's own position was probably somewhere between these two views. This suited Matt who was still unsure about his own ambition: whether to try and lead change; or whether to seek to merely influence it. His own studies took him further into exploring the impact of political decision making on communities that had been reliant on single industries. There were many of these around in the north Midlands and South Yorkshire as a result of the closure programme in the mining industry. Towns and villages that had been largely self-reliant were becoming increasingly desperate and many families were struggling to cope with the impact of the change. What employment opportunities there were, were often short term or low skilled and assistance to support those affected to re-train often seemed at best misplaced, or at worst misguided. "Exactly how many painters and decorators does one village need?" one former miner had told Matt, as he began his fieldwork, referring to the training that he and his former colleagues had been offered since their pit had closed.

Alongside his PhD work, Matt became directly involved in the work of the Centre and found the atmosphere and support within the team both challenging and helpful. Jane moved on to a new job with a London based think-tank in early 1989, but by then he had new friends within the group and across the University. For him, it felt that life really was looking up.

Over Easter he and a couple of colleagues had gone skiing to the French Alps and it was on his first day back after the break and sporting a tanned face with what skiers often referred to as a panda look, that he first met her.

"Sorry," he said, tray in hand, as he turned away from the till in one of the cafés on the campus. "I didn't see you."

She'd been trying to jump the queue as she only wanted to pay for the banana that she was holding out. "My fault," she said. "I shouldn't have been trying to jump in."

Matt took his tray and went to sit down with his skiing friends. They were reminding each other of their exploits of the previous week both on and off the piste. Their laughter was dominating the otherwise calm of the café, the students still being on leave.

She'd sat at a nearby table and was trying hard to read a book whilst eating her banana. Their conversation intruded into her reading and eventually she sighed, stood up, noisily scraped her chair back under the table and pointedly walked past them. They gave each other a knowing look as their gaze followed her out of the room, sharing a stifled giggle.

Later that day Matt was working in the library when he noticed the time. It was the fortnightly Centre team meeting and he was, as usual, in danger of being late. He hurried out of the library building and across the campus to the Centre's offices. "Sorry," he said bursting in. "Didn't see the time."

"Take your seat Matt and get your breath back," said Pauline, looking at him over her glasses. "I was just introducing Charlotte here. She'll be taking Jane's job. She's going to be working on the follow up to the implementation of the Children Act."

"I think we've already met," she scowled, as Matt sat down. Charlotte went on to introduce herself to the team and told them a bit about her background. She was the same age as Matt having gone to university straight from school. She'd been working for an independent research group based in the south-west but her husband had recently got a job nearby and she'd consequently looked for a move as well together with their young daughter.

At the end of the meeting Matt had offered to put the kettle on and took orders for teas and coffees, making sure that he made Charlotte's last. "Really sorry about earlier," he said. "We must have sounded like right plonkers."

"That's ok," she replied, as she took her coffee along the corridor to Jane's former office closing the door behind her.

As it transpired, apart from Centre meetings, he didn't have much contact with Charlotte till a few months later. It was a casual remark from Pauline who suggested that Matt was the person to speak to about Scotland and the Edinburgh Fringe in particular, which led to the two of them having an in-depth conversation.

Charlotte's husband was keen on a holiday north of the border and they were looking for ideas. Matt had to admit that his knowledge of Scotland didn't really extend far beyond Edinburgh itself, but he was glad of the opportunity to share what he knew. Although she knew of the Festival she didn't really know much about the Fringe and said that it sounded really exciting.

Matt's studies took him deep into the summer that year and he didn't get much chance for a holiday. He did have a couple of weeks back in the Dale, but, in spite of his family making him welcome, it was increasingly feeling less like somewhere that he came from and more like somewhere he went to. His father though seemed less anxious about him not yet having a career when he explained the sorts of opportunities that he hoped would be available to him when he got his PhD two years later.

Back at the University that autumn, he'd initially forgotten about the advice that he'd given about Scottish holidays. That was until a Centre meeting a few weeks into the new term. He'd offered to clear away the dirty coffee cups, something that the others were happy to let him do. She'd hung back though as he collected the cups together and held the door for him.

"Thanks for doing that," she said. "My turn next time."

He stifled a laugh, knowing that he was the only person who ever tidied up. "Did you have a good time then?"

"Sorry?" she said.

"Edinburgh. You asked for .... "

"Oh, yes. I should have said thank you." The look on her face though implied that something was wrong.

"Was it something I said?" Matt asked, as he washed up the cups.

She didn't respond immediately. "No, it was nothing. Nothing you said anyway," she eventually replied.

He tried again; asked her where they had been. She answered 'here and there', though did admit that the Fringe had been good. It was clear to him that there was something that she wasn't saying.

In the event it was Charlotte herself who shared more. It was a few weeks later and she stopped him in the corridor outside her office and asked him if he'd got time for a drink after work.

"Great idea," he said instinctively. He spent the afternoon in the library struggling to concentrate on his research as he pondered why she had asked him and why now. Later he wandered back to the Centre and found Charlotte waiting for him at the door.

"Thought you'd stood me up," she said. She started walking towards the staff car park without another comment.

Matt followed. "We're going off campus then?"

"Yes," she replied. "Too many eyes and ears around here."

She drove north out of the town and into the country. Turning off the main road after a couple of miles, she pulled her car up at a canal side inn. There were no other cars in the car park. It was early for the bar meal brigade. She bought the drinks and they took the seats by the window overlooking the canal. Matt was happy to accept the drink but puzzled by what they were doing there.

"I don't really know you," she began "and that's why I thought I could perhaps talk to you." Over the next hour or so, Charlotte unburdened herself: about having a child, Sarah; who she had had shortly after starting university by a partner who she no longer knew; about her subsequent marriage to Ian; and about her aspirations and her dreams, that were very different from his. The holiday to Scotland had not gone well. It had rained, but that had not been the problem. Her relationship with Ian was increasingly difficult and for the sake of Sarah she was thinking of leaving him. She was lonely and confused.

Matt struggled to take it all in and particularly why she was entrusting him with all the detail. All he did know was that he was in company of a pained and troubled young woman who, at that moment, was extremely vulnerable and in the absence of anyone else, he instinctively wanted to help. His arm reached around her shoulders and she didn't pull away. He asked her whether her husband would be missing her and what about Sarah.

She explained that he thought that she was away overnight.

"Where are you staying tonight then?" he asked.

"Don't know I suppose."

Without thinking Matt offered her his settee.

Looking back two years later as he stood in line ready to go on stage to collect his PhD he realised that that was the moment that he had grown up. His decision to let her stay even that first night had implications and consequences that he would only realise as subsequent events unfolded. As his name was read out and he crossed the stage to receive the acknowledgement of his PhD, he knew that there were was more than one set of eyes in the audience that was looking on in admiration at his achievements, for not only were his parents there, but Charlotte had taken the Centre's allocated ticket in order to be present at the event and was sitting at the back. He made sure that he looked in both directions as he came down from the stage.

By then she had moved out of the home that she and Ian had lived in and had rented accommodation for herself and Sarah. Although they weren't living together and didn't really acknowledge even to themselves that they were an item, Matt had, in turn, become a regular visitor.

In summer 1991 and after his graduation, Matt had, as he had always hoped, been taken on by the Centre as part of the team responsible for studying the introduction of the landmark Children Act 1989 that autumn. Implemented by new Prime Minister, John Major's Conservative government, it was being trailed as one of the most comprehensive pieces of English legislation ever produced. Amongst its significant achievements was to make the welfare of the child paramount in all legal processes. It was an exciting first project for him to be involved in. The fact that he and Charlotte would also be working closely together was an added bonus, he thought, as he signed the contract that gave him his first full-time job.

CHAPTER NINETEEN - GOING HOME
(April and May 2014)

The Children & Young People (Scotland) Act 2014 received royal assent on 27 March and with Easter being in early April, Matt was looking forward to the break. Implementation was going to be a longer journey and its start could wait until at least after the holidays.

It was Good Friday and a Runrig CD was playing on Catriona's car's stereo as they drove up the A9, the main route north through the heart of the Highlands.

Catriona sang along with the words as they passed Drumochter, the sun rather than the moon guiding them northwards. "I always like to play this one when I make this journey," she said. "Do you know Runrig?"

"I've heard of them. Loch Lomond and all that. It's hard to miss at Scotland football and rugby matches. And, as for last New Year's Eve, I hate to think how many times myself and Aurélie began '*By yon bonnie banks and by yon bonnie ...*'"

"Aurélie? Who's Aurélie?" Catriona almost goaded him, her face both puzzled and teasing at the same time.

Matt paused, suddenly unsure. "Someone from the University. Works near the Centre," he said eventually. "She's from France. Hadn't been in Edinburgh for Hogmanay before. We did it together." His staccato like responses betrayed his unease. A silence prevailed in the car, broken only by the music.

Catriona decided to stop for lunch near Aviemore and headed to Rothiemurchus just outside the village on the road to Loch Morlich and the Cairngorm Ski Centre. "Come on, Mr Centre Director, you can buy me lunch."

For the first time since Mothers Day the relationship between them was cool. Matt was uncertain about what to say. He realised that by saying nothing there was a danger that Catriona was going to believe there was something that he was hiding and yet he was struggling to find words to open the conversation. Matt chose his moment just as their lunch arrived. "Hogmanay was good. I'd never done Edinburgh before this year. It was good to do it with some friends as well." He paused, waiting for Catriona's reaction.

It didn't come. Instead she responded to the waitress's question as to whether they were enjoying their lunch. She commented on the soup saying that coconut, sweet potato and chilli was an unusual but complementary combination.

Matt tried again. "How long is it going to take us from here then?" he asked.

"Matt, I want to ask you something. No, actually I want to tell you something." Catriona paused herself. "I love my children and I've done all I can to give them the best since Nick left. It's not always been easy. To begin with I didn't know that he wasn't coming back. For some time I didn't know that I was in fact a single parent. Since then it's been me and them and I've kept it that way. Nobody else." She paused again. "Then you turned up."

Matt opened his mouth, but Catriona's expression prevented any words emerging.

"I've often said I wasn't going to fall for anyone ever again. I didn't need a man. Rob'll tell you that. He's asked me out more times than he can probably remember. But somehow you've been different. It was as though you were looking. Looking for someone. Like a fool, I've let myself start to think that that might be me."

Matt found himself nodding.

"If we're going to make it though, then there isn't going to be anyone else."

"There isn't," Matt replied. "Not any more." He paused himself, thinking of the significance of what he had just said. "I'd be lying if I said there hasn't been, but right now there isn't. Aurélie works nearby my office. In the French department at the University. We bumped into each other shortly after I started. She's been a friend; we've done a few things together, but she's got someone of her own." He couldn't bring himself to talk about Charlotte, that was still too painful and would have to wait he thought as he took his wallet out to pay for lunch and saw the ultrasound picture tucked in the back. That still hurt.

They left Aviemore and headed north again towards their destination. The sky was clear and the sun shone brightly on the snow that still clung to the tops of the mountains. Although there was a slight chill in the air compared to further south, the temperature was warm and there was very much a sense of new life rising around them as they ventured further north into the highlands.

The 'yes' posters were noticeably more common as they had journeyed up from Edinburgh and Catriona teased Matt that if things went in one direction then in future he might need his passport. 'Indieref' was something that they had never discussed and a silence quickly embraced the inside of the car. It was a subject that was increasingly putting a strain on established relationships, let alone emerging ones like theirs. Catriona turned the music up and the sound of Runrig accompanied them over the Slochd summit and down past Culloden towards Inverness.

After stopping on the outskirts of the city to do some supermarket shopping, it was late afternoon when they finally arrived in Lochcarron. Catriona parked the car on the verge opposite the cottage. The weather was calm and the quiet of the place was almost deafening as they got out of the car and gazed over the loch.

"Wow," whispered Matt. "That's incredible. Do you feel it as well? It's like waiting for your ears to pop on an aeroplane."

"Aye, I know," Catriona replied. "It can be amazing. It never fails to get me as well. But it also encroaches on you, reminds you that it's there, and takes you over. It's what made some of us leave."

"How could you want to," Matt began, but Catriona was already at the other side of the road opening the front door. "Not locked, then?"

"Why would you? We never do round here. 'Locks are only for incomers and tourists', my Dad used to say. No, Magdalena left it open for us anyway."

"Magdalena?" enquired Matt.

"Yes, she looks after it for me. Cleans it between guests. Let's me know if there's anything needs doing. She's Polish. Been over here since 2007. Her children are now learning Gaelic. It's a real sign of the times. Makes a mockery of some of the 'indieref' arguments though. Scotland for the Scots and all that. Magdalena and her family are probably more local to this area than I am now." Catriona paused, one foot inside. "Come on, let me show you round."

Together they entered what had been Catriona's family home. The late afternoon gloom meant that they had to let their eyes grow accustomed as they went from room to room. Catriona apparently did not want to turn the lights on as they explored. As she showed Matt round she was describing a time some years off and it was as though light would somehow curtail that illusion. They paused on the landing.

"This was Mum and Dads' room," she said, almost tip-toeing into the room on the right at the top of the stairs.

Matt suspected that the ubiquitous birch wood furniture that was a feature of the room and that had become standard in many self-catering cottages the country over, had not been there when her parents had last slept in it. Catriona was by the window looking out over the loch. Matt approached her from behind and put his arm gently round her shoulders, her ponytail falling over his elbow. She took his hand. "Am I forgiven?" he asked.

"Just don't cheat on me Matt."

They stood for a moment, each in tune with their own thoughts.

"Hello, Hi," a voice called from below.

"Magdalena. We'll be down in a minute," answered Catriona.

Downstairs, Catriona and Magdalena discussed some work that needed to be done to the house leaving Matt to explore by himself. There were two bedrooms and thus he quickly concluded that the one to the left must have been Catriona's when she was a young girl. There were two single beds, again in a modern birchwood design and it was difficult for him to get a sense of what the room would once have looked like. Closing his eyes he touched the walls and drew in a deep breath. For a moment he could hear voices, a mother calling her daughter; a teenager groaning a response; a father reproaching her. But he opened his eyes and realised that such thoughts were his own imagination. He had no comprehension of the relationship that Catriona had had with her parents. As he stood, a voice called his name bringing him back to the present.

"Matt. Come and give us a hand emptying the car." They unpacked their supermarket shopping into the kitchen and eventually went back for their cases.

A few minutes later Matt found himself standing uncomfortably at the top of the stairs not sure which room to enter.

"Sorry, just shutting the car," Catriona called as she came into the house closing the front door behind her. She climbed the stairs with her own case and found Matt apparently paralysed. "Something wrong?" she asked. A broad smile crept over her face as she realised his predicament. "I know, I used to find it tricky at first sleeping in Mum and Dads' room.

Didn't seem right. But, hey, it's the biggest room so that's where I put the double bed. Are you ok with the left, I really do prefer the right?"

Matt was visibly relieved and unpacked his own case into the wardrobe and chest of drawers.

"Come on, let's get done here and then we can head along to the Hotel for something to eat. Lunch was a long time ago."

Ten minutes later, they were walking along the Main Street beside the shore of the loch to the Hotel, Catriona's arm firmly through Matt's. Even though it was dark, Catriona was recalling who used to live at which house and in particular those that her childhood friends had stayed in. "That was Callum's. In fact it still is. He lives where his Mum and Dad did. You'll meet him at some point". But most had moved on and most of the houses were now holiday lets. Even those that were occupied permanently tended to be outsiders, incomers, she said. Time had moved on from when the blasting from the new road had caused her and her friend Shona to hide on the brae above the village.

The smell of wood smoke from the open fire met them as they entered the Lounge Bar of the Hotel drawing them in on what had become a cool evening. There were a number of people gathered in the bar laughing and talking, clearly relaxing for the Easter weekend.

"Welcome to Lochcarron," Catriona began. "Home of the mighty Kishorn Camandoes!"

"The what?" Matt asked.

"Oh, it's the local shinty team. It's a big thing over here. None of your namby-pamby football or rugby in the north-west! Now, my treat, what can I get you?"

"A pint of ... whatever's in the hand pump," Matt pointed to the real ale pump on the bar.

An hour or two later and both of them were more relaxed. They'd eaten from the hotel's range of pizzas and Catriona had speculated about what her parents and particularly her father would have made of such apparently foreign food being available in the Hotel. She recalled that during her childhood, the Hotel was somewhere that her father went along to with the other men of the village. Rarely was it place for women to go except for family occasions such as christenings and weddings. "Hatches, matches and dispatches," her mother would say, "that's the only time you'll get me in that place." Seemingly it was even less likely for children to have been allowed to cross the threshold.

But that was a different time, Catriona suggested, one before tourism had become central to the economy of the area, a time when men like her father had sustained a living in the village without the need to rely on outsiders. Catriona's father had apparently been a joiner and had made much of the furniture in their house, although he had mainly worked repairing boats for local fishermen as well as general odd jobs in the village. Matt wanted to know why, if that were the case, the house contained so much modern ubiquitous flat pack type furniture and what had happened to the hand crafted pieces that she would have known as a child.

"It was time to move on," Catriona said. "It's not what tourists want any more. A bit like hotels, they expect all self-catering cottages to basically look the same. At least, that's what the agent said. I've got some of Dad's bits down the road and there are one or two things still in the house. The rest went to auction."

Matt found it odd that Catriona seemed so nonchalant about her family's past and about the beautiful area that she had grown up in. Although he was not as regular a visitor to Hattondale as he would like, he still considered it to be where he was from, in spite of what he may have said at Helen's dinner party in January.

"Come on, let's get back," Catriona said. "There's places I do want to show you tomorrow, although I need you to help me with a couple of things in the house first thing."

They both slept long and woke together taking in the calmness of the morning. Matt suggested that in the absence of Bobby he would make breakfast in bed and the coffee and croissants that he produced took them another hour to consume; the croissants giving Catriona another cause to speculate what her father would have thought about the crumbs in the bed!

They spent the morning doing a few of the jobs that Magdalena had identified, but by lunchtime Catriona decided that they'd done enough. Instead she said that she wanted to take Matt to somewhere just outside the village that was very important to her. It was a place that she visited every time she returned. After they'd eaten, they walked for about a mile out of the village back along the road from Inverness. Past the

Hotel, and the new developments further up the hillside, past the school and out towards the golf club. There sitting by the side of the road was the village's old graveyard shrouded by trees with the ruined old parish church in one corner. Catriona pushed open the rusty kissing gate and they entered the graveyard.

"It's over here," Catriona said, pointing at a relatively small gravestone towards one corner behind the old Kirk. She stooped down, pulling some moss away to read the inscription. "*To the memory of Elizabeth MacLeod. Born 4 April 1886, died 6 September 1971, aged 85. Gus am bris an lá, agus an teich na sgailean.*" A single tear rolled gently down her cheek.

For a few moments only the noise of the gentle breeze could be heard.

"She was my grandmother. She was everything you would want a grandmother to be. She was my inspiration. Even as a small child, I used to love listening to her voice and her stories. They went back years, to the islands and to a time and a place where her family, my family, came from."

Matt tried to put his arm around her shoulder but she pulled herself away.

"No Matt, I don't need comforting. That's not what it's about."

"I'm sorry," he said. "I was only ...

"I know. But, you should know with your knowledge of children and families. Don't they call it attachment?"

Matt nodded. "You're right."

"My grandmother Elizabeth knew too. She worked hard to keep her family together. She'd raised my Dad by herself you see. Along with his two older sisters, my aunts. Granddad was killed in a fishing accident in 1930 when my Dad was just a few months old. There was no grave for her to remember her husband at. He left her to bring up the children by herself. She was a wonderful woman. I'm not sure any of us could be as strong as she would have needed to be."

"What was that you said in Gaelic?" he asked.

"It's from the the Song of Solomon in the bible: *Until the day breaks and the shadows flee away.*"

They stood apart, Catriona gazing into the distance, her ponytail swaying gently in the breeze. Matt looked at her and slowly began to understand what drove her, how she had come to care for her own children as a single parent, and from where she had drawn her determination as well as why she had not needed help to raise her children. He began to imagine the contrast between the beauty of the landscape in front of him and the hardship that it must have brought to previous generations. He saw for the first time its contrasts and recognised the need that Catriona and others had had to get away from it to places like Aberdeen and beyond.

Yet, somehow it continued to draw her back. A part of her that was; that part that was her grandmother would always be here. He recognised it himself. He too had spent years escaping Hattondale, in spite of the fact that he hadn't lived there since he had left school.

"Come on then. I'm done. Let's go," she said, interrupting the silence and Matt's contemplations. "How are you on a bike?"

"I haven't ridden for years," he replied. "Why?"

"It's a beautiful afternoon. Let's cycle down to Strome. Callum and Morag should be able to lend us a couple of bikes."

Callum Smith was someone that Catriona had grown up with. They'd gone to school together. Yet he had stayed in the village, had married Morag from nearby Plockton whom he had met at the High School there and they'd raised their family locally. After a few minutes reminiscences and Callum gently teasing Catriona that she'd found herself another Englishman, Matt and Catriona were peddling out of the village along Church Street, round Slumbay and on towards the mouth of the loch that gave the village its name. It was only four miles down the old single track road that had become virtually redundant since the building of the new road on the south side of the loch in 1970. The afternoon was glorious and the warmth was beginning to bring the gorse along the roadside, into bloom. Soon the bushes would be ablaze with their vivid yellow flowers and the pungent smell of coconut would be everywhere. Catriona recalled that her grandmother used to have a habit of putting coconut into much of her cooking and for years, never having seen a coconut herself, she used to think that her grandmother went out harvesting the gorse to supplement their diets.

They reached the castle at Strome in less than an hour and looked across at the village on the south shore still called Strome Ferry, even though no ferry had plied the route for over forty years. They chatted for some time each recounting childhood stories and it was early evening when they decided to head back. In the gathering gloom the ride back seemed harder than it had been on the way down. By the time they had returned the bikes to Callum and he and Catriona had laughed about cycling to the village primary school many years before, it was nearly dark. Catriona lit the fire whilst Matt cooked. They decided to eat on the sofa by the warmth of the fire rather than more formally at the table. Afterwards they cuddled up together on the sofa watching the dancing flames of the burning logs in the dark of the room and draining the bottle of wine that they had opened with their dinner. Both of them were finally relaxed.

....

Matt had begun to fall asleep his head resting in Catriona's lap when his phone rang. It was in his back trouser pocket. He sat up quickly, causing them both discomfort. He answered, his eyes not focusing in the gloom on the phone's display announcing the caller's identity.

"Hello," he answered.

"Is that Mathew Fawcett?" said the voice at the other end.

"Yes," he replied. "Who's calling?"

"This is Sergeant Ireland of North Yorkshire Police. I'm afraid that I have some news that I need to pass on to you."

Matt felt his heart stop.

"There has been a road traffic accident this evening near Ripon, we believe involving a car belonging to and being driven by your father. A Mr Frederick Fawcett."

"Was anyone else in the car," Matt cut in.

"Yes. I believe his wife, your mother."

"But how are they; where are they?"

"Is anyone with you," asked the police officer.

"Yes, but why?"

"Would you mind handing the phone to them?"

"No, I'm fine. I'll put you on loudspeaker though."

Catriona and Matt listened in silence, their arms around each other, as Sergeant Ireland described what had happened. Matt's parents had been driving south from Ripon towards Harrogate. A tractor with a trailer had been turning out of a side road. Their car had collided with the tractor. His father had been pronounced dead at the scene, whilst his mother had been taken by air ambulance to hospital in Leeds. After exchanging further details Matt pressed 'Call end' on his phone promising to contact his sister.

It was some minutes before either of them uttered a sound. Catriona held Matt and let him come to in his own time. From his silence, a gentle sob emerged, accompanied by a slow tear down his cheek. He stared blankly at the fire. Slowly, the sob became a cry and the single tear became a trickle and then a flood. His face was distorted with pain as the grief took over.

Catriona continued to hold him, the experience bonding them closer in the tragic circumstances. She thought of her own mother and father, of their deaths and of how bereft she had felt at the time. She thought of her grandmother. She knew the pain that was now so close to her.

It was nearly an hour before Matt could react. The wine that they had both consumed meant that neither of them was in a position to drive that evening. They decided though to make an early start for Inverness on the Sunday morning aiming to get the 10 o'clock London train. Matt would get it as far as York and then a connection to Leeds. He phoned the hospital and was told that his mother was comfortable but in a critical condition. However, there was nothing to be gained by trying to get to Leeds before the following day as she was heavily sedated. He wasn't looking forward to what he did next, but finally he phoned his sister.

Her reaction was that of anyone getting such tragic news late on a Saturday evening. In amidst her own tears though, she asked a one word question: "Edgar?"

There had been nothing about the family's pet in the information from the police.

Much of the journey to Inverness the following morning was in silence. Catriona dropped Matt at the back of the Eastgate Shopping Centre next to the station. They embraced quietly and kissed each other before Matt headed for the train. He promised to stay in touch and she said that she'd speak to Nick about continuing to look after Bobby if he'd like her to come down.

The train ride through the Highlands is normally reckoned to be one of the finest in the world. That Easter Sunday morning though it could have been through an industrial wasteland for all Matt knew. He checked with the hospital and with Fi and stared; stared at the grey of the seat backs, at the grey of the people on the train and at the grey of the day outside, even though in reality the sun shone. Just after one o'clock, Edinburgh, his home, came and went. As the train passed the depot at Craigentinny, he looked beyond it to Portobello. He thought of those who were now so important to him, in particular the woman who he had so recently left behind and wondered when he would be back.

By the middle of the afternoon the train pulled slowly out of Darlington station. Matt knew that the next station, about fifteen minutes further on, was Northallerton. Although not due to stop the train slowed, caught by signals, to allow another train to cross on to the Middlesbrough line. Almost in deference to an earlier journey and its passenger, the romantically named Highland Chieftain that had brought him all the way from Inverness rolled slowly through the station. He gazed at the northbound platform that he'd first known from that day that his father had left for university. A little boy and his mother standing there smiled. His own face broke into a grin, momentarily relieving him of his grief and his hand proffered an almost imperceptible wave.

After a change in York he duly arrived in Leeds shortly before five o'clock. Fi had travelled up from London by train as well and met him at the station. They got a taxi together to the hospital. Easter Sunday 2014 would live long in their memory.

Neither of them really knew what to say. For all that they were there to see their mother, it was the thought of their father lying dead in a mortuary somewhere that oddly most concerned them. As they stared at their mother still sedated and unresponsive, connected to a multitude of machines and with attentive nurses, their minds were taken up with thoughts of their father alone, unloved and by himself.

Fi, who by her nature would normally have taken charge, was by contrast quite reticent. It was Matt who discussed the situation with the care team. Their mother had serious but not life threatening crush injuries to her chest and stomach, but was expected to make a full recovery. She would probably need to spend at least a week in hospital. And no, she hadn't yet been told that her husband was dead.

Matt and Fi spent a couple of hours at their mother's bedside before deciding to head for a hotel which Fi had booked for them on the journey up. She had also managed to make contact with their parents' neighbours, the Claytons, and given them the sad news. To her surprise and delight she had found that Edgar was safe at home and that the Claytons had been feeding him.

Although it was Easter Monday, the following day was a whirlwind of emotions and responsibilities as they contacted the police, hospital, undertaker and a host of others all of whom offered their condolences but seemed to treat the situation as routine, almost ordinary. "Too ordinary," Matt later told Catriona when he called her from the hotel that evening.

Nick was heading for Norway the following day and had therefore brought Bobby back as originally planned. This meant that she wouldn't be able to join him as they'd hoped. Matt thanked her anyway and she promised to try and be there for the funeral. It all seemed so staccato like after the way that their relationship had been developing. Both of them were struggling to cope.

It was Wednesday before their mother was sufficiently awake to be told the news about their father. In the mean time, Matt had been in touch with the office and Helen had told him not to hurry back. She would look after Centre business in the mean time. "Oh, just one thing," she said. "That French friend of yours was in yesterday looking for you. I said you'd be in this week, but I dare say you won't now."

Aurélie, Matt thought. Always the wrong time. It had been like that since the first day he had seen her.

The doctor had offered to break the news to their mother if they wished, or to get the chaplain, but the brother and sister felt that it was their responsibility. It wasn't something that they found easy though. They tried to rehearse it but in the end Matt blurted it out. "He's dead Mum. Dad's dead."

Their mother stretched out her hands and her children took them. The three of them convened in silence. To a stranger it might have seemed odd that there were no tears, but Matt and Fi had probably shed most of theirs. Their mother's would follow once the effect of the medication had worn off. There would be a time and a place yet to come for them.

They continued to visit their mother during the week as she began to make a recovery and eventually they were able to contemplate the funeral arrangements. It was their mother's idea. "Hattonbridge. Why not? It's what the daft beggar would have wanted. And I'd like it there as well. I don't know if the old burial ground is still in use. I dare say it isn't, but if it isn't I'd still like the funeral itself there. Can you look into it Matthew?"

He promised he would, though it would have to wait until the start of the following week now and in any event he was going to have to head back to Edinburgh to get some more clothes. He arrived at about half past eight and Catriona met him in Market Street at the side of Waverley Station. Matt was tired and they drove back to Portobello in silence. Dylan and Bobby were at home together so Catriona went up to Matt's flat with him. This time they both stood at the window looking up Bath Street. Matt filled her in with the details of the week and told her that he planned to go back to York and Leeds on the Monday. Catriona suggested that he come round to Lee Crescent for dinner on the Sunday afternoon.

It was a nice day for late April he thought as he made his way round the following day and the four of them had a pleasant time. Matt even found himself laughing at some of Bobby's jokes, something he later told Catriona that he had found particularly helpful. As he was leaving Fi called him to say that the plan from the hospital was that their mother could go home on the Tuesday if there was someone to look after her. They agreed that they would both aim to stay with her until after the funeral.

The train journey back to Yorkshire on the Monday wasn't as bleak as it had been the week before. They stayed another night in the hotel in Leeds before arrangements were made to move their mother on Tuesday. Fi's husband Graham had driven up from London with their car and the three of them arrived at their parents' house shortly before their mother did. The Claytons had put the heating on and done some

244

shopping and even though it was sad it was a dignified homecoming nonetheless.

It transpired that the old burial ground in the village was no longer able to accept new burials and instead they agreed to have a funeral meeting in the village hall followed by a cremation. It was arranged for Friday May 9th.

Over the intervening week, the four of them shared many happy memories, including Fi's arrival in the world, of birthdays, holidays and their graduations, most of which Graham had heard many times before. He contented himself walking Edgar and doing the cooking. By the middle of the week before the funeral Ella joined them.

It was the day before the funeral though when a car drove up outside the house and there was a knock on the door. Fi and her family were out. Getting to his feet, Matt went to answer it, saying to his mother, who was sitting near the fire, "Mum, I think that this is someone I'd like you to meet." He opened the door and Catriona entered the house. "Mum, this is Catriona. We were together when the police called me. She's a very special person, Mum."

The funeral meeting was what their father had always wanted. 'No religion, just friends' is what he'd always said. The village hall in Hattonbridge was packed with many of them, as well as relatives and former colleagues from the estate. Many spoke, recounting happy days and the achievements that he had made in his life. There was laughter as well as tears and at the end of it there was a sense of joy and of a life fulfilled.

"What was it that was on your grandmother's gravestone?" Matt asked, his arm around Catriona, as they stood outside the hall at one point looking out over the Green.

"Gus am bris an lá - until the day breaks."

He nodded, smiling.

Afterwards some of them made their way to the crematorium where Martin, his cousin, led the gathering through the solemn proceedings. Then it was back to the Hattonbridge Inn for what Matt's grandmother used to call 'the ham tea'. Everyone agreed that it had been an uplifting day.

Catriona, who was staying in a nearby hotel, headed back to Edinburgh on the Saturday whilst Matt got the train from York the following day. He needed to get back to work and normality. Fi gave him a lift to the station and they agreed that she would stay on but would try and persuade their mother to go back to London with her to convalesce.

CHAPTER TWENTY - A MERRY CHRISTMAS?
(Winter 1995)

It was Christmas Eve and Matt, Charlotte and Sarah were heading north. Traffic on the A1 was particularly heavy around Doncaster and beyond towards the M62. Sarah and her Mum were virtually word perfect with the lyrics to Wonderwall by Oasis. They began singing it for the umpteenth time on the journey.

"Oh come on, give me a break," Matt objected. "Think of the driver!"

He'd only passed his driving test that summer and wasn't yet that confident about long distance driving. When his grandmother had died she had left him some money from the sale of the family haulage business. He'd invested it, with the intention of one day being able to buy his first car and without it, he would probably have been unable to afford it.

He had been at the Centre for four years and his salary, he recognised, was not going to earn him his fortune. He really should have moved on to a new job in Whitehall or with one of the London based think-tanks, like the one that Jane now worked for. The problem was that he had become attached to Charlotte and more importantly to her daughter. His skiing friends suggested that he felt sorry for them, which he strenuously denied.

He'd eventually given up his own flat earlier that year and moved in with Charlotte and Sarah. His contribution to the rent had been appreciated and when he had talked of taking driving lessons and buying a car he had been welcomed within the family. He had had his doubts though. He knew that he and Charlotte were still relatively young and, although they had had a close relationship now for a few years, he wasn't convinced that he wanted to make a long term commitment. Except, there was Sarah.

Christmas had been his mother's idea. His parents had visited him a few times at the University and he had been quite open about his relationship with Charlotte. They'd even sent Sarah a birthday present that year. But it had still come as a surprise to him when his mother had come right out on the phone one evening in early November and said: 'why don't the three of you come for Christmas? We'd love to have you.' Charlotte hadn't taken much convincing, which surprised him, as ever since he had known her, she'd always spent Christmas with her parents in Oxfordshire. Sarah, who by that autumn was in her first year at Secondary School, had been happy with the arrangements as well.

"It'll be fun," Charlotte had said. "And besides, I've never been to Yorkshire." She regularly teased him about him being a Yorkshire Pudding, which he didn't always appreciate.

The sun had made little appearance all day and it had been a dismal drive. It was late afternoon when they turned off the A1 at Leeming and headed up the Dale. The sky was dark and menacing to the west as they approached Hattonbridge. The first few flakes of snow began to fall as they pulled up on the Green outside the house.

"A white Christmas!" Sarah squealed as she got out of the car.

"That's what they're forecasting," Matt's Dad said coming out to greet them. "You must be Sarah and this must be your mum. Charlotte isn't it? Come on in. Matt'll get the bags, I'm sure."

Matt looked around him as he took their bags from the car. The village hadn't really changed much since he could first remember it, he thought. In fact, compared to the urban environment within which he lived and worked, he was quite happy to think of this place as home after all.

He went inside.

The house, by contrast, was not immediately recognisable. There was a larger than usual Christmas Tree and more decorations than he had remembered from when decorating the living room was his responsibility. Fiona, who had graduated that summer and was training to be a teacher, was already in deep conversation with Charlotte. The two of them looked as though they'd known each other forever. His mother had taken Sarah through to the kitchen, suggesting that she might like to help finish icing the Christmas Cake.

Matt stood in the hall surrounded by their belongings.

"We thought it probably best if Charlotte and Sarah had your room and you had the sofa in the living room," his father said. "You've probably seen. We've bought a new one. It folds out into a really comfy bed, we believe. You can leave your things on the landing for now."

Matt looked at the cases. His 'things', as his father had called them, were packed together with Charlotte's. She'd seen to that in her usual efficient way. How did his father think they lived, he wondered?

Five minutes later, after he'd moved everything upstairs, his mother called him down. "Matthew? Are you coming? We've got the chocolate log."

It had been a family tradition for as long as he could remember that they always had a chocolate log on Christmas Eve and it had always been his job to cut it. He came downstairs and walked into the living room expectantly.

"I hope you don't mind," his mother said. "I thought it would be nice if Sarah cut it." She was already portioning it out.

Later that evening, after dinner and with Sarah persuaded to go to bed, his parents suggested that Matt, Charlotte and Fiona might like to go to the Hattonbridge Inn. It was snowing when they stepped outside but the wind that had got up made it anything but magical. As they entered the pub one of those propping up the corner of the bar gave them an icy stare as they brought a cold draught in with them.

Matt went to the bar whilst the other two found the last remaining stools near the fire. Returning with the drinks, he stood awkwardly to one side of them with his pint of beer whilst they were deep in conversation. He'd known better Christmas Eves he decided. Outside, on the way back, there was already enough snow to scrape together snowballs and Matt threw one in his sister's direction. It caught her on the shoulder.

She turned and looked at him. "Thanks for nothing!" she said as snow stuck to her coat and scarf. Charlotte scowled.

It was not a comfy sofa, Matt decided a few hours later, as he lay there in the sitting room lit only by the glowing embers of the earlier fire. He slept fitfully and it was still dark outside when he was suddenly conscious that there was someone else in the room.

"Hello," he said, peering into the darkness. "Who's that?"

"It's me Matt. Are you awake?" It was Sarah. She explained that she couldn't sleep but that her Mum was fast asleep and snoring. She was also probably a bit excited about it being Christmas, she admitted.

Matt sat up, reaching for his dressing gown. "Come and sit here a moment then."

The young girl walked over to the sofa in the darkness and sat down. A feint glow still shone out from the hearth. "It's nice here," she said. "I like your Mum and your Dad's quite funny."

Matt feigned surprise, but then acknowledged that they were good parents.

"Could they be my grandparents?" she asked.

Wow, he thought. The implications of that had not crossed his mind. Sarah did have one set of grandparents in Charlotte's own mother and father, but having never known who her father was, he realised that she was missing out on another set. It underlined for him though, how order was so important to children and how it was wrong to assume that these things didn't matter to them. Implicit in Sarah's question though, was something that he had often contemplated but had never discussed with anyone: should he marry her mother? "We'll have to see," he said. "Maybe.

Maybe one day. But they can still be like your best friends you know."

He suggested that she went back to bed and he escorted her back upstairs. Before going back down he stood momentarily in the dark on the landing. Even though it was not the same house he imagined he could hear his mother calling from downstairs, calling for him to come and help her as she was in labour. Being a parent never was easy, he concluded, as he tiptoed back down.

Christmas Day was largely uneventful. Presents were distributed; too much food was prepared; and too much was eaten, although less than the amount that had been prepared! Importantly though, no one fell out with anyone. Matt's mother continued to spoil Sarah and Charlotte seemed happy for her to do so. The weather across the country as a whole had deteriorated and parts of Scotland were experiencing very heavy snowfall. As he watched pictures of the snow laden streets of Aberdeen on the television news, Matt realised that, as time had gone on, his love affair with Scotland, and Edinburgh in particular, had waned. He couldn't immediately recall the last time he'd been there.

By Boxing Day it had stopped snowing in Hattondale and Matt's father suggested that those who wanted to went sledging. His mother excused herself, saying that she'd get dinner ready. His father dug out the children's old sledge from the shed at the end of the garden. The Skelton road had been partially cleared and he carefully drove up the Dale past their old house to the slopes where Matt and Andrew had once played in the summer. It was an invigorating experience as they took it in turns to hurtle down the hillside. Fiona was keen to show Sarah how to get more speed and distance, leaving Matt and Charlotte to stand and watch. Charlotte cuddled into him, admiring the view and contrasting it with those in the Cotswolds that she knew.

"There's something about this place though," he said. "I keep trying to leave it behind, but somehow it doesn't seem to want to leave me."

"But you wouldn't want to live here again, would you?" she asked. "You know where the work is. You'd need to be a bit closer to London."

Matt looked puzzled. "I know, but I wouldn't want to live there either. We're probably quite well placed where we are at the moment I suppose."

"Maybe at the moment, but not for ever. We will need to move in the next couple of years. I don't think that Pauline is going to get all of the work if there's a new government."

It had been obvious for some time that the Conservative government under John Major was in decay and the likelihood of a new Labour administration with the appeal of its youthful leader Tony Blair, was increasingly being contemplated. The implications for social policy, as well as both direct and indirect investment in communities, was eagerly awaited.

"Let's give it a couple of years and see what," Matt said. "If Blair does get in, it could mean big things." He paused and squeezed her to him. "Come on, race you down."

The other three had stopped sledging and had made their way back to the car at the bottom of the slope. Matt and Charlotte half ran, half stumbled down the hillside, whooping and laughing, the two of them picking up snow and throwing it at each other as they did.

"You two look happy," Matt's father said as they rejoined them.

"Yes, why not?" Matt said.

Charlotte smiled.

Later that afternoon they all went round to the church to see the decorated pews. His mother's Mothers Group had made one of the decorations which impressed Sarah. Afterwards they sat in front of the fire to cut the Christmas Cake.

"I think Charlotte should get to cut it," Fiona had said.

Matt made no comment. He had already accepted that his traditional roles within the family were being usurped.

The following morning, with the promise of clear roads during the day, but more snow forecast for later on, Matt, Charlotte and Sarah left shortly after breakfast to drive back to the Midlands. They stopped for lunch at a roadside restaurant on the A1 near Lincoln. To others there, they probably resembled a happy post-Christmas family content with their presents and content that they were on their way home. To themselves, they were each looking forward in their own way, to what lay ahead for them, each conscious that their destination may not be the same.

As they turned back onto the road, lunch consumed, Sarah and her mother again picked up Oasis's Wonderwall.

"Give me a break!" the driver exclaimed.

CHAPTER TWENTY ONE - FULL CIRCLE
(June/ July 2014)

It took time for the hurt to recede; the feeling of finality, of emptiness that comes after grief. Some suggested to him that it would never quite go completely, but Matt was more sanguine. On the journeys into work on the bus he thought more of his father and the loneliness that he must have felt in the city, his wife and young son so far away. By contrast, he had been here barely a year and he had begun to establish himself in a way that his father had never quite achieved. He liked where he had ended up, even if the circumstances by which he had got there were not what he had planned.

Days were growing longer and the weather was distinctly milder. He and Catriona were seeing each other nearly every day, although he hadn't yet quite moved in to Lee Crescent. She had been very supportive in the weeks after he had returned to Edinburgh and had reflected on her own experience of losing her parents. Those around about them, including Rob and the others in the Espy, commented on the glow that the two of them exuded. Recovery was slow, but it was also rejuvenating. Matt promised that he would take her back to the Dales as soon as the opportunity arose. He was keen that she should see them in a happier vein. He also wanted to share them in the way that she had been keen to introduce him to Lochcarron. Fi had indeed been successful in persuading their mother to go back to London with them and their parents' house was empty for the time being. He hadn't heard from Aurélie now for nearly two months in spite of sending her text messages and leaving a note for her at the French Department in the University.

The activity of the Centre was gathering apace as the work to plan the new Act's implementation began. There had been a late drive, led by groups campaigning on behalf of care experienced young people, to include support up to the age of 26 for those formerly looked after by local councils, something that Matt wholeheartedly supported, though he and others questioned how this, and indeed other commitments within the Act, were going to be resourced. It was becoming clear, as the government in Edinburgh grew in maturity and confidence, that some of its determination to make Scotland a different and more socially responsible place were going to be thwarted by its lack of control over its budget. The volume of the 'indieref' in this respect was getting louder and the arguments were becoming more cogent. To Matt though, the one very large question about how the country would cope in the event of another banking crisis remained. No one seemed to have addressed that rather fundamental issue.

It was a particularly fine morning in early June and Matt had been complimenting Alison about the fact that on such days she often cycled into work.

"You should try it," she said. "It's only five miles or so to yours via the cycle route round the back of Arthur's Seat."

Matt had seen the blue direction signs advertising the cycle routes within the city but, without a bike, had never explored them. By chance, later that week he saw an advert on a notice board in the office for someone selling a mountain bike. Spurred on by Alison's comments and also by the memory of the day that he and Catriona had cycled down the loch to Strome, he contacted the seller and by the Friday was once again the owner of his own means of transport.

The Innocent Railway linking Edinburgh with nearby Dalkeith was opened in the 1840s. The origins of its name were disputed but what was not in question, Matt quickly learned, was that the old track bed, and particularly the old tunnel under a corner of Arthur's Seat, was an ideal escape route for cyclists. It helped them to get away quickly from the city centre and out towards the south-eastern suburbs, whilst at the same time avoiding the congested traffic routes leading out to the A1.

Matt thanked Alison for inspiring him, although noted that, as yet, he hadn't been caught in the rain.

"Welcome to fair weather cycling," she said. "In reality, most of us are."

One evening he was leaving the Centre's office slightly later than planned and after locking up had stood momentarily whilst he adjusted his back pack and put his helmet on.

"Bonsoir, Matt," a familiar voice said.

Matt turned and looked at the person who stood in front of him, a person who earlier in the year he had been besotted by.

"You have become a cyclist then," she said in her unmistakable French accent.

"Yes, I suppose I have," he replied, "although I've not gone as far as Lycra or anything!"

Aurélie laughed. "How are you Matt? I spoke to your colleague when you were off. She explained that you had had a tragedy."

"Yes, we did," he said. Matt told her what had happened and also about his mother's recovery.

"I'm so sorry to hear that," she said. "It must have been awful."

Matt began to push his bike away from the office and the two of them walked slowly up the side of the square. Aurélie explained that she'd been back in France for much of the last month or so as her grandmother had also died and her mother had found it hard to come to terms with.

Matt felt an inner despair as he recalled having doubted her so many times when she had talked of her grandmother being unwell and how he had assumed that this was some pretext for not wanting to contact him. They parted on the corner by the coffee kiosk where he had first observed her, agreeing to meet for lunch. As he cycled home through the tunnel his earlier realisation that their relationship was never going to be more than friendship was reinforced when it occurred to him that, whilst he had lost his father, Aurélie had lost her grandmother. They were he accepted, a generation apart.

It was the following week before they met for lunch and when they did they seemed strangely more relaxed with each other than they had ever been. They recalled Hogmanay and the Australians that they had met on the Meadows. They talked of their ski trip, although Aurélie admitted that she thought that it would be some time, if ever, before she went skiing in Scotland again. The cold clammy mist of the

259

Highlands was not something that she ever envisaged replacing the crystal clear slopes of her own Alps. She also talked of Jean-Louis and how he had helped her following her grandmother's death.

"He's been good to me Matt," she said. "We've talked a lot about ourselves and I like him."

It occurred to him that she was talking to him as if to her father. She was seeking his support, his approval.

"I've decided to go back. To leave Edinburgh. Jean-Louis has a new job in Paris. He's going to be a Sports Editor on one of the tv stations. We're going to get a flat together. I've applied for a job at a University in Paris to teach English."

Matt leant forward and kissed her on the cheek. "That sounds absolutely wonderful," he said. "I'm so happy for you. When are you leaving?"

"That's why I was trying to find you," she said. "I leave next month, once term has finished and all the marking is done. But there is one thing. You always told me about the place that you are from. Yorkshire. Well I don't know if you know, but the Tour de France is starting in Yorkshire this year. I wondered if you wanted to go. You show me Yorkshire and I'll show you France, all at the same time."

"Wow, I'm not sure what to say," he replied. "We could ... ," he paused. "There is one thing though. Since we went to the rugby together a couple of things have changed for me as well." Matt went on to explain that he too was now in a relationship and that, although it had only been a few months, it already meant a lot to him.

They looked at each other in silence, realising that their joy and grief had given them a shared experience that neither could have imagined only a few months ago. Matt said that he would first talk to Catriona, as he had promised to take her back to the Dales in happier times.

As it was it took Matt a few days to find the opportunity to talk to Catriona. He was open with her about the relationship that he had thought that he might have with Aurélie. He told her about their shared passion for skiing and of his for all things French.

"I bet you thought your number had come up, when you saw the incident with the coffee," she had said.

Matt had looked suitably abashed.

He'd suggested though that they could plan to go to the Dales for a long weekend. Although he'd had time off after the accident and for the funeral, he did still have holidays to take. They looked at the calendar and realised that 'Le Grand Départ', as the start of the Tour de France was known, was going to be at the end of the second week of Bobby's school holidays. He had apparently had such a good time at Centre Parcs that there'd been talk of him seeing Nick again on his way back to the States from Norway. After a subsequent conversation with his mother, Matt had agreed to call in at his parents' house as she was concerned that the place was being neglected and that she was not yet well enough or ready to go back.

"I'd like it if you could go and stay there, if you could," she'd said.

"I'll have Catriona with me, Mum," he had replied.

"I'd hoped you would. I'm glad for you. She's a nice woman. Look after her Matt."

He knew how much his mother had liked Charlotte and how sad she had been when he had told her that they were separating and that he was moving to Edinburgh. At the Hattonbridge Inn after the funeral, Matt had noticed Catriona sitting with his Mum and that at one point they were holding hands deep in conversation.

The Tour de France was due to start from Leeds on Saturday July 5th. The first day's stage was to take the riders up Wharfedale into Yoredale and through Hattonbridge and the northern Dales, including an ascent of the Buttertubs Pass, before a sprint finish that would take them back to Harrogate. When Matt enquired, he discovered that the whole event had taken a grip of Yorkshire's collective imagination. There was no room at the Hattonbridge Inn or at any of the farms and other local Bed and Breakfasts. Many local people were moving out for the week and renting out their houses. In the end, it was Catriona's suggestion. She'd put Matt on her insurance and he could take her car and go on ahead. He'd stay near Northallerton on the Friday and Saturday. Aurélie was staying in a hotel in Harrogate with Jean-Louis, but she'd get to Northallerton first thing and she and Matt would hope to get to Hattonbridge before the race did. He'd then drop her back in Harrogate on the Saturday evening once the roads were open again. Catriona and Bobby would then get the train to Darlington on the Sunday so Nick could collect him and for Matt to meet her.

It seemed to have been remarkably simple to arrange in the end, he thought, as he locked the back door to the Centre one evening. He'd phoned Aurélie before he'd left and she'd been fine with the plans. Fixing his helmet, he mounted his bike and set off for the old railway tunnel, a broad contented grin on his face.

The tunnel mouth opened in front of him like a yawning chasm, similar to the limestone caves of Hattondale that he had explored as a child. But this cave had streetlights through it, sufficient to guide the rider through whilst still leaving small pockets of darkness. As he gathered pace on the downhill slope water dripped on him from the roof of the tunnel and his previous grin left his face. There was something chilling about it that evening and he decided that cycling that way once the evenings started to get darker was perhaps something that he would not be doing too regularly.

He was glad to be out into the light again and cycling along the old track bed past Duddingston. In a short while, he thought, there would be Asda on his right and then he'd be at the A1 and the retail park next to Brunstane Station from where it would be turn left and downhill into Portobello. He'd be glad to be home that evening. It had been a busy few days.

In the distance he could see the green logo of the supermarket but his eyes were instead distracted by a group of young people pushing and jostling one another up ahead. Voices were raised and, from what he could make out, an argument was underway. He slowed his own pace as he warily approached them. He could see that there were two on cycles whilst another was trying to push what appeared to be a motor bike.

Getting closer he realised that that young person was Dylan and the motor bike was his own nemesis, the Wasp. He could also see that, even if the others were his friends, they were not being exactly friendly. Almost ignoring the others, he called out "Heh Dylan, how you doing?"

The young man turned, momentarily ignoring his tormentors. "Matt?"

Seizing the opportunity, one of them pushed out at Dylan knocking him and the Wasp to the floor. The two of them laughed and kicked out at Dylan and his machine as they lay on the ground. Matt threw his own bike to one side and confronted them. A punch was thrown which Matt parried, then a kick which he caught turning the assailant on his heel as he did so causing him to lose his balance. Dylan had stood up by this point and with Matt they faced the two assailants.

"What are you going to do now?" Matt shouted. "Not so big now, eh?"

The two young men made to lunge but withdrew laughing. Picking up their own bikes they started gesticulating and shouting a series of obscenities, but as Matt and Dylan stood their ground, the two of them started to cycle off.

"Thanks Matt. I owe you one," said Dylan.

"What was happening there then?" Matt asked.

"They're just two nedds I know from college. I was coming this way back from the shops at Fort Kinnaird and they caught up with me, just as the bike failed. I've been having a bit of bother with it recently. A mate's Dad looked at it the other day, but I think it's done. Those two were just having a go at me about getting a proper motor bike. They're always going on about the noise that it makes."

Matt smiled to himself.

"I was sorry to hear about your Dad, Matt," said Dylan. "I don't really know mine, well not properly, but I guess some of them are special."

"Yeah, you're right. Some are. Some just are."

The two of them pushed their two wheeled machines the remaining mile to Portobello. It was odd, Matt thought, how life's experiences brought people together.

Twenty minutes later Catriona opened the door to them at Lee Crescent. "My God, what's happened to you two? And Matt, what are you doing here anyway?"

The two most important men in her life looked at each other as if to say 'are you going to tell her or am I?' Matt's slight nod to Dylan indicated that it was his story to tell, which he duly did.

"And these nedds. Do you know them?" his mother asked.

"Yes, but don't worry about them Mum. They're just wasters. They're going nowhere at College. They're not even in there every day."

Matt withdrew down the path slightly and said that he needed to get home. Catriona hugged him and thanked him for being there for her son. They stood on the pavement and looked at the Wasp, scratched and bent in places. The once proud scourge of Matt and his neighbours at the bottom of Bath Street was looking a shadow of its former menacing self.

"He'll need to talk to his father about getting it fixed," Catriona suggested, "though he's been talking about getting his car licence. Frightens me, just the thought of it. It only seems a couple of years ago that he was playing with toy cars on his bedroom floor. They grow up too quickly Matt." Her eyes began to well as she thought fondly of her son's childhood. Pulling herself out of her momentary melancholy, she asked when she was going to see him next. He said he'd come round the following evening. They embraced again and he cycled away finally able to get home.

Later that evening though, after a phone call to his sister, during which he'd talked to his mother, he found himself thinking long and hard about home and what was now important to him. It wasn't living by himself in a rented flat that was for sure, he concluded. He'd quite looked forward to it at first. Being a student again. Being free to do what he wanted, when he wanted. But that itself was limiting. The last year had shown him that. He wanted recognition, he wanted acknowledgement, but above all he wanted love.

Alison was the first to notice the following day that he was not on his bike and he gave her a very brief outline of what had happened on the way home the previous evening. What it meant though was that as he got off the bus on the High Street in Portobello later that evening he was, he realised, unencumbered. Should he go left down Bath Street, or cross the High Street to he right and head to Lee Crescent?

It was Bobby who let him in a few minutes later. "Mum, Matt's at the door," he called.

"Well let him in then," Catriona's voice came through from the back of the house.

Matt went through to the kitchen, dropping his bag in the hall.

"Hello, Mr Director, you'll be stopping for your dinner then?" she said, kissing him on the cheek as she prepared the food.

Later on and after they'd finished eating, the two of them were sat out in the garden, the bottle of wine that they'd opened with the meal nearly finished. It was the longest day of the year and it was a particularly mild and still evening with only some very high cloud in the sky. After a while the sound of a train from the south heading through Craigentinny and into Waverley broke their silence.

"Matt, there's something I'd like to ask you. And I'd like you to think about it if you don't want to answer it straight away. I've been thinking a lot since Lochcarron and then your Dad dying. I've enjoyed living here for the last few years. Just me and the boys. It was important to me to know that I could be a good mum. But I guess it's meant that I've not always looked out for me."

Matt began to interrupt her, thinking that it was the fact that she stood out in the group of other school mums that had first drawn him to her and that on all those evenings in the Espy, for him, she was always the most glamorous.

"No Matt, let me finish. It's that being with you has shown me that I do want something else. I wake up on mornings when you haven't been here and think there's an empty space where you should be. The other pillow isn't touched or out of place. And you know what, I've decided that I want it to be."

"What are you asking?" he said.

"I guess I'm saying would you like to move in? Let's give it a go and see where it takes us. If we decide it's not going to work out, then ..."

"You mean, like a trial get together?"

"If you want to put it that way," she laughed.

"I'd like nothing more," he answered, a tear breaking onto his cheek.

"Are you sure you don't want to think about it?"

"Not at all."

They embraced and were wrapped in a close and fond kiss when Dylan came to the door. "Bloody hell you two. Can you not put each other down?"

"Dylan, come here a moment, can you?" his mother called.

Dylan walked over to them.

"There's something I want to check with you. I've been thinking about this for some time and I've talked to Matt about it just now."

"What, about him moving in?"

"Well yes, but how did you..."

"Come on Mum. Get real. It's the way it's been going for the last couple of months isn't it?"

"Well ..."

"Look Mum, if that's what you want, I think it's great. You're a nice guy Matt," he said turning towards his mother's lover. "And I still owe you. Are you going to tell Bobby though, Mum?"

"Yes, I'll do that tomorrow when he gets back from school. Why don't you fetch the other bottle of wine out of the fridge and another glass for yourself?"

Dylan went to the door but paused at the step. "By the way, that was Nick on the phone. He's going to pay for driving lessons and he's said that he might help me with a car as well."

....

For the next two weeks the two of them were noticeably more animated. After telling Bobby they had also told a few of their close friends. Work was busy though and a lot of Matt's time was taken up with consultation over the guidance that would accompany the implementation of the new Act. This was proving an even bigger challenge than many had anticipated. Matt increasingly reflected to Helen and others that it demonstrated that by contrast to the UK, Scotland was still a very young nation. Compared to Westminster, those in Victoria Quay were still relatively inexperienced in the craftsmanship of legislation. Independence, if it was to be achieved, that September or whenever, would bring with it many challenges, some of which could not even be contemplated by those who were becoming ever more vocal in the build up to the referendum itself.

Matt left Portobello on the day before the start of the Tour de France. As he drove down through the Borders, he couldn't help thinking, ironic though it was, about the good fortune that he'd had following his father's tragic death. A sad smile crossed his face though, as he reflected that his father would never get to meet Catriona, or to know that his son had apparently finally found the happiness and fulfilment that he had been seeking for too long. It was also ironic, Matt thought, that he had finally found that in Edinburgh, the city from where his father had sought his own so many years earlier.

Matt arrived at Northallerton in the early evening and after checking into his bed and breakfast strolled up the High Street and round past the old cattle market. It had always been a prosperous town as could be seen by the range of independent shops that continued to thrive there. He ate in one of the pubs and engaged in a conversation with a couple of old men at the bar whose accents brought back happy memories of his own childhood and upbringing in nearby Yoredale. For the second time in a few weeks he found himself feeling very much at home.

Saturday morning was sunny and warm and it seemed like the whole of Yorkshire was turning out to watch the race. Yellow painted bicycles were appearing everywhere and were almost as ubiquitous, Matt thought, as the 'Yes' posters north of the border. After picking up Aurélie from the station they fought their way through the traffic heading for the Dale, Matt's knowledge of the back roads helping him round the bottlenecks that were forming through the larger villages. They finally got to Hattonbridge shortly before the roads were closed and they managed to park Catriona's car in the field behind the pub.

"You must thank her for me," Aurélie said. "It was very good of her to let you use her car."

Matt said that he would. Quickly they merged with the crowd lining the route outside the Hattonbridge Inn.

When the idea of the Tour de France coming through the Yorkshire Dales had first been proposed, Matt had thought that it seemed as plausible as Scotland winning the World Cup and yet here it was. They watched as the caravan came towards them, the vans of the sponsors' vehicles handing out free samples of various French products. They grabbed some sweets and laughed as they thought of the childishness of it all. It was some time later though that they first heard it. The noise of the race and the vehicles of the entourage that followed in its wake could be heard coming along the Dale. It was like an on-rushing tsunami, a tidal wave of humanity and machine merged into a single entity. The noise increased with the helicopters overhead providing the television coverage. Then it was on them. A lone rider came first with motorcycle outriders. He rode confidently, majestically they thought, possessed as he was on his personal mission to get to the Buttertubs climb and claim the first red spotted jersey for king of the mountains. It would be his tonight if he kept on like that with the rest well behind and left in his wake for the time being, or until the team orders dictated the later sprint stages of the day's race.

Matt had his phone in his hand and was taking photos. Others were doing the same. This was going to be a selfie for posterity. Everyone looked excited, uncertain what was going to happen next. The noise turned into a roar as the peleton itself approached. The crowd of villagers, swelled by the visitors who had been camping at the back of the pub, clapped loudly. And then it was on them as they swept through and over the bridge. The bikes' wheels were a blurr, as were the multi-coloured lycra clad cyclists piloting their machines. Then the support vehicles, all driving far too quickly for the narrow Dales roads. What would Sergeant Woodward have made of this, Matt thought. Arrest them for speeding? He'd have had some job trying to keep up with them on his 1960s police issue bike that he used to patrol the village on.

And then it was gone. The whole thing was over and done with within a matter of minutes. What had been nearly two years of anticipation had barely lasted twenty minutes in total. Some of the crowd melted away to get on with their Saturday afternoon life; others headed straight back into the pub to resume their drinks and to watch the rest of the race on the big screen. Some suggested heading for what had, for the day, become known as Côte de Grinton Moor the last hill climb that the Tour would take on its way towards Leyburn, but others said that the roads had been shut hours ago and it would be a waste of time. Matt and Aurélie chose the pub.

The atmosphere inside was still electric and even though the whole thing had been over in a matter of minutes, the day, or rather the moment, that Hattonbridge, let alone Yorkshire, was the centre of Europe, was clearly going to live long in the village's memory. As the afternoon wore on and it was known that the riders were on their way to Masham and onwards to Harrogate, roads began to reopen. Matt and Aurélie joined the slow moving traffic heading south, eventually arriving in the spa town in the early evening. They met up with Jean-Louis near the Conference Centre which had become the temporary media headquarters for the race.

Suddenly, it occurred to Matt that this was going to be 'goodbye' for himself and Aurélie, for himself and the young woman who had beguiled him all winter. It was a day that had come on him as a surprise. And yet he did not feel sadness because, with Catriona's arrival the following day, he felt a sense of a new life opening up in front of him. Nevertheless, there was a tear in both of their eyes as he and Aurélie air kissed and said goodbye for the last time. They promised to stay in touch. And if he ever wanted a proper day's skiing then she would show him how it was done in the Alps. He laughed. Jean-Louis and Aurélie turned away hand in hand. Matt stood silently and watched for a moment as the young French couple blended into the crowds of Harrogate tourists and he could not make them out any more.

He turned and made his way back to the car. He drove north out of Harrogate and passed groups tidying up the road in the aftermath of the race, removing the signs and sponsors adverts from roadsides. He was back at Northallerton by late evening and called Catriona to check that everything was still okay for the following day. He went to bed feeling very proud. It had been a proud day for Yorkshire and he was proud to have been part of it.

The following day the Tour de France headed south from York to Sheffield, but Matt's interest in the race was over. His interest lay to the north and he headed to Darlington to meet Catriona. By the time he arrived, Nick had already collected Bobby. They left Darlington and headed south. They smiled at each other as they crossed the Tees at Croft. It was going to be different from the last time that they had been together in these parts. After stopping for a late lunch in Thirsk the afternoon was nearly over when they arrived at Matt's parents house. "Welcome to Yorkshire," he said. "Home of the mighty Tykes!"

CHAPTER TWENTY TWO - STARTING OUT AGAIN (1997 - 2000)

"Matthew. Are you coming? It's time to go."

"Give me a minute," he replied. "Just checking the back bedroom." He looked out of the window of the house that he had lived in since moving in with Sarah and her mother. But as he gazed across the roof tops of the terraced houses in the direction of the University, he reflected that by contrast it had always been their home. He could only hope that with the move, things were going to be different: like the words of the new Labour anthem, that had become an inescapable earworm in the run up to the General Election that was now only a week away, put it: *Things could only get better*!

It was late April 1997 and Matt and Charlotte along with Sarah were on the move. A new Research Unit was being established in the south-west and the two of them had successfully applied for jobs on the team. The Unit, which was funded independently through a charitable bequest, represented a new challenging, exciting and stimulating experience for both of them. Charlotte had wanted to go independent, but Matt had persuaded her to take a regular job, at least until Sarah had finished school. At their joint leaving-do though, knowing that Matt had always said that his next move would be to Scotland, Pauline had questioned whether he had checked a map recently! It was, he knew, a compromise.

A week later they were still unpacking boxes in their new home in Bath as the polling stations closed across the country. The television news was forecasting a landslide victory to new Labour. Matt poured them a glass of wine and they sat down to watch the drama unfold.

"What difference do you think it's going to make?" asked Charlotte, cuddling up to him on the sofa.

"Investment, I guess," he replied.

It had been six years since the Children Act 1989 had been implemented. However, the research that they had been involved in had often shown that in spite of it being well intentioned, the range of services that the Act envisaged had not always materialised. Cuts in local authority services had made it difficult for them to always put children's needs at the centre of decision making about services for them, in the way that the Act's ambitious architects may have dreamt of.

Like many of their new colleagues they were bleary eyed the following day when they got to the office. It was a mild sunny day, and although no one seemed to really know why, everyone seemed to have a smile on their face. The mood continued into the weekend and was even noticeable in the Saturday morning supermarket queue when the three of them went out to do their first big shop in the city.

"Can we have a picnic?" Sarah had beseeched them.

As the Monday was the May Day holiday, and buoyed by the sense of optimism that they all shared, they decided to get some bits together and head for the beach, a destination that had meant a long journey from where they used to live.

However, when they woke two days later, the weather had changed. The warm spring like conditions of the previous week had given way to late winter. Snow was even forecast for overnight into the following day. They went out for the day nevertheless and headed for the coast. It was not the day that they had anticipated and the outdoor picnic had been consumed inside the car. They headed back a lot earlier than planned and as they reached Bath the foreboding sky that enveloped the city added to their changing mood.

Sarah, who was now thirteen and due to start at her new school the following day, slammed the car door as she got out. "Why did we have to move anyway? I don't see what was wrong with the way things were."

Later that evening, Matt was trying to phone his parents to let them know that they had settled in. His call was frequently interrupted by a disgruntled teenage girl who was reluctant to go to bed and an increasingly frustrated mother who was losing the struggle. He learnt that there was also a frosty wind in the Dales, for even though it was May it had been snowing that evening in Hattonbridge. Things could indeed only get better, he thought, when he eventually put the phone down and realised that the house was now silent and that Charlotte had herself gone to bed without telling him.

Bath was a beautiful city, Matt quickly decided. The Georgian architecture, the way that it was crammed into a deep sided valley, the sense of history, all things which endeared it to him. But as the spring turned towards the summer and optimism continued, something seemed to be missing from his life, although he wasn't sure what. It was one evening as they were settling down to watch the news that he was reminded. With their landslide victory behind them the Labour government had lost no time in following through on its pre-election promise to hold a referendum on Scottish devolution. It was almost as though he'd neglected his love affair with Scotland.

Gradually over the next month or so he found himself sowing seeds with Charlotte and Sarah about the virtues of a holiday in Scotland that summer. Charlotte had needed some convincing given her memory of the time that she had spent there with her former husband. But she had, she admitted, enjoyed the Edinburgh Festival and in particular the Fringe. Sarah was on side when Matt promised that they could stop off at his parents on the way. She was fond of her 'Yorkshire grandma' as she continued to call his Mum.

"And I'm fond of her," his mother had said when Matt had phoned to check if they could stay on their way north. She'd also asked again though about when he and Charlotte were going to get married and have children, her grandchildren.

"No pressure then Mum," he'd replied. "See you in a couple of weeks."

Their first few months in their new jobs had been busy as the Unit had sought to capitalise on opportunities from the new government to prove the value of the planned investment in public services and along with their move, by August they needed a holiday. They were exciting times.

They were also clearly exciting times ahead in Scotland, Matt decided, if the conspicuous 'Yes' posters that adorned the road side from almost the moment they crossed the border at Carter Bar on the way to Edinburgh. They'd stopped there in the lay-by, eaten the picnic that Matt's mother had put together and posed for pictures against the 'Welcome to Scotland' sign. Even Charlotte conceded that the view to the north was stunning. It was just a shame that, by the time that they arrived in the city an hour or so later, the rain had set in.

Matt had rented a flat for them just off the Grassmarket and by the time he'd unloaded the car he was drenched. He pushed the door of the flat closed. "I think that's everything," he said.

Sarah and her mother were looking out of the window as the rain bounced off the glass. The castle rock loomed large above them, its grey shape dominating the view. It was far from being a romantic one.

Their time in Edinburgh though was generally positive and the three of them entered into the spirit of the festival and its madcap diverse environment. They saw some excellent shows and some new comedians, as well as doing some of the tourist things. Matt even persuaded Sarah to climb up the Scott Monument with him, although he was sure that a few more steps had been added from the time when, as a boy, he had climbed it with his father. By the last night, as they were walking back down the Grassmarket towards the flat, they had to admit that they had enjoyed their holiday and each other's company.

"I think I get it," Charlotte said to Matt putting her arm through his and her head on his shoulder. "I get what this place does to you. It sucks you in, makes you want more. Shame our jobs are at the other end of the country!" It had been very different from the previous time with her husband.

They laughed as they watched Sarah struggling to eat a crepe dripping in cream and chocolate that she'd bought from a food stall.

"Come on I want a bit of that!" Matt said chasing her down the pavement.

Charlotte admired the good natured relationship that Matt had with her daughter. Perhaps, she thought.

After the holiday, they quickly settled back into work and also into the social life in Bath. It was a more prosperous place than where they had lived in the Midlands, and its tourist industry, meant that there was always something happening. Charlotte, in particular, found it her sort of place and she made new friends very easily. One consequence was that Matt found that Sarah increasingly came to rely on him. The two of them would spend evenings together, when Charlotte was out, watching television or a DVD, looking at her homework, or putting the world to rights, whether that was Sarah's in Bath, or Britain's in the world.

Their friends began to tell them that they should take their relationship a stage further. It would give Sarah added security they said. It was something though that Matt and Charlotte had repeatedly said that they didn't need to do. They were happy, they maintained, with things as they were. The problem was though that they probably weren't, for although they'd never actually acknowledged it, Matt and Charlotte's relationship had to an extent always been one of convenience.

In the still of the evening, when Charlotte had gone to bed, Matt would stand at the window of their flat in an old

Georgian property on Bloomfield Road on the south side of the city, looking out over the roofs and wondering how he had ended up here. True, it was a great place to be, but how had a lad from the Dales, whose life had, for so long, been entwined with Edinburgh, ended up here in the south-west of England? He was not at ease. Charlotte was also far from content, although for different reasons. In spite of their jobs being assured, at least for the foreseeable future, her ambition was to set up her own business. He was not convinced. The risks involved seemed too great compared to the guaranteed income that the Unit offered, which was important if they were to buy the house together that they planned.

What also often bothered Matt was that Charlotte seemed to be more relaxed when his sister Fi was around. Fi had graduated as a teacher by the time that they had moved to Bath and had got a job in London. This had meant that, initially at least, she'd been a regular visitor and the two women became friends, often exploring the night life of the city whilst Matt and Sarah contented themselves with a night in and a DVD.

However, after a year of living and working in London, Fi had met Graham, a fellow teacher, and in summer 1999 they were married. It was a modest affair back in Hattonbridge at which Matt, Charlotte and Sarah had been present. It was the first time that he had seen many of their older relatives for some years and he sensed a tension from some who assumed that Sarah was his daughter and that he and her mother were not married. He was proud of his relationship with Sarah, after all he had been her Dad for much of her life, and it infuriated him that some were so quick to judge without knowing the facts. By contrast, others had been open in their encouragement to him to make what they called 'an honest woman' of Charlotte.

Matt had found his mother more reassuring. She had taken him to one side at the reception in the evening and told him that whilst she had always been taken by Charlotte and also had grown used to the idea of Sarah referring to her as her 'Yorkshire Grandma', whatever they did had to be right for the three of them, something that he'd reflected on over the following months.

In early 2000, Frederick Fawcett surprised everyone by announcing that he was going to retire from the estate. He turned sixty that year and decided that trekking around the Dale and checking on the tenant farmers and the other land users was no longer for him. He also acknowledged that the increasing computerisation of the role was something that he didn't fully understand. It was thirty years on from when he had gone to university and from when most of the job was still recorded in long hand in ledgers.

What was more surprising was that his parents decided to take the opportunity to move away from the Dale and from the village where they had first met. They bought a bungalow in a village on the outskirts of York. It would be more convenient for travelling to visit their children, his mother had reasoned, and the weather would be less harsh than it could be up the Dale, particularly during the winter. Frederick though, felt that he was too young to retire fully and he took on a part-time job as a business manager at the local primary school. "A sign of the times," he said to those who asked why a primary school needed a Business Manager. To everyone's surprise, never previously having had a pet, the couple acquired a Red Setter puppy, which they called Edgar.

In some ways the lives of those in his family were falling largely into place, Matt reflected one warm evening in early July as he gazed out over Bloomfield Road and the city below. If only things were as easy for him. Fi had been on the phone to them earlier in the evening. Having got married less than a year earlier she was calling to tell them that she was pregnant and that she and Graham were really excited. He'd congratulated her and said that he couldn't wait to be an uncle. Later on though, he'd been absorbed by the television news of the events that day in Edinburgh. It had been the state opening of the Scottish parliament. There had been crowds lining the route from Holyrood to the Assembly Building on The Mound and children from across Scotland had followed in the procession, symbolic of the new nation's future. Matt was wistful. He had wished he had been there.

Charlotte had suggested that he should go if it meant that much to him, but in the end work had intervened as the two of them were to make a presentation at a conference in London the day after the ceremony was due to take place. The immediate problem though, Matt accepted, was that they were due to move into the house that they had just bought. It was closer into the centre of the city and it had stretched them to the limits. Money was going to be tight for some time. Going to Edinburgh on a whim would have been a difficult one to justify he had acknowledged.

The conference was a challenge as there were problems in London with transport that day. It had meant that some participants were late; whilst others wanted to get away early in order to guarantee their journey home. In the end the two of them had left early themselves and had taken the opportunity to do some shopping before heading back to Paddington. Given their financial position and his sacrifice, Matt was surprised that Charlotte seemed preoccupied with jewellers' windows.

As the train pulled out of Paddington for the return to Bath later that afternoon, they looked forward to getting home. It had been a long day.

"Matt," Charlotte said, sitting closer to him and pausing to stare at the concrete expanse of west London as it slipped effortlessly by. "Can I ask you something? If you had to choose between someone and somewhere to love, which would it be?"

"What sort of question is that?" he laughed.

"Well I know that you wanted to be in Scotland yesterday for the opening of the parliament thing, so let's say 'me or Edinburgh', which would it be?"

He pondered for a moment. The sudden woosh of a train heading into London made them jump. He didn't answer.

CHAPTER TWENTY THREE - LOOKING BACK
(July 2014)

They spent the first part of the week at his parents' house. They cut the lawn as well as the hedges, which had always been the bane of his father's life, although the tomatoes in his father's greenhouse, which had been neglected, were beyond recovery. His father had always been proud of his greenhouse and his tomatoes. They took Edgar for long walks around the village and but for the circumstances of them being there, they felt like a proper couple. Mrs Clayton even said as much when Matt handed the keys back as they were leaving. "Your Mum's ever so happy for you Matt. I spoke to her the other day," she said.

Matt suggested that he should show off the Dale itself and he phoned the Hattonbridge Inn. After the commotion of the previous weekend when rooms couldn't be obtained within 20 miles of the Dale, things were different a few days on. Consequently after saying goodbye to the Claytons who continued to look after Edgar, they travelled from York to Hattondale, the reverse of the fateful journey that his parents had so recently made. Catriona suggested that she should drive. Matt didn't need much convincing. They stopped at the site of the accident and paused for a few minutes. Holding each other's hands they paid their silent respects. Then it was on to Hattondale. Matt was excited and as keen to show it to Catriona as she had been to show Lochcarron to him.

Childhood memories abounded: the Dale where he and Andrew had played; the former workshop that had been their Den; the primary school, now a holiday cottage; the Church, sporting a floral yellow bicycle rather than the decorated Christmas Trees; and the building that had been Taylor's grocery shop, sadly long since closed. There was also the Hattonbridge Inn, where they were staying, just keeping going in spite of last Saturday when the world's most famous cycle race gave it and other Dales landmarks their moment of fame in the sun. And there was their house, the house that Matt and his mother had lived in together whilst his father was at university in Edinburgh. It was all starting to make sense for Catriona.

That evening in the pub, she told him of the love that they shared. A deep rooted love bounded by their childhoods and by the very places that surrounded them. A love that would endure, would always be there, and was stronger than any passing love for a human being. That was transient love, she said, a love which had to be worked for. They sat by the open fire planning the rest of their week before going up to their room. They made love together before falling asleep in each other's arms.

A few hours later Matt awoke. He looked at the clock at the side of the bed. It was still early. He looked at the woman asleep beside him and smiled. As he lay there though, her words from the previous evening came back to him. Maybe she was right, he thought. He needed to see it for himself. This place in which, as a child, he had first experienced the love of a parent and that had spent a lifetime reaching out to him. He slipped out of the bed and crept as quietly as he could through the old building. Letting himself out he crossed to the car and collected his boots and jacket. Although it was daylight there was little sign of the sun and the clouds overhead suggested what might be to come. He almost tiptoed through the village, not wanting to disturb anything or anyone. Bunting still hung from the cycle race. He walked beyond the houses, past the farm at the edge of the village, past the 30 mph sign and out into the Dale. He paused for a moment at the house that he had grown up in, staring up at the window of the room that had been his bedroom. The air smelt sweet as the first rain began to fall on the summer grass. Different from the storm driven rain that had fallen the night that his sister had been born and when he had had to go for help in the dark.

Half an hour later he had walked well up the Dale itself. He reached the spot that, during the winter, had been their sledging field and which, during the summer, he and Andrew had rolled down through the buttercups. It was a liberating feeling, one that he had known all those years ago, but one that years of living in cities and urban environments had deprived him of. He stopped to get his breath and to take in the view looking back down Hattondale and to the village that he had known since he was a boy. The village from which his father had left 44 years earlier to go to Edinburgh, the village that had been his home, the village to which he had brought the woman that he had come to love and the village that now embraced her within its midst.

In spite of the rain which was getting heavier and beginning to prove a challenge even for his North Face jacket, he could still make out the limestone buildings and dry stone walls behind which sheep were already tucked up in their lee, sheltering from the weather. Although the prospects were looking bleak, he thought, there was still a natural beauty to the place, the place in which in an earlier time a mother had first loved her son.

He turned into the rain and continued head down, up the road towards Skelton, struggling to recall the translation of the Gaelic inscription on Catriona's grandmother's gravestone, whilst trying to get the view of both the village and the Dale as well as what lay beyond. What was it that had always drawn him on? But today there was nothing to see. Instead the low cloud from which the rain poured, hugged the tops of the fells and kept a lid on Hattondale. It was as though all he could now see was his old world. He paused and stared down at the village. Was that what it had all had been about? All those journeys. All those opportunities. All those people. He had always sought to move on, to move further away, but instead he was back where it had all begun. Newcastle, Bath, and the other places he'd worked or studied, even Edinburgh, they were not destinations after all. What he had learnt over the last year, as he had told Dougie, was the significance of the question 'where do you stay?' It was different from 'where are you from?' Even Geoff Newlove had appeared to know that, he realised.

A land rover was coming down the road towards him. It slowed when it saw him and came to a stop when it drew alongside. The driver opened the window and grimaced as the rain lashed into the relative warmth of the vehicle's interior. Matt recognised him instantly. It was the man who had been the boy all those years ago when they had swung down from the playground wall, when a game of British Bulldog had distracted the teacher; when they'd turned Calvert's outhouse into their den; and when Sergeant Woodward had nearly arrested them for breaking in.

Andrew Tait spoke to him. "Eh up, Matthew. It is thee, i'n't it? You know, I haven't seen thee in forty odd years. I knew you'd be back though. One day. You lot always are. You lot who try and get away. Tha knows tha's hefted to this place just like all these bloody sheep round here. It'll never let you go, tha knows! Jump in tha daft wazzock, tha'll catch thee death of cold standing out there in this."

Matt smiled, remembering the night that Andrew's father had uttered almost exactly the same words. He gratefully climbed in to the embracing warmth and dry of the land rover. He smiled at Andrew and together they laughed. There was going to be much to say. But for now the day had broken, he was home, his love intact and for now the shadows were fled away. Portobello, EH15 and all that it held would be for another day.